Flash Point

Midlife in Aura Cove Book 4

Blair Bryan

xoxo
Blair Bryan

The best place to buy books by Blair Bryan and Ninya is https://tealbutterflypress.com/

There you will support the author and find the best pricing as well as exclusive options like autographed paperbacks and hardcovers.

To my favorite Marine, my father, Jim, and all our military members and their families: Thank you for your service and sacrifice. Your dedication and bravery warm my heart, and I am endlessly grateful for the sacrifices you make to ensure our freedom.

Ooh-Rah!

READ MORE BY THIS AUTHOR

Use the QR code below to access my current catalogue. **Teal Butterfly Press is the only place to purchase autographed paperbacks and get early access.** Buying direct means you are supporting an artist instead of big business. I appreciate you.

https://tealbutterflypress.com/pages/books

Also available at Barnes and Noble, Kobo, Apple books, Amazon, and many other international book sellers.

Find My Books at your Favorite Bookseller Below.

Books by Ninya

Books By Blair Bryan

ONE

"This is why I love Florida," Katie mused to Arlo, who was sitting in the passenger seat of her green Volkswagen Beetle while she drove to Kandied Karma. It was late February, and with the top down to allow the gentle breeze, the sun was deliciously warm on the crown of her head. The wind ruffled Arlo's fur as Katie navigated to a parking spot near the rear entrance of her grandmother's artisanal chocolate shop in downtown Aura Cove. Katie quickly unbuckled her seatbelt but then froze when she saw her reflection in the rearview mirror.

"Holy cow. It's *all* white now," she remarked, leaning in and whipping her chin from side to side to confirm her entire head of hair was now as white as the driven snow. The change happened so quickly that it sometimes felt like she was staring at a stranger when she caught a glimpse of herself in a mirror.

"I think you look beautiful either way," Arlo offered, barking once for emphasis.

"*I* think you're trying to get back in my good graces with flattery."

"But is it working?" he teased, batting full-tilt puppy dog eyes up at her.

Katie laughed. "Nope." He whined in dismay, and she scratched under his chin to comfort him. "You're cute, but you're still in the doghouse for spying on me. Besides, I'm not the kind of girl who needs ego boosts from others anymore. I can genuinely say I like who I am."

"What an evolved creature you've become!" Arlo exclaimed. "Even just a year ago, you would have never made that claim."

Katie nodded. "True. I've come a long way, but there is still so much further to go."

"You'll get there," Arlo encouraged, confident in his owner. She patted him on the head and then reached over to open the car door to lead him into the back door of the shop. Once her eyes adjusted to the lower light inside, her jaw dropped, and she stopped dead in her tracks. Following too closely, Arlo whined when his nose hit her heels, then quickly backtracked, quivering in fear and hiding behind Katie as he looked up at the woman standing there.

Zoya rolled her eyes at their over-the-top reactions. "You're going to have to get used to seeing me on the regular around here. If I'm supposed to make those crotchety witches in the eternal coven happy, I'm going to need to find ways to be more altruistic. Hence, I decided to search out my two favorite do-gooders." She waved her gloved hands to indicate Yuli and Katie. "Got any ideas?"

"Step one might be to stop referring to the eternal coven as crotchety witches," Katie offered, trying to be helpful, but Zoya shot her an incensed glare that made her last few words trail off at the end.

"Historically, doing good has not been your strong suit," Yuli reminded her.

"True," Zoya admitted with a shrug. Her white hair was gathered in a loose braid that flowed down her back. She wore an aqua-colored sundress that reminded Katie of the color of the sea surrounding the Castanova Compound. "I've far preferred delivering comeuppance, but maybe it's time to turn a new leaf."

"Pfft." Yuli's disbelief was clear. "New leaf! Ha!"

"I thought after the *Fioletovy Mahiya,* we decided to let bygones be bygones." Zoya challenged her reaction, leveling her eyes on Yuli, who refused to back down, testing her grandmother. The *Fioletovy Mahiya* was a once-in-a-lifetime lunar event that temporarily lifted the veil between the living and the dead. During last February's full moon, Katie, Yuli, and Zoya discovered the only way to step into the fullness of their supernatural powers was to unite the mortal coven. It was a task that still seemed monumental, even after the healing they'd individually received during the event.

"In that case, since we open in fifteen, why don't you start your good deeds by stocking the truffle case?"

Yuli boldly asked in her typical direct fashion, making Katie grin at her audacity. It was obvious, Yuli was not pulling any punches and was ready to test this magnanimous version of herself Zoya was trying to claim.

Zoya scoffed at the idea, balling her hands on her hips. "Ana Castanova can't be seen engaging in manual labor," she huffed. "It's dangerous to her brand."

Yuli palmed her lined face with her hand in frustration. "It's far too early, and I am *not even remotely* caffeinated enough to deal with you and *your brand.*" Her annoyance was palpable.

Zoya plowed on, "Ana Castanova is a celebrity. How about I make a post on Instagram that I'm signing autographs at Kandied Karma? Just think how much that will increase business around here."

"No, thank you. We already have more customers than we can serve. We don't need you posturing for social media like some geriatric influencer," Yuli scolded, rolling her eyes. Instead, she walked over to a section of the wall and struck it three times with a closed fist. Katie gasped when she heard a soft click and part of the wall opened up to reveal an organizer lined with amber-colored bottles, mason jars, and clumps of dried herbs hanging upside down.

Like a moth to a flame, Katie was drawn to the hidden treasure. As she walked closer to the cabinet, her jaw dropped in awe. She thought she knew every inch of the chocolate shop by heart. "Has this secret hidey-hole been here the entire time you've owned this building?"

She walked over to it, marveling at the discovery, and ran her hands over the edge of the organizer.

"I had to have a place to stash our ancient ancestral ingredients away from the prying eyes of health inspectors," Yuli explained.

Zoya wandered over and surveyed the contents of the rows of jars and bottles.

"That's a pretty well-stocked pantry," she confirmed, looking over the available options on the shelves. "I know! How about I teach Katia how to create some of our family potions since you haven't gotten around to it yet?"

"Pardon me, but we've been a little busy around here lately," Yuli defended, sensitive to Zoya's criticism. Then, realizing Zoya always had an ulterior motive, her eyes narrowed as she asked, "Why? Are you planning something sinister that I should know about?"

"Not at the moment," she admitted with a sly grin and one arched eyebrow. "Though that's always subject to change."

"I don't have time for this insanity." Yuli shook her head and left the kitchen with two trays of truffles to stock the case herself. The door swung back and forth on its squeaky hinges in her wake.

"If you're looking to help, I received flashes from a woman yesterday who I believe is my next assignment from Karma." Katie began to explain, and an interested Zoya strode closer. Katie felt a flutter of fear well up inside her and tamped it down. Her body was subconsciously responding to the ramped-up interactions she'd already had with Zoya, but she pressed past her initial qualms. Zoya *was* powerful. She'd seen the havoc her great-great grandmother was capable of with her own eyes, but having a mighty ally to help her assignment with Rox could prove invaluable. Her daughter, Lauren, had fallen head over heels with Rox's son, Tom, and Katie received flashes of a possible wedding that could unite their families by marriage. There was a lot on the line, so she decided to put aside her misgivings and take as much help as she could get.

"I saw a future where Rox could be Lauren's mother-in-law."

Zoya pursed her lips and narrowed her eyes as she considered Katie's revelation. "It's a definite possibility."

One of Katie's eyebrows arched at her answer, and her intuition tingled. "I feel like you're leaving some vital information out. Do you know something I don't?"

"Do your best to quell the paranoia, darling," Zoya responded. "Not everything I say or do has an ulterior motive. What did you see?"

"Flashes of Rox in a military dress uniform and then a velvet-lined box housing a Purple Heart medal slamming shut," Katie said.

"Hmmm." Zoya deliberated over the information. "That's a very underwhelming report."

The tips of Katie's ears burned in embarrassment. She should have waited to bring it up when Yuli was present. Zoya was a formidable presence, and it was easy to be intimidated in the presence of her unflinching confidence.

"We are going to need to gather more intel. I'll see what I can muster up."

"What does that mean?"

"You're going to have to learn to trust me. I do my best work solo." Zoya effectively dismissed the rest of the conversation and strolled over to the secret stash of ancient ingredients. She mumbled under her breath as she inventoried the items on the shelves. A few minutes later, she turned toward Katie with a triumphant grin on her face. Yuli had returned to the kitchen as well.

"We have all the ingredients we need here for Verity Oil," Zoya announced.

"What does it do?" Katie asked.

"Ordins are notorious liars," Yuli explained. "When this oil is administered to their skin, it makes them unable to tell a lie."

"Ooh! That could come in handy with a few people in my life." Katie smirked.

"Please respect the magic, Katia, because it's very powerful. A single eyedropper full will render an ordin unable to tell even the tiniest fib for up to twenty-four hours," Yuli explained. "The closer you can administer it to the brain stem, the more potent it becomes."

Katie chewed on the inside of her cheek.

"What is it?" Yuli asked, instantly picking up on her energy shift.

"Isn't it playing God a bit to force an ordin to tell the truth? Aren't we taking away their free will?"

Zoya sighed in frustration. "Fantastic. We've got another bleeding heart in the mortal coven."

Yuli shushed her. "Let her speak."

"I'm torn. Recently, magic has helped me much more than harmed me, but we could not say the same about Jefferson."

Zoya threw up her hands and talked over Katie. "What more did you want? It was an effective Karma rebalance!" she huffed, then admitted, "Did I get a little carried away? Possibly." She shrugged off the supernatural spell she'd executed that left Katie's ex-husband financially and physically impotent. Irritated, she gripped her hips with the palms of her hands, thrust her shoulders back, and stood up for her decision. "No! I did not get carried away. If given the chance, I would do it again," she declared.

"That's my point," Katie said. "Just because we can, does that mean we should?"

Yuli mulled it over. "I've always advocated using our supernatural powers when it accomplishes the end goal and harms the fewest people necessary."

"Sometimes harm is unavoidable," Zoya chimed in. "And sometimes, it is just plain satisfying."

Katie shivered. "I hope I never become the kind of witch who savors the suffering of another human being, no matter how evil they are."

"I think we're going to have to agree to disagree on this," Zoya added. "There are some ordins who just won't learn any other way."

Katie didn't agree but bit back her reply. She wasn't confident enough in her abilities to stand up to Zoya yet.

"Things are getting heated. We should table this discussion for now," Yuli said, ever the diplomat. "Ultimately, Katia, you will have to answer these ethical dilemmas for yourself. I do believe it is worth a discussion before any of us makes a decision on our own that will affect the coven."

"So we're deciding by committee now?" Zoya scoffed at the idea. "I refuse to work that way."

"As always, you can exercise your free will." Yuli knew Zoya wasn't the kind of witch to question her motives or walk through past experiences looking for ways to improve. "But your stubbornness to change will not help you earn your reincarnation."

Yuli's judgment made Zoya press her lips together in a straight line. Picking up on her discomfort, Katie offered a carrot. "Tell me more about Verity Oil."

Eager to change the subject, Zoya turned toward her. "It takes seven moons to reach its peak state of efficacy."

"Why?"

"Seven is the sum of the spiritual and physical realms. It's a sacred number," Yuli explained.

Katie rubbed her hands together, excited to learn more about her supernatural lineage. "How do we make it?"

"Stick with me, kid," Zoya offered. "I have so much to teach you." She pulled out a dried satchel of lavender and a brown glass bottle filled with a thick, viscous liquid.

"Not the myrrh," Yuli said as she dug deep into the recesses of a drawer and pulled out an antique hardcover book Katie had never seen before.

"Yes. It's cinnamon, mugwort, vanilla, and myrrh," Zoya said, relying on her memory.

Yuli shook her head in disagreement. "You're wrong." She opened the book, and it crackled to life. Golden sparks shot out of it and flowed down onto the countertop. Awed, Katie walked over to the ancient book and glanced at the page Yuli was reading.

"It's blank," Katie said, confused.

"No, Katia, you're just not knowledgeable enough to be able to read it yet." Yuli explained, "Soon."

She walked it over to Zoya, delighted to prove her error. "See, it's cinnamon, mugwort, vanilla, and *mandrake.*" She tapped on the page and handed the book over to Zoya. "Your mind is not the infallible steel trap you claim it to be."

A sheepish look flashed over Zoya's features for a microsecond. "I'm never wrong." She read the page slowly under her breath. Her forehead knit together in confusion, and she shut the book and then opened it again, rereading the same page. Several long minutes later, she finally mumbled in the smallest voice imaginable, "You might be right."

"What?" Yuli asked, her eyes twinkling with unconcealed mirth as she cupped one hand to her ear and leaned toward Zoya.

"I said, you're right," Zoya repeated, the smallest fraction louder.

"I can't hear you," Yuli gloated, beaming with pleasure.

"Alright! I said you were right!" Zoya's eyes flashed in anger, and Katie gasped when she felt a wall of heat flash through her center then immediately fall away.

Yuli held up a hand. "Calm down. There's no need to get pissy about it!" Consulting her watch, she said, "I'll open up. You two get started on the Verity Oil in the double boiler. It needs to simmer for a week before it's bottled, anyway. Then, Katia, I'll need your help for the commuter rush."

"You got it," Katie quickly agreed.

"The *celebrity* can slink out the back door to protect her *brand* from the stink of menial labor." Yuli used finger quotes to convey the absurdity she felt.

Zoya rolled her eyes when Yuli left through the swinging door. "She's a tough old bird, your grandmother," she remarked to Katie.

"She is." Katie nodded. "You are both more similar than either of you will ever admit."

"Stubbornness runs in the gene pool, darling."

"Speaking of the gene pool," Katie began shyly. "I was wondering if you'd be available to come by for a family dinner and meet the rest of my brood."

"Oh?" Zoya's green eyes locked on her great-great granddaughter's.

"As Ana Castanova, of course."

"Yes, that would be awkward if the children found out, wouldn't it? We'd have a lot of explaining to do."

"Especially since they saw their dad grinding on you at the Autumnal Equinox Ball on TV."

Zoya blanched and visibly wilted at the thought of seeing Jefferson again. "He won't be there, will he?"

Katie laughed. "No way. We have zero contact. Though I might run into him a bit more when the kids get married, or when there is a baby on the way. But for now, he is blessedly in my rear-view mirror."

"Thank Lilith. I couldn't stand the man, and I wasn't even married to him."

"Did you really give him a micro penis?"

"I'd never lie about a micro penis, darling." A wicked grin broke out on her features, and Katie dissolved into a pile of giggles.

"You're an original. They broke the mold when they made you."

"They did." Obviously pleased by the compliment, Zoya added, "I like to think I am a crusader for feminine justice. Women get minimized and stepped on all the time. I'm just righting a few of the wrongs in my own special way."

"You can say that again."

Zoya glanced around the kitchen. "Now where does that woman hide the double boiler?"

Two

The Adapt4Heroes Foundation was bursting at the seams of the unassuming brick building it inhabited in downtown St. Pete's Beach. Since Rox had assumed the helm of the organization four years ago, it experienced exponential growth. She was proud of the foundation's upward trajectory and the lives she'd directly and indirectly impacted.

Currently, all twelve offices were filled to capacity, some of them shared, and even the storage room had been converted into a makeshift office for her administrative assistant, Keith. The board was pushing for a real estate acquisition to expand, and Rox's days were filled with scouting various locations when the agent could nail her down long enough to look.

She far preferred the other hands-on parts of the job where she was in the field, shoulder-to-shoulder with a veteran and his family and offering a hand to help them rebuild their lives after a devastating injury. Rox excelled in those tender, hopeless moments inside a hospital room with a service member whose entire world had been shattered in the span of a second.

After doing the work to put herself back together after the loss of her leg, she became a remarkable rehabilitation guide. When you'd walked a mile in a wounded veteran's boots, and experienced the same terror and loss yourself, it was easier to gain their trust and light a pathway to their new future. Soldiers were trained to follow their mentors into battle, and she could tap into that instinct. It was the juice that gave her life purpose, and she was driven by the mission of the foundation.

That morning, she arrived at the office with a smile on her face, renewed with fresh vigor, and couldn't wait to start the day. It was 0800, and she was sipping on a cup of coffee when Keith knocked softly at her office door.

"Come on in," she said, leaning back into her chair as she hoisted her mug up. "I was just finishing my coffee. Want a cup?"

"Coffee gopher is my job," Keith replied. He'd served in the National Guard and did volunteer work at the foundation until Rox snapped him up to manage the deluge of paperwork and travel arrangements that overwhelmed her as the foundation grew.

"I would respectfully disagree," Rox said as she reached for a mug and poured him a steaming cup. As a leader, she'd always approached the position with a desire to serve. She believed no task was too small, and keeping her team happy contributed to making them productive far more than domination tactics. Accepting her offer, Keith's pinched expression relaxed, and he rewarded her with a tight-lipped smile, reaching for the warm mug.

"Thank you." He took a small sip as he settled into his chair. His eyes darted around the room, and she couldn't help but notice the dark circles that were smudged underneath. Keith sat on the edge of the chair and jiggled his legs up and down, expelling tension. Rox tipped her head to the side, studying him, picking up on his anxiety.

"You seem a little on edge. Is everything okay at home?"

Keith raked his freshly shaven jawline with his fingers, letting out a sigh. "Alicia's meds are now over a thousand dollars out of pocket each month."

"Wow, that's a house payment," Rox exclaimed. She drummed her fingers on the desk as she chewed on a solution.

"She doesn't do as well on the generic," he offered as he took another sip.

"God, it makes me sick when an insurance company thinks they should make these kinds of critical care decisions."

"It's big business," he admitted. "There isn't much we can do. We've exhausted the appeals process."

"Bullshit!" Rox pounded her fist on the desk for emphasis. "There's got to be something we can do." She sat back in her chair and glanced around the room before lurching forward, snapping her fingers, and shooting him a finger gun. "I got it! We evaluate the health plan annually. I am going to personally see that we find a better plan with name-brand pharmaceutical coverage. Or maybe I can negotiate with the board to include a pre-tax match on contributions to your flex account?" She was spit-balling solutions on the fly, thinking out loud.

"You would do that?"

"Of course." She leaned closer to him, her warm eyes crinkling in the corners. "Besides, I need all your brain cells reserved for the work we're doing for the foundation. Alicia deserves to feel better, and you deserve some peace of mind." His eyes became watery and darted to the side to hide.

"That would be a huge burden off my shoulders." Keith bit back the emotion that threatened to overwhelm him. "Thank you."

"Make a note in my calendar before next month's quarterly review. I find it's best to ease the board into decisions like these."

"Will do."

"Anything else I need to know?"

"I don't think so," Keith said as he opened his laptop and clicked on the calendar. "You've got a packed schedule, as usual. There's the golf event on Wednesday, and we've secured the venue for the annual fundraiser. They want to talk menu as soon as possible." He scrolled further down, engrossed in the screen. "The contractors are wrapping up modifications on three residences this week, and your presence has been requested at the VA Hospital on Friday. A patient is being fitted for his first prosthetic."

Rox nodded solemnly. "That's the most important task of the week." She glanced down at her own prosthetic, and all the emotions she felt the day she'd been fitted came rushing back. She'd been forced to accept a new normal and had struggled with it alone. When she joined the foundation, she made a vow never to let another serviceperson suffer the same fate.

"Well," Rox sat back in her chair, "looks like I need to cram a week's worth of office work into today."

"As usual." Keith gave her a weary smile. He stood to leave, and Rox pulled a sheath of receipts from a basket on her desk and placed them in his capable hands.

"Let me guess, you'd like me to file your expense report?"

"You know the drill." She grinned. "I manage the people, you manage the paper."

"You got it, boss."

———

Later that afternoon, the soft glow of a desk lamp on the corner of Rox's desk illuminated her determined expression as she sat in her office with a phone pressed to her ear. The fading sun cast shadows on the wall behind her as she tapped the pen in her hand in tune with the Muzak on the other end. She was grateful when a soft knock at the door gave her something else to focus on.

Seeing a familiar face, Rox smiled as she waved in one of her oldest friends and colleagues, Sergeant Major Samuel Williams. On the phone at her desk, she pressed the mute button and said, "These D-Bags got me on hold again." She offered him a sunny smile. They'd first met on deployment for Desert Storm when he was a critical member of the squad during her final mission. Saying yes to his offer to join the board at the Adapt4Heroes Foundation was a no-brainer.

Physically, not much had changed since they'd enlisted. He still wore the high and tight haircut he adopted right after basic, and the ironed creases in his dress khakis were still starched and ramrod straight, but his sandy blond temples were now gray.

"Do you have time to sign checks?" He sat down in the chair in front of her desk and made direct eye contact, speaking in a hushed tone. "Our net 30s are due." He laced his hands together on his lap, and relaxed capability oozed from him. It was one of the first traits she'd appreciated so long ago. In the face of terror, he had an iron will and remained cool-headed. Roxanne glanced over, gave him a quick nod while holding up one finger, and redirected her focus to the phone call.

"Listen closely." Rox's voice was steady, stretched drum-tight with determination. "We've got a veteran here who lost both his legs in service to our country," Rox paused to let that grim reality set in, then continued, her tone unwavering and her grip tightening on the phone in her hand. "And *now* he's confined to his own home because there's no wheelchair ramp. This is not about charity; it's about honoring the sacrifices he made. It's about restoring mobility and giving this exemplary soldier a better quality of life."

In front of her, Sam nodded in complete solidarity. His acknowledgment served to strengthen her resolve. She punched the speakerphone button, and the bureaucratic voice on the other end came through the speaker. It was cool and business-like veering toward dismissive. "We understand your concern, Colonel Sullivan, but there's a process we need to follow to qualify a service member for the Specially Adapted Housing Grant. It takes time, and we can't just make exceptions for one case."

Rox's jaw set, her frustration simmering beneath the surface. "You're adhering to a process that's so rigid it's failing those it's meant to serve!" She let the legitimate outrage she felt infuse passion into her voice. "This veteran doesn't have time to wait while we cut through bureaucratic red tape. He needs this ramp now. He needs a bathroom adapted to fit his needs *today*, not six months from now. What would you do if this was your son?"

There was a pause on the other end, a weighty silence that spoke volumes. Rox knew she had struck a chord, that she had managed to break through the callous veneer of this gatekeeper's indifference.

"Look," Rox's tone softened just a touch, her voice

now a blend of empathy and focused determination, "I know you're doing your job. But this isn't just about a ramp; it's about the values we stand for as a nation. It's about showing the world we take care of our own. So much has been taken from this man and his family. You and I can restore some semblance of dignity back to his life. He deserves that much."

She could almost hear the cogs turning in the government official's mind. She intimately knew the delicate dance he was required to engage in daily between protocols and compassion. It was a bureaucratic struggle, something Rox understood from her years of service.

"Let's be clear," Rox's voice took on a renewed edge, "I will not back down on this. I'll rally support, wrangle the media, and use every resource at my disposal at the Adapt4Heroes Foundation to shine a light on the plight of this family while they wait for the VA to do the right thing. They deserve more than our empty promises."

The line crackled for a moment, and then a sigh echoed through the receiver. "Fine, Colonel Sullivan. We'll make it happen. We'll expedite the process and allocate the resources for the wheelchair ramp and bathroom retrofit."

"See?" Roxanne leaned back in her chair with a grin on her face. Across from her, Sam raised a fist in shared triumph. "You made dreams come true today. How does it make you feel?" Rox grinned.

"Fantastic, ma'am," the voice said.

"I'll be in touch to make sure the project stays on track and the grant funds as expected. Thank you for your flexibility."

As the call ended, Rox exhaled slowly, her shoulders relaxing for the first time since she'd dialed the number.

"Nice job!" Samuel stood and thrust his hand out to her. "I knew the VA was no match for Ricochet!" He used Rox's nickname from her days at West Point when her stilted, obnoxious laugh got the attention of her superiors.

"No man ever is!" Rox agreed with a disarming smile. Over the course of the phone call, the bustling office at the foundation had emptied. Her assistant, Keith, popped his head in. "Is there anything else you need today, ma'am?"

"Actually, there is. I need you to stop calling me ma'am," Rox teased the man.

He shot her an embarrassed grin. "Can't help it. It's the way I was raised."

Sam piped in, razzing her, "Me too. It's a sign of respect for your elders."

"Shut it, Williams!" Rox didn't miss a beat. "I've only got a few years on you."

Keith crossed to the desk and handed her the black leather password journal and the monthly receipts all organized into neatly labeled file folders.

"Your expense report has been filed."

"You, sir, are a gentleman and a scholar." Rox tucked the black book into her top drawer, locking it inside. The file folders, she set on the corner of the desk.

"I'll file those for you first thing," Keith added.

"Thank you," Roxanne said before straightening up with a warm smile.

"We're going to have a cold one to celebrate a win. Want to join us?"

Keith declined. "Maybe some other time. I've got to get home to get dinner started."

"Come on, just one," Sam prodded. "Fifteen minutes isn't going to kill Alicia." Keith's jaw tightened, and he blanched at Sam's insensitive comment.

Rox shot Sam a look, and his cheeks pinked up. He cringed and quickly apologized, "Sorry."

"Stop busting his balls. At least he has someone waiting at home for him," Rox said. "You don't even have a cat."

"Cats are overrated." He shrugged off the insult with ease.

"Have a great night, Keith," Rox called as he offered her a wave, shut the door quietly behind him, and then left.

She glanced down at her watch. "It's close enough to beer thirty. Ready to celebrate?"

"Absolutely! I'll grab the checks and you get the beers. We'll make it a working celebration." He left the room and returned with a thick stack of invoices and white envelopes with windows.

She crossed the room to where a small refrigerator stood and pulled out two beers, popping the tops off and walking one over to Sam. He held his brown bottle out and clinked the neck of it against hers. "To Monty and

Peabody and the rest of the squad," she said and poured a little of the beer into the empty mug on her desk.

"Hooah!" they cheered together. In between sips, she scribbled her signature on the invoices and checks, grateful that each one meant securing significant resources to improve the lives of soldiers with whom she was deeply invested.

There wasn't a month that went by that she didn't remember the two men they'd both loved like brothers. She dedicated her work at the foundation to them. In her mind, they would live forever, and it was always a relief to be in the presence of Sam, who intimately understood what they'd been through and the significant loss they'd suffered.

Her short active duty history had left scars that cut deep, both physically and emotionally. As she sipped her beer, she glanced over at her best friend. She was grateful for Sam, for their friendship and mutual respect for each other that spanned decades. While there were always good and bad days, she acknowledged that at least she didn't have to walk through them alone. She always had Sam.

THREE

A few days later, Katie walked into the Starfish Bar and Grille and over to the table where Rox was scrolling on her phone with a pair of olive green reading glasses perched on the end of her nose. Seeing Katie approach, she promptly whipped them off and tucked them away into a black crossbody bag.

Rox stood up with an engaging grin and extended one open palm, offering her a seat in the booth across from her.

"I'm a hugger," Katie warned as she circled her arms around Rox, her shoulders tensing as she braced for the jolt that always accompanied skin-on-skin contact with her current assignment from Karma. She closed her eyes as vivid images filled her brain. A man dressed in battle fatigues carrying a much younger and bloodied Rox in his arms. She was unconscious and her eyes were closed. Then Katie heard popping from a spray of automatic gunfire, and it made her flinch and jerk away. Her eyes squinted as they adjusted to the saturated colors around her.

"You okay?" Rox appraised her with a concerned eye as she pulled back from the hug and leveled her gaze at Katie.

"Sorry." Katie laughed at herself as she turned away and sat in the booth. "I guess I shouldn't have had that last espresso!"

"No worries. I'm just glad we're finally sitting down and breaking bread together," Rox said with a warm, easy smile. "I've been waiting a long time for Tommy to find the right woman, and by the looks of it, he finally has."

Katie burst with pride and returned the compliment honestly. "Tom is a wonderful man. You did great work there."

"And Lauren has a good heart and a great head on her shoulders," Rox added.

"I'm happy to hear you say that!" Katie leaned in and confided, "I am so proud of the woman she's become."

"You should be. She's wonderful." Looking directly into Katie's eyes, she said, "Strong women raise strong women."

The sentiment tugged at Katie's heartstrings. "Thank you. Although I have to admit, strength has come later in life for me, but I appreciate you seeing it in Lauren."

Rox waggled one finger at Katie. "Not so fast! I see it in you, too," she softly added. "Look at us! A couple of four-star generals in the mothering department."

Katie chuckled as their server sidled up to the table, and Rox wasted no time getting right down to business. "I'd like a Blue Moon." She glanced over at Katie. "What would you like? The first round is on me."

"No. You can't do that!"

"I can! And I insist. Taking no for an answer is not my strong suit."

"Okay. Well, then… how about a pineapple vodka soda?"

Rox cut in before the waitress could leave. "And…" She pointed over to a table where two men in their early twenties wearing fatigues and combat boots were devouring chicken wings. "I'd like to take care of their tab. Here." She pulled her credit card out and handed it to the waitress.

"Do you want me to tell them you bought their lunch?"

"Nope." Rox's lips curled up in a secret smile. "Just thank them for their service."

Katie glanced over at the unsuspecting young men. One of them had obviously said something funny by the way the other one was chuckling. "That's really kind of you." Roxanne was proving to be a warm, generous woman, and Katie instantly liked her.

She shrugged off the compliment. "It's a family. Brotherhood isn't quite the right term. Damn those gender stereotypes!" she cursed with a grin. "But you catch my drift?"

"I do."

"The Army always takes care of our own."

"It's admirable." Katie smiled kindly and then made an awkward transition to bring the focus of the conversation back to Rox. "So, tell me more about yourself." Karma had given her a puzzle to solve, and she needed more details to put the pieces together.

Rox let out a half-snort, half-laugh. "That's the most boring topic on the planet! Next!" She banged her fist on the table for emphasis and let out another abrupt chortle that Katie couldn't help but join. She was rougher around the edges than the socialites Katie was surrounded by in Aura Cove, but she found Rox's honesty refreshing. It put Katie right at ease.

"You're too humble," Katie told her as the server dropped off their drinks and Rox's credit card.

"What do you want to know?" Rox asked, taking a long sip from her beer.

"Whatever you want to tell me." Katie didn't want to define the conversation with her own agenda. She already knew it was better to let Karma do the heavy lifting.

"I grew up an Army brat. My dad moved us all over the world from base to base, so I guess the Army is in my blood."

"I bet that was hard."

"It was, and it wasn't. I learned how to thrive in any environment and to enjoy every day like it was my last because someday it might be," she said wistfully, looking down at her bottle before her tone lowered and she admitted, "Female friendships took a hit, though."

"I bet." Katie took a sip of her fizzy cocktail.

"When you're the new girl in school every couple of years, it's hard to build lifelong bonds created when you grow up with your classmates since kindergarten. But it's all I've ever known." She brought the bottle to her lips and gulped it halfway down. "When I lost my leg in Desert Storm, I thought I lost everything." She picked at the label of the bottle in her hands. "The career I signed up for vanished, and I had to regroup. Man, that took a toll." She was lost in her own heavy thoughts for a moment.

"Starting over is hard," Katie commiserated. "I can't imagine what it would be like when you're physically missing a part of yourself, too."

Rox took another sip. "It's a battlefield all on its own. The loss of identity is crippling. Literally!" A halted, "Ha!" left her lips as she was amused by her own choice of words. Then she continued, "But it's like any loss. You go through the five stages of grief, and many times, PTSD takes hold and makes the journey back to yourself even more challenging. The silver lining in surviving all that bullshit is understanding. I can meet other veteran amputees on a level playing field. It helps when they see an officer who has climbed the mountain they are currently standing in front of. It builds instant camaraderie and trust. I love helping soldiers navigate their new challenges."

"So, in a way, you're still leading soldiers through battle—but it's their emotional wars," Katie remarked.

"Well said!" Rox mused, "I never looked at it like that!" She nodded, turning over Katie's words in her head. "I was one of the lucky ones. Since I'd graduated West Point and was firmly on the officer track before my injury, my rank was high enough that I was able to take on a support role on base. It allowed me to stay on and retire with a full military pension." She shifted in her seat. "And the other consolation prize was it gave me the opportunity to become a mother. Tommy was born almost two years later. He got a shot at a real life where we weren't moving around from base to base every few years." She offered Katie a curt nod. "Truth be told, losing my leg was hard on my marriage. I guess it was just another casualty of war. We thought having a baby would fix us. It didn't."

"I'm sorry to hear that." Katie reached forward to pat Rox's hand.

"I'm not," Rox shot back with a snorting laugh. "Not really the marrying kind over here, if you know what I mean! Tommy was the best product of our union. Few men like to be ordered around at home, and after being trained to lead soldiers into battle, I didn't know what to do with that energy. I couldn't turn it off, and it was the end of us. Garrett volunteered for deployments and didn't come home from his sixth one." Her voice cracked, and she averted her eyes.

"I'm so sorry for your loss."

"Tommy was the one who suffered," Rox said. "We

weren't a good match from the start, but it took me far too long to recognize it."

"We've walked down a similar road, it seems." Katie gave a tight-lipped smile. "I got divorced several months ago, and I'm still trying to figure out the ropes."

"You'll get there," Rox encouraged. "It helps to find your purpose."

"I totally agree." Since she'd discovered her true purpose in life was to help women get a Karmic rebalance, she felt more alive and driven than ever. "Lauren's father is a prominent defense attorney in St. Pete's Beach."

Rox snapped her fingers together. "Jefferson Beaumont! Of course, he was on a billboard I used to drive by every day on the freeway."

"Yeah." Katie laughed, wrinkling her nose. "Seeing his face larger than life plastered to a billboard you could zip by on the interstate was a bit much, but he's always loved the limelight. When I discovered he'd turned into a midlife crisis cliché by banging his twenty-something assistant, I had enough."

"Good for you!" Rox crowed. "It takes balls to leave after all those years. So many women decide to turn a blind eye and stay."

"It wasn't easy, but to be honest, I've been happier in the last year than I've ever been. I finally feel like I'm in the driver's seat of my own life instead of being a passenger forced on someone else's journey. It's been freeing, and I have learned so much about myself."

"Cheers to that!" Rox raised her bottle, and Katie clinked her glass against it.

"How long have you been retired? You're so young!" Katie exclaimed, eager to shift the focus back to Rox. She was rewarded with another burst of loud guffaws.

"You're too kind." Rox pursed her lips, making mental calculations. "Coming up on five years soon. God, I can't believe it's been that long," she said, taking another long sip of her beer. She set down the bottle and shivered. "Retirement is not for me. I floated for a year, gained twenty pounds, and watched everything worth watching on the streaming services, but I was miserable. When Sam reached out with the opportunity to be a crusader for our military veterans who have been wounded in battle, I jumped at it."

"Who's Sam?"

"He was one of the men in my squad during my deployment in Desert Storm. When I lost my leg, Sam saved my life and was awarded the Medal of Honor for his bravery, so when he asked me to interview for the CEO position at the Adapt4Heroes Foundation, I jumped at the chance to serve with him again."

"Wow." Katie was in shock. "Sounds like quite a hero."

"He's the real deal," Rox agreed. "When I say we go way back, it's legit. I'm talking all the way back to the sandbox. There isn't anything I wouldn't do for that man. He's closer to me than a brother. We've come up through the ranks together, and I've watched him excel and even outrank me."

"I bet that was hard to swallow."

"Not anymore." Rox shook her head. "I made my peace with my path years ago. I'm proud of him."

"That's incredible," Katie said. "Be sure to thank him for me. Because if he hadn't performed that heroic act, Tom wouldn't exist, and I wouldn't be sitting here today, enjoying your fabulous company."

"True story!" Rox nodded solemnly. "I thank God for him every day."

"No doubt," Katie gushed.

"Well, now that you know my entire life story, what's yours?"

Katie took another sip of her cocktail. "There's not much more to tell. My life is pretty low-key. You already know my grandmother owns Kandied Karma in Aura Cove. I've worked for her off and on for years." She paused for a moment, then added, "I spent the first half of my life taking care of my family, but now that my children are raised, the second act is unwritten. Now, I'm just trying to enjoy my life, spend time with my family, and help a few people along the way."

"Nothing wrong with that." Rox nodded.

"It's a beautiful life," Katie agreed and then couldn't resist adding, "Magical, you might even say."

"What a great outlook!" Rox said.

They shared a plate of raw oysters, and each ordered the shrimp fettuccine alfredo. When Katie left after their long lunch, she still wasn't any closer to answers. On her drive home, she went over the flashes she'd received already, but they were just too vague. Frustrated by the lack of progress toward understanding her assignment, she knew she'd have to be more patient and wait for the next steps of her mission to be revealed.

FOUR

At her beachfront home in Aura Cove, Katie nervously glanced down at her watch, checking the hour for the hundredth time in five minutes. "Looks like our special guest is running a little late," she explained to her family gathered in the dining room. The long wooden table was set with crystal, candles, and a gorgeous bouquet of spring flowers, including lush peonies and sunny daffodils. Seated in chairs waiting for the guest of honor to appear were Katie's adult children, Lauren, Beckett, and Callie. Also seated were Yuli, Kristina and David, and her best friend Frankie.

"The table is extra fancy tonight. What's the occasion?" Lauren asked, and Katie felt her cheeks redden slightly. She had pulled out all the stops to impress Zoya but hadn't realized she'd gone overboard until Lauren noticed.

A frustrated Yuli pulled out the gold pocket watch

she kept on a long chain suspended from her neck, opened it, and grumbled under her breath. "She gets five more minutes."

"That's fair," Katie conceded.

"Who gets five more minutes?" Lauren persisted, her curiosity piqued.

Before Katie could answer, the doorbell rang and saved her from coming up with a convoluted explanation. She crossed to the front door and opened it wide, taking in a magnificently dressed Zoya. Her driver, Higgins, was still seated in the car. "You can invite your driver in. He doesn't have to sit out there and wait. We have plenty of food," Katie offered.

"Don't get too chummy with the help, darling. Boundaries are important for all relationships."

Zoya's long white hair cascaded down her back, wild and free. She was dressed in a floor-length silver gown with a green jacket that enhanced the color of her enormous eyes. Katie glanced down at her basic cotton maxi dress, wondering if she should have put more effort into her appearance. There were three new dresses with the tags still on them sitting in the back of her closet, and she kicked herself for not putting one on.

"Don't wait for a special occasion to wear a new dress. Being alive is a special occasion!" Zoya exclaimed with a well-timed wink, reading her mind. "Shall we?" She stepped into the entryway and then followed Katie to the table. All eyes shifted to Zoya, and a confused hush fell over the guests at the table.

"Wait. Is that?" Beckett was the first one to gather

his wits enough about him to put words together. Around the table, every mouth fell open in shock as she neared. He turned to his sisters, and they exchanged a flurry of heated whispers.

"Are you… Ana Castanova?"

A warm smile lit up Zoya's face. "Guilty as charged."

"How do you know our mom?" Callie asked, clearly in shock with a celebrity in their midst.

"Yuli and I go way back."

"What?" Beckett glanced over at Yuli. "You never mentioned knowing Ana Castanova."

"You never asked." Yuli shrugged. "Besides, I have many celebrity clients. I didn't feel she was important enough to name." Undeterred by the not-so-subtle dig, Zoya went on.

"Kandied Karma truffles have been a staple at all of my fundraisers for years. Your mother spoke so highly of you all during my last visit that I simply had to come meet you in person."

Beckett and Callie ate up the explanation with a spoon, while a wary Lauren struggled to swallow it. She wrinkled her nose in disgust. "I think you're all forgetting she's the one who broke Dad's heart."

"I think *you're* forgetting he was stepping out on Mom before their divorce was final," Beckett reasoned, his allegiance always to his mother, and it made Katie's heart squeeze.

Like a dog with a bone, Lauren would not let it go.

"You led him on with that obnoxious yellow Ferrari." She folded her arms across her chest and narrowed her eyes on Zoya as Katie offered Zoya her seat at the head of the table. Katie pivoted to pull out the chair next to her and settled on it as an uncomfortable silence stretched out.

Zoya broke it and shrugged off Lauren's anger. "I would argue he made out like a bandit. How many men get a parting gift of that caliber after knowing a woman only a few weeks?"

"She's got a point there, Lauren," Beckett said. "I'd kill for a whip like that." He turned to Ana and lowered his voice to a much deeper register, attempting to inject bold sexiness, and asked, "Tell me, Ms. Castanova, are you attracted to *younger* men?" He leaned in with an engaging grin, arching his eyebrows at her playfully, and delivered a roguish wink that made Zoya chuckle.

Katie choked on the wine she was sipping and a barking cough caught in her throat.

"Gross, B!" Frankie said, jumping in to save the day. "You're punching way above your weight. First, you take a run at Marisa, and now, Ana Castanova? I appreciate the unfettered confidence of youth, but come on, dude!"

His cheeks pinked up, and he averted his eyes self-consciously.

"What happened with Marisa, anyway?" Frankie asked.

He'd fallen hard and fast for Marisa, the estranged

wife of a mafioso who invaded Katie's home months ago. The beautiful young woman had been her first assignment from Karma and had spent some time recovering at Katie's beach house after their escape. Her tender-hearted son had gotten his heart broken recently when Marisa moved out and decided to make a fresh start without him.

Katie cocked her head and shot Frankie a death glare that silenced her further questions. She knew the loss still stung and wanted to save Beckett from further embarrassment.

"Sorry," Frankie mumbled and reached for her glass.

Eager to change the tone of the evening, Katie declared, "Now that the guest of honor has arrived, let's eat!" She reached forward for the platter of short ribs and pot roast she'd been simmering together all day. The meat fell apart as it hit her plate, and she handed the platter to Callie. Zoya scooped minuscule servings of velvety smooth mashed potatoes and tender slices of roast onto her plate and handed the bowl to Katie.

After placing her napkin on her lap, Zoya speared a sliver of beef with her fork and put it into her mouth. "Utterly divine," she remarked, and Katie was amused by the surprised expression that settled on her face.

"It's Yuli's recipe," Katie offered, eager to give credit where it was due.

"You always make the best pot roast, Mom," Kristina gushed, weighing in.

"I'm sure it's not up to the caliber of your personal

chef." Yuli sniffed, yet she was secretly pleased by her praise.

"Well, yes. While I do employ a Michelin-starred chef at my personal residence, I would hold this dish to the same standard. It's sublime." She speared up another forkful of the tender beef.

Yuli's face softened from the permanent scowl that seemed to fill it when Zoya was around.

"A Michelin-starred chef?" David remarked, stunned by the admission. "You have a personal chef?"

"He does the bulk of the meal planning and preparation, but he also has other various personal duties to perform."

"Wow." David was in such shock, and Katie hoped he wouldn't feel compelled to dig deeper into the definition of personal duties. She felt relief, then embarrassment, flood in when he moved straight to the financials.

"If you don't mind me asking, what does that run you?"

Katie's cheeks pinked up. "Dad! That's none of our business."

"Jeez, Louise!" David said. "I'm sorry if I offended you. I was just curious."

"Hmm. I wish I could remember," Zoya answered, taking another bite and crossing her fork and dinner knife on the plate.

"I *wish* I was wealthy enough to have a personal chef on payroll and not worry about how much it cost me!" David laughed. "We are clearly living on two different planets."

To her credit, Zoya only nodded at the interaction.

"Your life is so glamorous," Callie's voice sounded dreamy, and she had stars in her eyes. "What's it like?"

Getting caught up in his sister's excitement, Beckett added, "Your parties at the compound are insane! Do you personally know Marshmello?"

"Let's suffice it to say that when I call, his people always answer," she confirmed, clearly enjoying the starstruck responses she was getting from them. "I have an idea. The Spring Equinox Ball is coming in a few weeks. How would you all like to be added to the guest list?" She was being magnanimous, and every person at the table, with the exceptions of Yuli and David, was under her spell.

"Seriously?" Beckett exclaimed with a grin.

"I'd be delighted to host you all for the weekend."

"For sure!" Callie said. "I could use a break to cut loose before finals."

"Finals, huh? What are you studying?" Zoya asked, surprising Katie by taking an interest in Callie's life.

"Animation and Movie Design, with a minor in Business Management," Callie said. "The double major has been a killer."

"But you're in the home stretch now!" Katie said.

"She almost made the Dean's List last quarter," Kristina offered. "She works so hard."

"Grandma, almost doesn't count," Callie admitted. She'd had to fight her way through the rigorous program. "I've been too focused on my education and haven't had enough fun," Callie cried. "With graduation in a few months, I'm running out of time!"

"I've always believed bad decisions make the best stories," Zoya said, dabbing the corners of her lips with the cloth napkin before setting it beside the plate.

"Yeah, they do!" Beckett called in agreement, nodding his head up and down enthusiastically.

"Someday, when we get to know each other a little better, I'll have to share a few of mine."

Katie cleared her throat in a warning to Zoya and met her gaze, begging her to change the subject. She could hear the niggle of thoughts from all the people surrounding her cueing up louder, and she stilled her mind against them. When they hissed and faded away into silence, she heaved a sigh of relief, grateful she'd finally learned to tune them out. When it came to Beckett's escapades, sexual and otherwise, she preferred to remain in the dark.

Zoya turned toward Callie and shot her a disarming grin. "In the spirit of fun, rebirth, and renewal, you must come to the ball. Callie, this might be your last chance to cut loose before graduation." She turned to the rest of the table. "What say you?"

David cut in, "In light of what transpired at the last one, I am sure you can understand why we don't think it's the best idea." He turned to his daughter. "Right, Katie?"

"I don't know," she considered. It *was* dangerous for the kids to be at the compound, but not in the way David expected. The idea of her supernatural world and her children's ordin one colliding was becoming too close for comfort. "He might have a point."

"Come on, Grandpa," Callie begged. "Mom? This is a once-in-a-lifetime opportunity."

"I don't want to see my grandchildren become tabloid fodder," David explained.

"We'll be on our best behavior," Beckett promised. "So boring any footage of us will be relegated to the cutting room floor."

"They *are* adults, Dad. It's not our decision," Katie said, and Callie's eyes lit up with excitement. Lauren was still holding out.

"I don't have anything to wear," Lauren mumbled, wary of the woman who had a sketchy history with her father.

"That's easy. I'll make some calls to some of my favorite designers and you'll have your pick. I'll even bring in your very own glam squad to make sure your hair and makeup are flawless."

Katie could see Lauren coming around despite her misgivings. The corners of her mouth quirked up at the mention of the glam squad. "Can I bring Tom?"

"Of course," Zoya answered.

"Okay." She finally relented, and Zoya clapped her hands together. "Yuli? Are you in? Maybe you can teach my chef a thing or two."

"I guess." She added, "If only to keep an eye on things."

"Kristina? David?"

"We're going to pass. Witnessing the grandkids sow their wild oats is not very appealing to us," David answered for them both, his nose wrinkling in distaste. "Besides, we're happiest at home and in bed by eight-thirty."

"Frankie?"

"Damn skippy! A night of hobnobbing with celebrities is right up my alley and I wouldn't miss it for the world. Can I bring my Harry Willey?"

Zoya's eyebrows arched up. "Excuse me, your what?"

"My guy, Harry Willey."

Zoya chuckled despite herself. "Of course. I'm sure he'll fit right in with all the other harry willies in attendance." Her eyes glittered in amusement as she chuckled at her own joke.

She got to her feet and prepared to leave. "Then it's settled. I'll send the plane for you. Your mother can inform you of the travel arrangements."

"Thank you for the invitation!" Beckett was thrilled at the prospect and was already mentally packing his suitcase. "I'm going to need to get a couple of new banana hammocks in an array of vibrant colors. You know, for the ladies."

"Nope!" Katie winced, covering her eyes. The idea of Beckett rocking a thong poolside made her stomach queasy. "Just nope, nope, nope!" She shook her head in protest. "That's a vision I can never unsee!" She waved her index finger at her children one by one. "Please make sure your bathing suits cover your cheeks, all of you!"

"You can't tell me what to do!" Frankie said in mock outrage. "You aren't my mother!"

"The rule still stands!" Katie said. "Yuli too!"

Yuli threw her head back and roared with laughter at the very idea. "Wouldn't that be a sight?"

FIVE

The next morning, Katie was at Kandied Karma and had just settled down after the morning commuter rush. She was in the kitchen washing dishes when a woman walked in the back door.

"Sorry, ma'am, the customer entrance is in the front," Katie informed, as both she and Yuli regarded the woman with confusion. She was dressed in retiree wear—a flowing linen bohemian skirt and a layered tank and cardigan with Birkenstocks on her feet. Her hair was gathered under the wide brim of a sun hat, and her enormous sunglasses covered most of her face.

"It's me," Zoya remarked as she pulled off the hat and the glasses at the same time. "Ta-Da!"

"Why are you wearing that get-up?" Katie asked.

Yuli chuckled. "Because her highness wants to mingle amongst the common folk undetected."

Zoya rolled her eyes and walked over to where the Verity Oil had been simmering. She pulled the lid off the pot and swiped a spoon down into the liquid to test the consistency. Curious, Katie walked closer.

"How do you know when it's done?"

"It's as thick as maple syrup," Zoya answered, "and it smells like an apothecary."

"What does an apothecary smell like?" Katie asked.

"Like laurel…"

"…and licorice," Yuli added, answering her question in unison with Zoya.

"Look at you two finishing each other's sentences!" Katie grinned as she scooped up her thick white hair in one fist and leaned over the pot to take a whiff.

"It's peppery, and I can detect a hint of nutmeg, too," Katie remarked.

Zoya's eyebrows rose in response. "Very good. New Yayas rarely have the ability to distill the more difficult olfactory markers with such conciseness."

Katie felt her heart swell with pride at the compliment.

"She's gaining powers and abilities at remarkable speed," Yuli offered.

Interested, Zoya's discerning eyes leveled on Katie's. "Tell me."

"Well, retrocognition came first." Katie explained, "On my birthday, I received flashes of past events from skin-on-skin contact with Jeff. Next, I started noticing auras around people. Color waves that would smudge and shift, affected by their emotions. Finally, when I was held hostage, I started to hear thoughts from the people around me and saw glimpses of possible future outcomes."

"Precognition," Yuli jumped in, giving the ability its proper name. The long list compiled in such a short time filled her with awe. "When you tally them together like this…"

Even Zoya was stunned, "…your powers are revealing themselves with remarkable speed."

Katie gulped. "Is that a good thing?"

"It's definitely a *thing*. Whether or not it proves to be good will be revealed later," Yuli explained.

Out in the shop, the bell jingled and Katie glanced through the small window in the door to see Oz walking in with his Pomeranian, Shasta, and a backpack. He had an extra spring in his step, and his buoyant mood was infectious.

"Want to see if that disguise of yours is any good?" Katie offered. "You have to meet Oz. He's my next-door neighbor. Great guy."

"Well…" Zoya dragged out the word, wincing as she drew in a breath between her tightened lips.

Yuli chimed in, "That's right, you introduced yourself to him already as the dog walker." With newfound glee at the obvious faux pas, she continued, "How about we make this interesting? If you can interact with him without detection *and* without resorting to magic, then I will…" She paused, lost in thought, trying to come up with an attractive offering.

Zoya snapped her fingers together. "I've got it! If I win, you have to spend an hour in my glam chamber at the compound to get rid of that nasty eleven that has been permanently carved into your forehead." Her eyes sparkled and shimmered with barely concealed mirth.

Yuli's lips turned down in a frown, and she rolled her eyes. "It is always about the superficial with you, but fine." She thought it over, and a knowing smile curved her lips and made her eyes twinkle. "And... if *you* lose, you'll have to work a full Saturday shift behind the counter at Kandied Karma," she added with a self-satisfied grin.

"It's a bet!"

She thrust out her hand and Zoya presented hers just as confidently, and they pumped up and down to seal the deal. Their feisty, competitive natures made Katie chuckle.

"Off you go now!" Yuli said with a grin and then pulled another tray of truffles out as they all walked out into the front of the store to greet Oz. Zoya grabbed her sun hat on the way. "No sunglasses!" Yuli called out as if she had eyes in the back of her head. Zoya grumbled but left them behind.

"Oz! How have you been, my friend?" Katie asked.

"Fantastic!" he answered as Yuli closed in.

"Good to see you!" Yuli said with a smile. "I'd like to introduce you to our friend, Esther Birch."

Zoya tugged on the front of her sun hat and extended a hand. "Cheerio, old chap! Nice to meet you." Katie detected a hint of an awful British accent and had to cover her mouth with her hand to hide her amusement.

All their eyes shifted to Oz as his head quirked to the side, taking in the woman.

"There's…"

"Yes?" Yuli encouraged, her eyes sparkling.

"Something familiar…" he added, his eyes boring into her. "Have we met?"

"What do you have there?" Zoya asked, pointing to his backpack, quickly changing the subject, hoping it would distract him.

Still trying to figure it out, Katie saw his forehead furrow into deep lines for a moment before turning back to answer her question. "I just published my latest podcast episode." He unzipped his backpack, pulled out his laptop, and set it down on the table.

"Podcast, you say?" Zoya asked again, feeling vindicated he wasn't able to put the pieces together, quickly veering toward gloating. She relied on the fact that whenever you asked a man about himself, he was always happy to become the focus. She was convinced she had this in the bag.

"Jimmie and I went to the El Conquistador again, and we made contact with a spirit!"

"Fascinating!" Zoya said, egging him on.

"Eureka! That's it!" He snapped his fingers and leaned closer to Zoya. "You remind me of Katie's dog walker." He reached out to tug up the brim of Zoya's hat, and she slapped his hand away. The man's cheeks reddened, and he laced his hands together in front of his stomach to prevent the urge to reach out again. "I only met her once, but I'm pretty sure she was wearing a disguise." He leaned closer to Zoya, narrowing his eyes.

"Dammit!" Zoya muttered under her breath, and then with one hand pushed Oz down into a chair and snapped her fingers. Gold sparks shot from her palms to him, and his head dropped to his chest as he went unconscious.

Yuli punched one thick fist into the air and shimmied her hips in a celebratory jig. "Victory tastes so sweet!"

"Well, savor the flavor, darling, because it's the last time you'll ever taste it," Zoya grumbled as she rubbed her palms together and pressed them out toward Oz. The golden light shot right through his closed eyes. She waved her hands up three times, and his head popped up and he opened his eyes and stretched.

"I'm sorry. Did I doze off?" he asked, confused and embarrassed.

"No worries," Yuli said, tapping on the open laptop to remind him. "You were going to share your new podcast."

"Yes!" he enthused, picking up right where he left off, at first ignoring Zoya completely, then seeing an unfamiliar face, he introduced himself.

"Hi there!" Oz offered his hand. "I'm Oz, and you're?"

"Filled with contempt," Zoya mumbled with a scowl and then forced herself to smile at the man. "Esther Birch."

"Nice to meet you, Esther," he said. Katie waited for

recognition, but instead, a blank, neutral expression settled on his features.

The evidence of magic filled her with awe and reverence, and she was still blown away whenever she witnessed it unfold in her real life. But there was another feeling now accompanying it. Guilt. She'd always been a live-and-let-live person, but she was starting to see that magic was crossing lines she'd long drawn in the sand. Here was another example of using supernatural abilities to control the outcome and reality of an ordin, and it made her uncomfortable. It seemed on the cusp of godlike power, and she shuddered, thinking about all the ways it could go wrong if placed in the wrong hands.

He pressed play on the screen as the women gathered around the table to listen.

Melodramatic Intro Music Fades In

Oz: Welcome, dear listeners, to our inaugural episode of "Seven Minute Ghost Stories." I'm your host, Oz. In this chilling installment, we delve into a ghostly tale of darkness and desperation, where the ocean's furious embrace hides secrets that refuse to be buried.

Sound of the Ocean's Roar

Oz: Our journey takes place at The El Conquistador, one of the oldest hotels in St. Pete's Beach, Florida. It stands as a sentinel on the shoreline of the Gulf of

Mexico, its timeworn walls containing the secrets of a heinous crime committed over a century ago.

Since its inception, the El Conquistador has been a playground for the wealthy, catering to the affluent and celebrities. The ultimate in luxury, its opulent suites were only associated with relaxation and merriment, but its reputation was tainted when it became the scene of an unthinkable tragedy. In 1921, a young woman's naked body washed up on the hotel's private shoreline. Upon further investigation, it was determined the woman was a guest at the hotel and was staying with her husband, a highly decorated colonel from World War I.

Eerie Battle Sound Effects in Background. Oz's Voice Deepens to a More Theatrical Tone.

Oz: What happened to Isabelle Cartright? How did she end up on the shore of the gulf when, by all accounts, she was excited to be on holiday with her husband? We struck out to unravel a mystery that has eluded justice for decades. Armed with a friend's top-of-the-line ghost hunting equipment, we entered Room 313, the room Isabelle Cartright shared with her husband, Colonel Nathaniel Cartright. It was the last place she would ever rest her head. Once inside, I found it hard to breathe. There is a heaviness that engulfs you, and the air in the suite has a coppery scent.

Sound of Static and Whispering

Oz: We settled inside Room 313 and activated the EVP recorder, and it's red light cast an eerie glow in the low light of early evening. Hoping to record our interactions with any entities in the room, and not knowing what to expect, I tried to keep an open mind. As we introduced ourselves, the sound of a woman's voice emerged from the white noise and static—at first it was but a whisper, a haunting rasp that called out the name, "Isabelle." Goosebumps prickled my skin, and the atmosphere grew electric with anticipation.

Crackling Static Sound

Oz: Next, the electromagnetic field meter on the desk roared to life, and its lights began to flash erratically. The temperature in the room dropped, and a chilling sea breeze sent shivers down my spine. Pushing past the increasing terror, I clutched a Y-shaped dowsing rod in my hand, and when it twitched, I felt the gathering of energy and let it pull me to a mirror affixed to a bureau. Its shiny surface distorted like a portal into another realm.

In the reflection, I glimpsed a jagged, spectral figure – with hollow dark eyes that seemed to pierce through my soul. Tendrils of panic unfurled in my belly as my eyes drank in the essence of a man consumed by darkness. I felt a knot of dread uncoiling and tightness clawing at my throat. The mirror became a portal to the past and painted a nightmarish tableau of love twisted into hatred. The gruesome scene was reenacted like a film noir, and I watched in horror as the tragedy unfolded, and his hands encircled the throat of his beloved. He trembled with rage, staring deep into her eyes, as he choked the life from her body. Then he collapsed on the ground gasping next to her pale corpse.

Sound of a Muffled Scream

The next reflection was a vision of the Colonel's shadowy figure hidden in darkness. He gathered up Isabelle's slack remains and, in the middle of the night, after rowing her out into the ocean in a dinghy, he placed her corpse in its watery resting place.

Haunting Music over Splashes Intensifies

Oz: The dowsing rod trembled as I confronted the spirit's culpability in Isabelle's death.

Rapidly Increasing Heartbeat Sound Effect

Oz: My heart raced as the room closed in on me, and I felt the entity's anger rise. It compelled Jimmie to shout, "I implore you to release the spirit of Isabelle Cartright!" In the warped mirror, the Colonel opened his mouth to scream. "Colonel Cartwright, release Isabelle's spirit at once. Entity, remove your attachment to this place and release your stranglehold on the past."

Suspenseful Music Swells

Oz: (In barely a whisper) And then the walls started to throb around us as the oppressive energy reached a fevered pitch. In the mirror, the spirit shrieked. The mirror shattered, and in its web of cracks, we saw the Colonel's figure collapse into itself like a defeated shadow, then dissipate into the abyss. The room fell silent, and the weighted feeling lifted from my chest as the oppressive atmosphere drifted away like the aftermath of a tropical storm. My hands trembled as I switched off the ghost hunting equipment. An hour later, we emerged from Room 313, still haunted by the darkness we had encountered, but relieved the readings on the electrometer had lowered significantly. Jimmie was certain Isabelle Cartright's soul had been released during our encounter. As for the Colonel? We weren't as sympathetic to his spiritual imprisonment.

Atmospheric Sound Effects

Oz: Our bizarre conference with the two entities left me curious. It was such a surreal experience that, when I got back home, I decided to dig a little deeper and see if I could find any records about what happened next. It led me to the St. Pete Public library where a research librarian named Maude helped me put the remaining pieces of this sordid tale together.

A Ticking Time Bomb

Oz: One year later, the Colonel checked himself

back into the El Conquistador, and as you probably guessed, into Room 313. By all accounts, he'd moved on with his life. He was dating a local woman and was often in the public eye, photographed mingling with heads of government and military officials. Although he was questioned, he was never a suspect in the disappearance of his beloved wife, Isabelle. On the Anniversary of her death, inside Room 313, he poured himself a drink and there were reportedly loud sounds of wailing coming from the room. Guests reported the disturbance and the authorities were called to investigate.

Old-Time Police Sirens

Oz: When police broke through the door, they discovered the Colonel was dead. His naked body was sprawled out on the bed, and the word 'liar' was written on the mirror in red lipstick. The most peculiar clue as to what transpired was a glass tumbler resting on the nightstand. When it was tested, it was found to have traces of tetrodotoxin, a substance that is deadly to humans and is up to 1,200 times more toxic than cyanide. A substance that can only be found... in the ocean.

Another Crash of Waves on the Shore

Oz: How did it get in the glass? Was it Isabelle

exacting her revenge from her watery grave? That, my friends, is a mystery that remains unsolved to this day.

Oz: Dear listeners, this encounter shattered any illusions I had about the supernatural. It was my first foray into the earthly bonds with the afterlife, but I assure you it won't be my last. As I reflect upon this chilling tale, I'm reminded that some crimes are too heinous to be forgotten, too dark to be swept away by the passage of time, and that the desire for justice is eternal.

Reflective Pause

Oz: We may never have all the answers, and some mysteries are destined to remain unsolved. But in shedding light on a few of these dark corners of history, we honor the victims; we bring them the justice they deserve, and we remind ourselves of the thin veil that separates the living from the dead.

Outro Music Begins

Oz: Thank you for joining me on this journey into the unknown. Until next time, stay curious, stay vigilant, and remember that the past is never truly silent. When given the chance, the truth will prevail, and even when buried in the depths of the ocean, it will always find its way to the surface. This is Oz, signing off.

Outro Music Fades Out. A series of legal disclaimers

*plays. Seven Minute Ghost Stories assumes no
responsibility or liability for any errors or omissions in
the content of this podcast. The information contained in
this podcast is provided on an "as is" basis with no
guarantees of completeness, accuracy, usefulness, or
timeliness and is for entertainment purposes only.*

Oz reached out and shut the laptop with a satisfied grin on his face.

"Wow! It's your best podcast yet. Great editing!" Katie added, "And the sound effects really kicked it up a notch."

"Jimmie's got a bag full of tricks," Oz revealed. "It was the most surreal experience of my life. I still get goosebumps thinking about it!" He turned to Zoya and asked, "What did you think, Esther?"

"Absolutely riveting," Zoya deadpanned, the sarcasm so thick Katie had to turn away to hide her laughter.

"I might have embellished it a little," Oz admitted, "for dramatic effect. Was it too much?"

"No way!" Zoya said, her words dripping with false encouragement. "You, my good man, set a soul free!"

He waffled back and forth under the weight of her heady praise. "I don't know if it was really her or not."

"But you don't know it wasn't!" Zoya smiled, really trying to convince Oz he'd made contact with the long-lost spirit of Isabelle Cartright. "What an ending! Hearing the Colonel get his just dessert warms the cockles of my revenge-thirsty heart."

Oz's bushy eyebrows danced up his forehead. "I guess that's one way to look at it."

"Just goes to show you that when a man puts on a military uniform, he can get away with murder!" Zoya declared clearly getting swept away due to her own biases against powerful men.

"It was a different time. Now, with forensics and DNA, it would be much more difficult to get away with a homicide, but back before all that technology was available, it was easier to escape detection. Especially if you were an attractive, wealthy, and highly decorated war hero with friends in high places," Oz explained.

"The military draws two personality types—those consumed by a need for power and those who truly want to serve," Yuli said.

Katie considered her bold statement, already classifying Rox as the latter.

Zoya huffed, "I disagree. The uniform is about power and domination, pure and simple." She'd learned that lesson as a teenager at the hands of her father's military friends in Ukraine.

"Not always," Katie offered. "Tom's mother was a career military woman and has dedicated her retirement to serving at the Adapt4Heroes Foundation."

"Are you talking about Rox Sullivan?" Oz asked.

"You know her?" Katie was surprised.

"Everyone knows Rox. She's the real deal. The Adapt4Heroes Foundation is what it is because of her dedication."

"See?" Katie said to Zoya, trying to prove her point.

"She's about empowerment and rehabilitation. Rox is a fine example of living an exemplary military life of service."

"I'll be the judge of that," Zoya muttered.

"Such a cynical outlook," Yuli groused, and Zoya's eyes flashed a warning.

"If she checks out, she's in the minority," Zoya conceded. "I believe there are far more power-hungry predators hiding in plain sight behind the uniform."

"Some of them are." Oz tried to explain, "In any position of power, there are a few rotten apples."

"Rotten apples?" Zoya was flummoxed and huffed her frustration.

"Settle down, Esther," Yuli said pointedly, not wanting to rouse Oz's suspicion further and draw attention to their latest assignment. Changing the subject, she turned to him and asked, "The usual?"

"You know me well." Oz grinned. Katie packaged up his orange caramels and chocolate-covered espresso beans and handed the package to him with a smile, while Zoya slipped out the door undetected. She knew exactly what she needed to do next.

Six

Zoya smoothed her white hair and adjusted the vintage Valentino scarf knotted around her neck, exuding her typical air of overconfidence. She looked out the window of her town car at the brick building standing tall against the backdrop of the setting sun. Its sweeping windows reflected the final golden rays back down to the concrete sidewalk below. She knocked on the glass of the window, and seconds later, Higgins opened the door and she stepped out. While the heels of her leather boots clicked on the sidewalk as she strode to the front entrance, she hemmed and hawed over whether she should have been more forthcoming with Yuli and Katie about her plan. She'd been a solo act for decades, but to please the coven, she knew she had to change her tactics. Would it have helped build the trust and bridge the divide that still existed in the mortal coven if she'd clued them in? Maybe.

It appeared her granddaughter's ability to hold grudges had become as legendary as her own, and Zoya took a small measure of pride in that fact. Mere words would not sway Yuli; she was a woman of principles. Not the same principles that Zoya led her life by, but principals just the same.

She pushed the rest of her thoughts away to focus on the task at hand. The glass door was emblazoned with the Adapt4Heroes Foundation logo. She took a deep breath, and with a gloved hand, pulled it open. Once inside, she was greeted by the soft hum of hushed conversations and typical ambient office noise. Following the sounds, she entered the reception area. A gangly man sporting a crew cut manned the front desk. He stood, and when he walked around the desk to greet her, she glimpsed metal. The sun pouring through the window reflected off his prosthetic leg.

"Can I help you, ma'am?"

"Ma'am?" she asked with a disarming grin. "That's absolutely dreadful." She paused, then got right to it. "I'm looking for Rox Sullivan."

"Do you have an appointment?"

"I do not." She opened her handbag, pulled out a card, and handed it over to the man. "But she might want to make an exception." Seeing the name Ana Castanova on the front of it, his demeanor instantly shifted.

"Can I offer you something to drink?"

"No, thank you," she said, enjoying watching him flit around anxiously trying to please her.

"Rox is at a golf outing, but her right-hand man is here. I am sure he would love to meet you. If you want to take a seat, I'll let Sam know you're waiting."

"Fantastic." She muttered as disappointment set in, realizing this impromptu visit was proving to be a bust.

He disappeared behind the desk, and Zoya heard him murmur into the phone, "You're never going to believe this. Ana Castanova is in reception."

She didn't have to wait long. A handsome man strode confidently into the reception area and flashed her a grin that wiped twenty years from his features. Still in fantastic shape, Zoya appraised the man standing in front of her. With wide shoulders, rugged charm, and meticulously groomed, he was conventionally attractive. He had the air of a man who had seen depravity and human suffering in war-torn countries and had survived. There was a depth to him that most men lacked. Zoya extended her hand and shook his.

"Sergeant Major Samuel Williams, at your service." He wrapped her gloved hands in his and then pulled back to offer her a corny salute that he surprisingly pulled off as endearing. A deep dimple in his left cheek peeked out when he grinned and made Zoya's heart skip a beat. He had charisma, and she steeled herself against it, focusing on the task at hand.

"Let's go to my office," he offered as he led her down a hallway. Small offices branched out on either side of it, each filled with people working the last hour of their shifts.

"I didn't realize the organization was so robust," she acknowledged.

"We're the fastest growing non-profit in Florida," Sam stated with obvious pride as he turned into his expansive office and offered her a seat across from his well-appointed desk. He steepled his fingers together and regarded her with warm eyes. "What brings you to the Adapt4Heroes Foundation today, Ms. Castanova?" He barely got the question out of his mouth before his nervous energy peaked and his demeanor skewed boyish. Letting out a nervous laugh, he explained, "I'm sorry, but I'm going to need another minute. We don't get very many celebrities of your caliber around here, and I am a bit tongue-tied." She cocked her head at him, briefly distracted by the idea of his tongue, then shook her head to clear it. She watched him struggle to maintain eye contact, and it amused her. His gaze dipped down to her cleavage then back up more than once.

She grinned, watching him fawn all over himself, and wallowed in the power she lorded over his more basic instincts. "I don't know if you're aware," she batted her thick eyelashes at him to disarm him further, "but I fancy myself a bit of a philanthropist."

"Of course! Your generosity is legendary." He wiggled with anticipation like Terrance, her man-servant canine, had when she'd first turned him. Sam was obviously eager to please her and piled on the flattery.

"It's very important to me to personally vet the organizations the Castanova Foundation chooses to financially support." Zoya stood, ambling over to a wall of framed photographs and award plaques. "I'm sure you heard about the Blackwell Fertility debacle?"

"Yes, ma'am." Sam shook his head and whistled. "What a monster Damian Blackwell turned out to be!"

"Well, let's just say the foundation dodged a bullet there due to my personal research and due diligence process." She deliberately lingered on the word personal and got a thrill when she watched Sam gulp in reaction to it.

"I'm on a fact-finding mission here, gathering intel as you Army folk might say." She winked as she admitted the true reason for the visit. Lies were always best told when they were cloaked with the truth. "Tell me more about the work you do here."

"Absolutely," he gushed. "We provide a vast array of healthcare and rehabilitation services to military service members and their families who are injured in action, from helping make their homes wheelchair accessible, to restoring their mental health and physical wellbeing after deployment."

"Doesn't the VA handle those aspects of reintegration?"

He started laughing, his eyes crinkling at the corners, and his dimple made another appearance. "The truth is, they try, but since we're in the private sector, we have much less red tape to cut through. Our mission is to help the entire soldier. Oftentimes, we are a go-between to help them navigate and fully utilize their benefits at the VA. We understand the system because we exclusively employ veterans here."

He paused, then stood and took a step to close the distance between them, and Zoya felt herself flush with warmth the closer he came. "When an injured soldier comes home, they need many more resources than the VA can provide to integrate successfully back into civilian life. That's where we come in." The timbre of his voice warmed as he spoke with confidence about the work the foundation did.

While she listened, Zoya leaned closer to the wall of photographs that featured Sam and a masculine woman grinning with local celebrities, heads of state, and war heroes in full dress uniform. "Who's this woman?"

"Colonel Roxanne Sullivan. We served together in Desert Storm." His voice lowered and pinched with sadness. "The day Rox lost her leg, we also lost six brothers."

"My deepest condolences for your loss." Selfishly, she reached over to squeeze his arm and connected with a rock-hard bicep. It distracted her from her mission for a moment as she imagined her hands locked on them in the throes of passion. The vision sent tingles of delicious want down her inner thighs. She had to force herself to pull her hand away.

"We almost lost Rox, too," he added, "but I carried her out of there to the extraction point and was awarded a Medal of Honor for saving her life." His intense gaze met hers. She was hyperaware of the fact he was painting himself out to be a hero in her eyes, but it had a tang of conceit that didn't sit well with her.

"How very honorable of you," she said, then couldn't resist adding, "Isn't that one of the core values of the Army along with *selfless* service?"

A flash of embarrassment flashed briefly across his features that Zoya found delicious. Breaking the balls of an overconfident man was one of her guilty pleasures.

"Yes. Well, my apologies if it came across as grandstanding." He offered, "As I said, I'm a little tongue-tied in your presence. I'm sure I've bored you to tears."

Zoya stepped closer to Sam. The male ego was always so fragile. She cleared her throat softly and forced her tone to become warm and inviting, then offered him a heaping helping of flattery. "Sergeant Major Williams, I couldn't help but notice your complete dedication to the foundation's mission. It's commendable."

Sam looked deep into her eyes, and his gaze softened. "Thank you. It's important work."

"Indeed," Zoya replied, her voice carrying a hint of sympathy. "Helping those who have sacrificed so much for our country is truly admirable."

A faint smile tugged at the corners of Sam's lips. "Yeah, it's not easy, but it's worth it."

Zoya focused her energy, allowing her intuition to guide her. She reached out with her mind, brushing against the edges of his thoughts, seeking a point of entry. So far, he'd proven to be dreadfully boring in conversation, but physically desirable. Dominating a war hero in the bedroom did have its perks.

"I can sense that you have many stories to tell from the enemies you have faced and the battles you've waged. A warrior doesn't truly become one without sacrifice."

Ain't that the truth? Damn few of us left.

His first darting thought was yawn-worthy bravado.

Sam's eyes darkened with a hint of sadness, but he didn't look away. "I suppose we all do, but some stories are better left in the past."

Zoya lowered her chin and then looked back up at him through thick black lashes. "Sometimes the past can be a burden too heavy for one man to shoulder alone."

"I carry it so the others don't have to," Sam said earnestly. For the next hour, Zoya forced herself to sit down, lean in, and look attentive while he shared embellished stories of his glory days from a life lived on the edge of danger during a career of well-decorated deployments. He paced as he rehashed the terrifying details of his years of service in the Middle East and eventually landed on the desk in front of her, sitting on the edge of it.

As the one-way conversation flowed, his walls seemed to fade away, leaving them cocooned together in a more intimate bubble.

"There's something about you," he finally said, apparently exhausting the gamut of conversation one man could have about himself.

"I'm just a great listener, darling," she offered with a half-smile.

The tips of his ears pinked up. "Did I babble on too much? I just find myself at ease with you."

"At ease, soldier," Zoya told him, offering him a wink and a salute. The gesture made him grin, deepening the laugh lines on his face as the dimple surfaced again.

"I have a crazy idea," he prodded with a boyish grin.

"Go on," Zoya encouraged him, leaning in. "I happen to adore crazy ideas."

He cleared his throat, his cheeks faintly tinged with color. "Well, there's a black-tie event coming up in a few weeks. Salute & Soiree. It's our largest annual fundraiser for the Adapt4Heroes Foundation, and I was wondering if you'd accompany me."

Zoya's eyebrows arched, a mixture of surprise and amusement dancing in her eyes. "Me? Your date?" She grinned becomingly up at him through her lashes. The thought filled her with dread, but she forced herself to say, "Perhaps I could be persuaded."

Rox is going to shit if I land Ana freaking Castanova as a donor.

The name Rox got her full attention. Knowing she was going to be in attendance, Zoya made a rash decision, forcing a smile as she announced, "I'd be honored to accompany you, Sam. It sounds like a wonderful event, and I'd love to support the foundation."

It didn't sound wonderful at all. In fact, it would be utter agony. If listening to Sam recounting his glory days for the last hour was any indication, it would be an evening of pure torture. One man's diatribe was bad enough, but an entire ballroom filled with boring men and women stuffed into ill-fitting dress uniforms and formal wear, trying to one-up themselves to prove who was the top dog? That would be almost un-survivable. She stood and pulled off her glove. When her skin connected with his palm, she received a number. 12,454.

A quick calculation decreed Sergeant Major Sam Williams would be regaling all the women in the nursing home with the same tired battle stories thirty years from now. God save them all. She pulled a card from her small handbag and placed it on his desk. "That is my private number. I only share it with a select few. I hope you will be discreet."

Hearing that, he thrust his shoulders back with pride. He picked up the card to study it and then opened a drawer, took out a key, and locked it inside his desk.

"You're a quick study." She dangled a compliment at him. "I must go, but forward me the details of the event."

"Absolutely." Pleased with himself, he led her to the door. At her town car, Higgins waited outside and rushed to open the door when she approached.

"How did it go, my queen?"

"Not sure yet," Zoya mused. "It gets me closer to Roxanne, so I accomplished my goal." She pulled her gloves off and leaned back into the cushy seat of the luxurious car. Glancing upward, she said, "I know you can see me up there." She addressed the eternal coven.

"If you only knew the sacrifices I just made to help Katia's assignment from Karma. My ears are bleeding from Sergeant Major Williams' insufferable monologue. If this is what it feels like to do good, no wonder I've always chosen an alternative!" She untied the knotted scarf at her throat and flung it down on the seat next to her, mentally calculating just how inebriated she would need to be during the ball to make the night palatable in the presence of so many egotistical ordins.

"There aren't enough Vodka Gimlets in the free world!"

SEVEN

A week later, Frankie was rooting through the drawers in the bathroom, looking for sunscreen and a hair tie. The air was thick with humidity as Harry was already in the shower, and billowing clouds of steam were pouring out and hugging the ceiling.

"Are you almost done in there?" Frankie was dressed in a cover-up and rocking a tankini, ready to spend the day poolside at Katie's house. "We're supposed to be there in twenty minutes."

"I might need a little help in here," Harry goaded from behind the shower curtain.

"Why didn't you put out the bat signal earlier? You know I'm always down for sexy shower shenanigans with you." Frankie grinned as she whipped off her cover-up and suit in record time, reducing them to a wadded-up pile on the tile floor. A naked Frankie yanked open the shower curtain to reveal a sheepish

Harry standing under the stream of hot water, his hair soaked and dripping like a wet dog.

"Not that kind of help." Harry laughed as he pulled a triple-bladed razor from the shower caddy and handed it over to her. "This kind." He turned around, exposing a thick swatch of dark hair on his back. Frankie reached out and tangled her fingers through it, then tugged on it playfully. Beads of water broke free from his shoulders and glistened, then trailed down his back, getting lost in the sea of dark hair.

"Can you shave my back hair? I can't reach it."

"Wow. We've reached this level of comfortability with each other already?" Frankie pretended to be appalled, but secretly she loved the fact he felt uninhibited enough to ask her to help. "Come here, my little Koko," Frankie teased. "Do you need your emotional support kitty?" She winked and pointed to her freshly waxed lady garden.

Catching her 80s reference, and getting into the spirit of it, he hung his arms down like a gorilla and started to bang on his chest and hoot and grunt for the next few minutes, dissolving Frankie into giggles.

"Shave my back now, woman!" Harry bellowed, then offered her a smirk and a wink. He dropped his voice to a lower register and added, "Hashtag romance."

She snorted, "Right! All this grooming talk has me swooning into a puddle of pure romance over here, Willey," Frankie shot back, matching his sarcasm note for note. She gave in to his request and set the razor on the ledge of the tub, bending down to gather up her clothing. "Okay, but let me get dressed first." She wiggled back into her suit and cover-up. "Hand me the conditioner," she requested.

"For what?"

"Do you want razor burn or a smooth, hairless back?"

"Uh... door number two?"

"Then hush up and do what you're told." Frankie smirked, pushing her luck with him and loving every second. He placed the bottle in her hands, and she shook it rapidly, then squirted it without warning directly onto his back with an evil chuckle.

"Ooh! That's freezing!" Harry yowled. "Would it be too much to ask you to warm it up in your hands before you put it on my nice, warm skin?"

"Fine, you big baby." She swiped her hands over his back to gather up the thick liquid, then rubbed her hands together and spread the conditioner evenly over it. Frankie picked up the razor and then made her first cut, beginning at his shoulder and shaving straight down to his left cheek in one long swipe.

"Ewww," she groaned, wrinkling her nose at the hair-filled goop that now rested in between the blades of the razor. Running it under the stream of water to clear it, she shook it off before adding, "I knew it! You *are* a G-O-rilla!" She turned him away from the shower. "Roll your shoulders forward. The muscles across your blades are bumpy," she told him, dragging the razor in a perpendicular line. Pleased with herself, Frankie smirked, as she washed off the hair and added a little more conditioner to his back. A second later, the she-devil on her shoulder whispered in her ear, and she couldn't stop herself from executing a playful wayward swipe of her fingertip between his butt cheeks that sent him leaping into the air. Turning to face her, he covered his backside with his hand protectively. "Hey! What are you doing back there?"

"Just making this task more fun for me," Frankie answered, laughing. "You know, looking for that element of fun in every job that must be done."

His eyes twinkled with laughter as he shook his head, chuckling under his breath, "You're the worst."

"True," Frankie said, adding, "But you love me."

"Also true. God help me." He sighed dramatically before dropping his shoulders in mock defeat.

"Turn around," she directed, and he complied, giving her one quick, suspicious glance over his shoulder. Frankie had to press her lips together to stop the laughter from escaping as she dragged the razor across his back parallel to the last stroke. She took a step back to admire her handiwork in its full glory. An enormous "F" was practically glowing in the exposed bright pink of Harry's skin against the sea of black hair. Pleased with herself, she sang out, "All done!" and then tried to repress the laughter deep in her soul.

"What? No way!" Harry turned around and narrowed his eyes at her. "Why do you look so guilty?"

Her eyes widened, and she snorted, then pressed her lips together as he unsuccessfully tried to get a glimpse of his back over his shoulders. Twisting from side to side, he couldn't make out the reflection in the steamy mirror.

"Wipe it off and give me a hand mirror," he demanded.

Knowing the jig was up, Frankie wiped down the mirror with a towel and put a compact in his hand. Seeing the "F," for the first time, he burst out laughing. "Marking your territory?" he asked with a smug grin. "I mean, I don't blame you. I *am* a total catch. It's only natural you would want to brand me with your initial since this rocking hot body is going to be shirtless in an hour poolside. If only to stop Katie or her daughters from…" His eyes widened at the over-the-top suggestion.

Frankie laughed. "Dude, that's gross." She cringed and pushed his shoulder playfully as he laughed at his own joke. "Fine. Guess I'll take one for the team and finish it."

She spent the next several minutes on the task and, when it was complete, washed the conditioner off his back. But she found herself unable to stop from sliding her slippery finger in between Harry's exposed cheeks a few more times. Each time she did, it made him laugh harder.

"Stop making unauthorized withdrawals from my prison wallet," Harry teased.

"Your prison wallet?" Frankie snorted with laughter. "That's going in the vault."

"The vault?"

"It's where I keep our deep cuts."

"What?" Harry was confused.

"You know, the good stuff only true fans know about."

"Hmm. The vault. I never had one of those before," he admitted, and Frankie melted. She wasn't used to a man being upfront and honest with his feelings, and each time he was, it made her heart clench. Each time, she could see a little further down the road to forever with him.

She rinsed his back off one more time with the handheld sprayer. "There. My Willey is far less hairy now." Frankie snickered at her own joke and took pride in a job well done. Unable to stop herself, she slid one final slippery finger down Harry's back and swiped it between his cheeks.

He whipped around, yanked the shower head from her hand, and clipped it back on. "That's it! You have assaulted my crack for the last time. You have the right to remain silent." He grabbed her wrists and pinned them at her hips while she giggled, then he yanked her into the shower fully clothed. Ignoring all of her further protests, he silenced them with his tongue. His stubble was rough on her neck as he smothered her with kisses. Giving in to the delight of the sensation, her legs buckled, and he caught her at the waist. She wrapped her arms around his broad shoulders and gave in to the pleasure, letting him undress her in the shower. "How about we get dirty again before we get clean?" he murmured into her ear as he pressed her wet body against the shower wall.

Half an hour and three orgasms later, they pulled themselves together enough to pack a pool bag and some towels and head over to Katie's. It was a balmy early spring day, and after Frankie let them inside using the door code, they found Katie lounging on a chair by the pool with Arlo curled up at her feet. She was wearing a huge sun hat and a bright pink and orange cover-up.

"I figured we could start the grill when the kids get here," Katie mentioned with a lazy yawn as she soaked up the sun.

"I don't like to brag, but I might know my way around the briquettes," Harry was quick to offer.

"Really? Then it's all yours!" Katie acquiesced with a grin. "Anything that will stop me from smelling like grilled meat for the rest of the day. The only one who finds that even remotely appealing is Arlo. Right, boy?" He quirked his ears up hearing his name. She absentmindedly reached under her chair and scratched his chin, and he blissed out, enjoying the warm sun on his fur.

"The Spring Equinox Ball is coming up," Katie said. "Are you two getting excited?"

"For sure. Now that my gorilla is shaved, we're all set," Frankie blurted, then pinched her lips together when Harry shot her a look.

Katie's forehead wrinkled up in confusion. "Is that another euphemism for your lady garden?"

"Yeah. We'll go with that." Frankie giggled, offering Harry a carefully concealed wink as he busied himself digging two towels out of the bag and handing one to her.

"Two days and two nights of wicked debauchery on a tropical island?" Frankie enthused. "Sign me up!"

"How does that work for you, Harry?" Katie asked, genuinely wondering. "You're a police officer, and I've heard some rumors about the partying that happens at events like these."

"I always do some research before I make travel plans," Harry said. "Ana Castanova runs tight security at her parties. She goes to great lengths to make sure consenting adults can have the time of their lives, but all necessary protections are in place to ensure the safety of her female guests. Leslie Stahl did an episode on her female forward philosophy after the Epstein allegations surfaced."

"That's pretty cool," Frankie added as she reclined back in her pool chair.

"And since the compound is in international waters, it's technically out of the jurisdiction of the Aura Cove Police Department."

"Ah. That didn't even cross my mind," Katie said.

"Besides, police officers can go on vacation just like anyone else," he justified. "Now, if I witness a felony in progress, or there is perceived danger to my loved ones or the public, then I would act, not because it is required, but because it's the right thing to do."

Katie nodded. "Great answer. You're a good egg."

"He is," Frankie answered. "He's the best egg." She settled back on her chaise lounge, happy that the sunglasses on her face obscured her vision. It still took her breath away when she realized how deeply she was falling for Harry. Her wariness and distrust of the entire male population had morphed into a focused irrational fear of losing the last good one. It didn't make sense, but the human heart never does.

"Get a grip," Frankie mumbled under her breath as she nodded off in the sun. "It's okay to let yourself be happy."

Eight

In the dead of night and asleep in her bed, Roxanne was restless. She cried out, tossed and turned, and then bolted straight up. Panic roared in her chest, and it took several long seconds to get her bearings and calm her hammering heart. A sheen of sweat covered her body, and she reached out to turn on the ceiling fan using the switch by her bed, shivering in the cooler air, trying to catch her breath. Eventually, her heart rate began to slow, and she fumbled for her liner and prosthetic leg. Not bothering to wrap her exposed limb fully, it was a quick and dirty middle-of-the-night solution that gave her the greatest chance of successfully getting back to sleep after a bathroom break. She got to her feet and walked a few steps to her ensuite bathroom.

Exhausted, she collapsed on the chilly seat of the toilet and tried to calm her racing thoughts. Though the nightmares had decreased in frequency, it was impossible to escape the handful she was practically guaranteed every year. Hating to complain, she didn't even bring them up at her appointments as there were so many other soldiers with severe PTSD who were seriously debilitated and needed extensive psychological treatment. Rox hated the idea of having precious resources wasted on her more manageable ones. She stood to flush and then walked over to the sink to wash up. Studying her bloodshot eyes in the mirror, she bent down and scooped up handfuls of cool water and splashed her face to wash away the remnants of the night terrors that lingered. She tugged the hand towel from the ring it was draped on and wiped her face dry.

Slowly, she made her way back to the bed and tried to settle down enough to fall back asleep, but her mind kept drifting back to that one hellish day when her entire world changed.

———

In 1990, after graduating from West Point, Rox was several months into her first deployment in Iraq during the Gulf War. It had taken time to acclimate to the punishing climate, but she had. The desert of the Middle East was the devil's playground, where the sun's scorching glare and tireless winds sandblasted every object they touched. Grains of sand wiggled their way into every nook and cranny inside her clothing, chafing her skin raw in patches, into her gear, and underneath her fingernails. It obsessively burrowed in, driven by the

wind, finding clearance in the tiniest of spaces, adding a
gritty film to every surface. The unrelenting heat and
dust storms of the desert were as far away from the
ever-present humidity and lush greens of Kansas where
she'd last been stationed, and she couldn't think about it
too often without becoming homesick.

Even though, at first glance, the desert appeared
barren, Rox quickly learned it was bursting with life.
Scorpions skittered across the waves of sand dunes,
leaving transient tracks that dissolved into the gusty
breeze seconds after they were created. Snakes searched
out pockets of cooler shade in the rocks, lying in wait
for their next meal, and conserving their energy until
they found it. Rox was continually awed and amazed at
a living creature's natural instinct for survival even in
the harsh conditions of the desert.

She was twenty-two years old and eager to prove her
worth and leadership skills in the field. As a female
officer in the Army, Rox had to work twice as hard as
her male counterparts to earn half of the opportunities
for advancement, but Rox was a driven woman. One by
one, she'd overcome any challenge that was thrown her
way at West Point, and every goal she'd set since
graduation put her on the track for Major by thirty.

While the combat exclusion policy prevented
women from being assigned to combat units in Desert
Storm, Rox knew the nature of war often blurred the
definition of combat and that the needs of the unit
always came first. Rox was looking for a way to step up,
volunteering to participate in the most complicated

missions, knowing that being under fire and in extreme circumstances, her commanding officers would be forced to tap the person best qualified to carry out orders, even if they were female.

Since becoming a Second Lieutenant, she'd strung together a quick series of victories on her first few reconnaissance missions. Each operation was increasingly more difficult than the last, and she excelled quickly, drawing the attention of her commanding officers.

Rox had just received her latest orders. Her next mission was infinitely more dangerous. She was part of a squad of eight sent to gather intel on where the locals were rumored to be hiding high-ranking members of Saddam's army in the area. It was to be a fact-gathering tactical mission only lasting forty-eight hours, but being deep in enemy territory came with much higher risks. Rox excelled in the field. Being a vital part of the squad provided an adrenaline rush that kept her fully engaged and presented opportunities she could leverage for future advancement.

After several months in the punishing sun, her skin was leathery, deeply tanned, and blasted raw. Her lips were cracked and her uniform was perpetually drenched with sweat that never cooled her body. Dressed in full fatigues and combat boots, she surveyed her supplies and her rucksack. She religiously checked over and assessed her gear as she packed necessities. The body armor was scuffed and worn, and she spent her last evening before they rolled out cleaning her weapon and going over the game plan in her head.

The group of eight left in the early morning hours. After setting up a rendezvous point, they climbed into two Humvees and caravanned out into the desert. The first hour was uneventful as they jockeyed across the dunes and barely there roads.

Ahead, in the first Humvee, the Officer in charge and three enlisted were leading the way. Her vehicle followed behind and was filled with three other soldiers she'd come to love as brothers. Each of them had a special skill set—they were individual cogs in a well-oiled weapon of war. Rox sat in the passenger seat scanning the roads for threats. Her specialty was reconnaissance. In the driver's seat next to her, Sergeant Sam Williams was a communications specialist. A six-foot-tall pretty boy, he had the golden good looks of a surfer and was quickly garnering the attention of his superiors. He was ambitious, a go-getter, and a wizard at keeping the sketchy lines of communication open with the Army-issued equipment.

Corporal Michael Montgomery, Monty for short, was a sniper and a total hoss. Every muscle on his body was thick and sinewy, with the ebony skin of an African Prince. Specialist Pinnick, a.k.a. Peabody (after some barracks high jinks had him waking up in a pool of his own urine), was the explosives expert. He was a scrawny beanpole with a perpetual spark of mischief in his eyes and a sharp wit. He didn't pack on the muscle like the other two did, but he was tough as nails.

Hyper-alert, Rox scanned the area as Sam followed the Humvee ahead of them. In the gunner's position, Monty was poised and ready with his weapon. Outside of the vehicle, the wind howled, swirling up a cyclone of sand that sprayed the windshield in a gritty spray. They'd passed through two empty villages whose houses were reduced to smoking rubble. Every so often, they would pass the charred skeleton of a Humvee. Rox eyed those more closely, knowing it was easy for the enemy to hide explosives inside and detonate them from a distance.

"Listen up, guys." Rox's voice carried over the rustling wind as they neared their destination. The sun was beating down on them already, and her tone commanded their immediate attention. "We've got a mission to complete. Intel suggests an enemy encampment is just beyond those dunes. These are high-ranking officers in Saddam's army that Psyops wants to use as leverage. Our job is to gather information, assess defense capabilities, confirm precise location, sweep the area, and eliminate any…"

Her sentence was cut off by an explosion that detonated ahead. The Humvee leading them disappeared into a cloud of dust and fire, and their vehicle rocketed side to side from the blast. Stunned, Rox's head snapped back, and Sam slammed the brake pedal to the floor. They skidded to a stop just short of the fireball that consumed the Humvee ahead of them. Shrapnel rained down on the windshield as the ground shook.

In horror, she scanned the area for the source of the

bomb, her eyes landing on the burned shell of a vehicle ahead. It had become a fireball that completely obliterated the first Humvee. With the fate of the Officer in Charge unknown, Rox understood that, as the next highest-ranking officer, the squad would look to her for orders. Time stood still for a moment as she assessed the devastation and made a snap decision.

"Go! Go! Go!" she shouted, leading the way as she opened the door and jumped down onto the sand. "Cover us, Monty." She picked her way across the shifting grains that were burning hot. The fire died to a low roar as she covered her nose with her elbow to prevent the toxic smoke from choking her lungs, taking tentative steps to the burning Humvee. In the passenger seat, the Officer in Charge lay motionless after suffering a fatal head wound, but in the back of the smoking vehicle, she sprang into action when she heard a moan from one of the other soldiers. The other two had already lost consciousness.

"Get 'em out," she shouted to Peabody. "Williams, call for medevac!"

A sudden chatter of deafening gunfire erupted from the dunes ahead and to the side. Bullets whizzed past them, peppering the coarse sand and sending plumes of finer sand airborne, forcing them to dive for cover. The acrid scent of gunpowder filled the air, mingling with the smoke from the burning Humvee and sweat.

"Take cover and return fire!" Rox's stern voice barked orders, cutting through the chaos. She had no choice but to leave the wounded and hunker down behind a sand mound. Needing to secure the area immediately, her gaze intensified as her survival instincts kicked in, and she gathered intel around her. The sharp pop of close-range gunfire made her heart pound, and the metallic taste of fear welled up in her mouth.

Next to her, Monty scanned with his scope. "We're pinned down!" he yelled over the popping of more gunfire, his deep voice strained. "I don't have a clear shot."

"Williams! Call for back-up!"

Williams was huddled behind the wall of sand, his fingers flying across the radio's buttons. "I'm trying, but interference is heavy out here!"

Another volley of gunfire sprayed the sand around them, and Rox felt a sharp sting as a bullet grazed her shoulder. She clenched her teeth against the pain that seared through her like a branding iron.

"Got you," Monty growled, satisfied when three insurgents dropped to the ground after three shots from his assault rifle in quick succession. "It's like whack-a-mole out here. They just keep coming."

Rox's mind raced. "Peabody, we gotta move. Cover fire!"

Peabody nodded grimly and pulled out a grenade from his pack as sweat raced from under his helmet down his mutton chops.

"On my mark," Rox ordered. "Monty, cover us."

He fired off precise shots, and bodies started dropping around them.

"Peabody! Now!" Rox shouted, and he pulled the pin and launched the grenade. Three seconds later, the sand erupted in a series of explosions. The dunes shook, and the metallic smoke mingled with the scent of charred debris and human hair.

"Move, move, move!" Rox ordered, leading the charge toward the insurgents. Chaos reigned, and Roxanne's instincts kicked in. Her training took over as she shouted orders, guiding the men through the battlefield. Bullets zipped past, thudding into the sand with dull, popping sounds. The sand swirled around them, and a shower of debris rained down, obscuring Rox's vision.

A deafening sound of artillery fire erupted, and Monty dropped to the ground. Out of the corner of her eye, she saw Peabody rush for cover. With every sense on high alert, Rox turned to face him, when her brain registered a faint click that made her heart drop to her feet. Time seemed to stand still as she waited for the single second that would change her entire life.

"No!" she screamed into the hell-storm of bullets and flying chunks of debris that rang off her helmet. Peabody didn't even know what hit him as another explosion rocked the ground, this one much closer. Rox felt a searing pain roar through the lower right side of her body, followed by a deafening blast that sent her sprawling to the ground. The world around her blurred as she lay there in shock, waiting for the smoke to clear. Coppery blood filled her mouth, and the scent of burnt fuel and gun smoke lingered in the air. Her leg throbbed and her breath was ragged as she gathered her wits about her. She covered her mouth with her sleeve and sucked in air through it.

Blinking away the dust and in a daze, Rox glanced down, and her heart seized. What remained of her right leg lay mangled and bloodied, and shards of shrapnel were embedded deep within. Unable to comprehend the horror, she froze in terror, grateful the shock had delayed the agony that would soon arrive.

"Lieutenant!" Monty's shout cut through the chaos. Rox blinked twice and, through the hazy smoke, saw Monty lean over her, his face etched with fear. "We have to get you out of here."

"Peabody?" she asked.

"He's gone." The words cut through her like a knife. In shock, her mind drifted and thoughts raced.

"Get to the rendezvous," she told Monty.

"We're not leaving without you," he demanded. His jaw set in a firm line.

"It's a direct order." It would be the only one she would give that day, and Monty ignored it.

"Williams, carry LT. I'll cover you."

Pain disoriented the train of her thoughts. Sadly, she smirked at the irony that your life truly does flash before your eyes before you die, but she was instantly devastated to discover her highlight reel was seriously lacking. Knowing this was probably it, she wondered how her life could be over before it had even started? She'd had so many plans for her life, so many more mountains to climb, figuratively and literally. She'd arrogantly thought she could have it all. A long and highly decorated career in the United States Army and, when she was ready, a husband and a family. It was on her to-do list, but not until after twenty-five. But now she realized she'd waited too long. The agony of the injury combined with the loss of Peabody and the rest of her dreams flooded through her as her eyes fluttered and she drifted in and out in a daze.

From a distance, Rox heard Williams shout to Monty. Then she felt pressure under her arms and the sensation of being dragged behind a dune. She screamed as every grain of sand stung as it scraped against her exposed flesh, leaving a bloody trail in its wake. Behind the dune, lying on the ground, she heard Monty and Williams making a plan.

"We need medevac now!" Monty yelled in between scoping shots from his weapon.

She heard Williams rattle off a sit-rep. "We've been hit. Multiple casualties." Rox felt a tugging sensation and a relentless squeezing above her knee, and when the tourniquet was tightened, she almost passed out from the pain.

"The bleeding slowed, but we've got to get LT to the medic," Williams shouted. He'd taken one to the shoulder, but the adrenaline kept him fully engaged.

"Right behind you." Monty grabbed his rifle and lined up the shot while Williams gathered Rox up in his arms. A fiery burst of pain stole Rox's breath, and she felt her vision start to swim. Every step he took sent a jolt of agony through her body, and she moaned in the moments between consciousness and shock. Their voices became distant, intertwined with the shower of gunfire that continued to rain down.

Faraway in a dreamlike state, she could hear the rumble of the approaching caravan. Roxanne drifted out of consciousness in William's arms, the agony so overwhelming she was ready to escape the hell of Iraq. Even if it was in a body bag.

NINE

The next morning, Rox drove to the Adapt4Heroes Foundation early. Opening the door to her office, it surprised her to see Keith already seated behind her desk, studying the screen. When she entered, he abruptly stood, hurried to the other side of the desk, and began to file a stack of manilla folders into a filing cabinet.

"Sorry, I was getting the jump on next month's expense report for you."

"At 0600?" she questioned, stifling a yawn with the back of her hand.

"Early bird gets the worm." His glance darted over to her, then back to the task at hand. "My son has his first band concert today, so I thought I'd get an early start to make up the time. Remember I mentioned it to you last week?"

"Of course," she said. "Good on you! You can't get

those days back, and showing up for your children is important."

He winced, then added sarcastically, "Important, but excruciating. I mean, when will I get another opportunity to experience the auditory assault of an off-key clarinet?" He chuckled under his breath. "I thought "Hot Cross Buns" on the recorder was bad, but this takes it to a whole new level."

"Ha-ha-ha!" Rox's laugh bolted out like a shotgun, staying true to her nickname. "They are truly terrible at that age," she commiserated. "Tommy's brief six-month love affair with the violin were some of the longest days of my life."

"Well, I'll leave you to it," Keith said. "Did you want the door open or closed?"

"Always open." Over the next hour, she updated the current projects on her roster and made a list of phone calls she needed to make. At nine a.m., Sam strolled through the doors and into her office. He cocked his head to the side, studying her, as warm concern filled his features.

Sitting in the chair across from her desk, he said, "You look exhausted, Ricochet."

"Long night," Rox admitted, setting down the pen and folding her hands together. "It's pretty rare when I have the recurring battle nightmare when I lost my leg, but when I do, it guts me every time."

"The brain is a powerful thing." Sam reached out to put a comforting hand on her forearm. "War changes a person from the inside out. It can create the scariest hell and trap us in our own minds, but only if we let it."

"You're right. Thanks for the reminder." She looked down at her fingers for a long moment before asking, "How do you deal with the memories? You were coherent for all of it. I don't know how you've been able to carry the trauma of witnessing your battle brothers being killed in action. I consider it a blessing that my brain shut off from the shock and I was unconscious when we lost Monty and the rest of the squad."

"I have to take it day by day," Sam said, looking down. "The mission scarred us both. A day like that is seared into the fabric of your soul. They give you a medal for your bravery in battle, but the thing they don't tell you is that your toughest battles will be waged in your mind after you come home." He looked her dead in the eyes and continued, "For me, it's the survivors' guilt that rears up from time to time. Why am I here and they are not?"

"That's a hard question to wrap your head around," Rox agreed. "It's one I've tried to answer myself. All you can do is move forward and make your life mean something. Not a day goes by where I don't look up and tell the fellas that I'm going to make their lives matter, and when I'm fighting the bureaucracy for improvements, it's to make them proud of me."

"They *are* proud," He vowed, looking up. "Having a beer in heaven waiting for the rest of the squad to show up."

"What a reunion that will be!" Rox grinned.

Sam nodded in agreement. "Can't wait."

"Thanks for the pep talk. It definitely helps."

"Anytime."

An hour later, she was seated at her desk going through the mail when a thick, official-looking stack of paperwork was delivered to her desk. She pulled the letter opener from the cup on her desk and guided it into the corner to yank it open. A cashier's check fell out and fluttered to her desk, coming to a rest facedown. She tugged out a thick stack of legal papers from the envelope and set them next to it before turning the check face up.

"Holy shit," she whispered under her breath. "Williams!" She looked down at the check she held in her hands, shocked. At four-hundred-and-fifty-thousand dollars, it was the single largest donation the foundation had ever received.

Sam rushed through her door. "What is it?"

She handed the check to him, unable to speak, and focused on the pages in front of her. "It's from the estate of Officer Oscar Mendoza." As she read through the papers, the name felt familiar, and she ran over it in her head like a tongue searching for a lost tooth. Recognition finally dawned when she remembered he was a double amputee whom the foundation helped secure state-of-the-art prosthetic legs that would allow him to hike the Grand Canyon on his fiftieth birthday three years ago.

"He left it up to our discretion to use as we see fit."

Rox looked up after scanning the bulk of the document, still in shock. A huge winning grin spread across her features, and excitement welled up in her belly.

"We are going to help so many soldiers and their families with this!" She reached out to tug on the check to pull it back and laughed when Sam refused to let go. "It's a lot of money, isn't it?"

"It's the biggest check either of us will hold in our hands." He grinned, finally releasing it as he settled back down. "Ever think you got into the wrong field? What if instead of enlisting in the Army, you'd applied yourself and gone to college and majored in business? Or maybe ran an internet startup?"

"No," Rox admitted, then grinned at him. "And neither would you."

"You're right. Outside of the money, it would be a hollow victory," he claimed. "Everything happens for a reason."

"I used to hate that statement," Rox admitted. "It was the kind of trite psychological bullshit they used to trot out at the hospital when I was learning to walk again." She shook her head in disgust, and her expression turned grim. "Put it on a needlepoint pillow for Christ's sake, but no soldier with a career-ending injury ever wants to hear it."

After a long pause, she added, "Overall, I'm content with my life's path, but I wish I'd had a little more time to utilize the training I received at West Point in the Gulf before everything went FUBAR."

"But the men and women you've trained have gone

on to do amazing things. We're talking hostage rescues, successful counterterrorism operations, and even providing disaster relief stateside during Hurricane Katrina, the California Wildfires, and COVID-19. It's got to be a small consolation that you had a part in shaping their destinies, Rox. Even if you didn't get the glory on the front lines."

"True." She looked down. Though she'd made peace with it a long time ago, some days she felt like an NFL quarterback who was benched in the prime of his career. The skills she'd toiled for years to learn felt underutilized, and it had been a challenge to accept her limitations at first. Over the rest of her military career, she learned to let go of the expectations she'd carried and to accept the life she'd been given. It had been a forward-and-back exercise that forced her to grow up and acknowledge where she fit in.

It wasn't until she began working at the Adapt4Heroes Foundation that she could finally work through the myriad of unresolved feelings she'd carried since losing her leg. She intimately understood the struggle a soldier felt when they returned home, missing a limb, unable to walk or perform basic duties. She was empathetic to the sorrow and despair a soldier felt when they finally regained consciousness in the hospital and the reality of their new existence set in. It was the reason she often was the first military face wounded soldiers would see when they were stateside. Receiving a visit from someone who'd suffered the same fate and who had carved out a meaningful life helped them see a possible path through the limitations they now faced. She'd become their champion, cheering them on and giving healthy doses of tough love when it was needed. Being the CEO of the Adapt4Heroes Foundation was the highest use of her talents, and Rox was finally at peace with the road that had led her there.

TEN

Rox's office was empty at the Adapt4Heroes Foundation, as were most of the surrounding ones over the lunch hour. Knowing she was scheduled to attend a charity golf outing and wouldn't return until the following morning, he strolled into her office and over to her desk. From the pocket of his khakis, he pulled on a pair of latex gloves he'd helped himself to from the cleaning crew and tugged them over his hands.

Pulling open the drawer on the front of the desk, he scanned the contents, finding the small silver key resting in an organizer in the back of the drawer. He fished out the key and slid it into the lock on the front of her desk drawer. Rifling through the contents of the file, he finally found what he was looking for—a black leather book. Inside, indexed carefully in Rox's perfect penmanship, were all her logins written in pencil. Whipping through the pages, he noticed she had the same bad online security habits as most people in her age bracket, only changing passwords when she was forced to. Few of the entries had ever been altered.

He remembered asking Rox about the password journal the first time she'd handed it to him, shocked that her passwords were stored at the office in written form. Her response was naïve and misguided. "They can't be hacked if they aren't online. I only need to concern myself with the thirty or so people in this office instead of the billions online." That odd tidbit she'd willingly shared when she'd been brought on board had planted a seed of an idea that was now a sturdy oak tree. It was like having an affair. The first one was a challenge requiring you to wrestle with your morality. Subsequent conquests were simpler, and you had to claim the title of cheater.

Not wasting any time, he jiggled her mouse to wake up the desktop and then opened the cracked cover of the password journal. Navigating to the bank account for the foundation, he initiated a wire transfer of two hundred thousand dollars.

The windfall would solve so many of his current problems, and he felt a fizzy surge of dopamine rush up from his core after completing the brazen act. Instantly, the wire transfer was completed, and the light from the monitor washed over his features. He shut down Rox's computer and placed the password journal back into the drawer. Using the key, he locked it and tucked the key back inside the back of her top drawer in the organizer.

Checking to make sure the desk was exactly as it

had been when he entered the room, he pulled off the latex gloves, walked out of her office, left the building, and headed down the street. Strolling down the sidewalk, he waited until he was a quarter of a mile away before depositing the gloves into an already overflowing trash can.

He'd put events in motion, and in about thirty days, when the next bank statement arrived, the first shockwaves would hit. All he had to do was play it cool for a little longer and wait it out. He felt a wave of regret but tamped it down. It would do him no good to go soft now.

ELEVEN

The morning of the Spring Equinox Ball, Katie sat in a long limousine filled with her family, speeding toward Aura Cove Aviation. It was a private hangar used by the East Coast elite and had a much different vibe than the pedestrian Tampa Airport only twenty minutes away. Zoya's plane was ready, its yawning stairway awaiting their ascent, and their driver eased the car to a stop near it. It was a surreal moment of outrageous visible luxury that made even cynical Lauren speechless.

"We are riding on Ana Castanova's private jet?" Callie asked, exiting the vehicle and standing in front of the jaw-dropping aircraft.

"Sweetheart, close your mouth. You might swallow a fly, and you remember how that ends," Katie said, laughing at the memory. Callie had spent the better part of her fifth year turning *There Was an Old Lady Who*

Swallowed a Fly into an earworm and drove them all crazy.

"Don't get her started," Beckett cautioned. "Perhaps *I'll* die if she starts in with that nonsense again." He grabbed his mother's carry-on and followed Katie up the steps into the aircraft.

"Whoa!" Lauren's jaw was the next to drop as she slid into her cushy seat. "A girl could get used to this."

Tom was just as shell-shocked by the opulence of the sleek interior of the jet. "Now this is the way to travel," he enthused as he accepted a warm wet towel to freshen up and snuggled into the seat next to Lauren.

Katie considered Lauren's words. *Could a girl get used to this?* Eventually, the Castanova fortune and all it entailed—the private island, the estate, and the fleet of planes would be passed down to her. It was the craziest notion. To have so many resources at her disposal would be mind-blowing, but knowing they would come at the price of outliving her children was a bitter pill to swallow.

First, Yuli would be deeded the estate when Zoya passed on after the birth of the next supernatural generation when one of her children started a family. It wouldn't be long before Yuli would have to follow in Zoya's footsteps and assume a new identity so as not to arouse suspicion with the ordin members of the family. Yuli would outlive her daughter, and the transition would be more difficult, requiring a rebirth and total isolation. The thought raced panic through Katie's chest, and she felt her breath quicken. She didn't know if she'd be strong enough to stay away from the ones she loved most when the estate and mortal coven were officially her responsibility.

Katie pushed away the anxiety of the future as she watched Yuli settle into her seat while Frankie and Harry boarded the aircraft. They took seats next to her, sighing when they sank into the ivory-colored leather. Frankie brushed her thumb across the burled wood grain of the cup holder and mini table next to her.

"This is so fancy!" She leaned in to whisper to Katie, "If this is mere transportation, I can't wait to see the compound!"

A bubble of fear welled up in Katie's belly. "Keep your wits about you," she whispered. "Especially around the kids."

She mimed zipping her lips shut, locking a key next to her cheek, and tossing it out the window.

Gosh, I hope she can. Katie tried to let go of the fear and tension she felt from keeping a secret of this magnitude from her children, but she had her doubts.

In the small kitchenette on the aircraft, the flight attendant popped a cork on a bottle of champagne and started passing around crystal flutes perched on a silver tray to each traveler.

"Don't mind if I do!" Frankie accepted hers with a giggle and pointed her pinky finger over to where Harry was seated. "My Harry Willey loves a nice glass of champansky, too." The attendant placed a flute in his hand, and they chimed them together before Frankie chugged her entire glass and held it out for a refill.

"Pace yourself, woman," Katie cautioned.

"Fun hater." Frankie pouted.

"Geez, Mom, don't be such a buzz kill," Beckett huffed.

Katie held up both her hands. "I'm sorry. You're right. Mom is officially off-duty." She left them alone and walked over to where Yuli was seated. She'd spent most of her time staring out the window, and Katie was concerned.

"You seem rather pensive," Katie acknowledged as she sat down in the seat next to her.

Yuli leaned close to Katie's ear and spoke quietly to avoid being overheard. It wasn't necessary as Frankie's natural volume increased while she double-fisted champagne and egged the kids on to keep up with her. It was an effective decoy that gave them a chance to speak candidly.

"The Spring Equinox is always a time for reflection for Yayas. You'll feel a pull toward nature and a desire to connect even more powerfully with the elements. It's a time of rebirth when we celebrate the Earth's fertility and our own creative energy that can birth new life into the world."

"Hmm." Katie considered her words. They especially resonated as it deepened her understanding of herself. Of all the seasons, spring was her favorite. It was a reawakening she savored. When new leaves sprouted on dormant branches and, once again, the cycle of life began. Hearing Yuli reaffirm her experience connected her even more closely with her grandmother.

"There is a balance and harmony on the Equinox where the light and dark seek equilibrium. Figuratively and metaphysically."

"Maybe that's why Zoya's edges are softening," Katie offered.

"Perhaps," Yuli said gently.

"She's trying," Katie whispered.

"She *is* making an effort, but I need to see sustained change before I believe it."

"That's fair." Yuli was making progress, slowly, but it was still progress.

An hour later, the plane touched down, and they gathered their luggage and rolled it toward a waiting group of golf carts. Higgins loaded their luggage on the back of two, and then they climbed on board and eased down the pathway to the estate in a caravan. Katie watched her kids experience the same awe she had when she'd seen the compound for the first time.

"This is better than any five-star resort I've ever been to," Lauren proclaimed, and sitting next to her, Tom was just as blown away.

"I wonder what it's like to live here every day?" Callie asked as they rounded the corner and the oceanfront property came into view. "Wow. To get to go to sleep at night to the soundtrack of the sea? That's my dream!"

She leaned her head on Katie's shoulder, an endearing gesture that still melted Katie's heart. She was always the one of her children who needed reassurance the most. "You have no idea how much I need this right now, Mom. With finals coming up soon and then getting my resume ready and out into the real world, I am freaking out."

"Take a breath, sweetheart. This is the perfect opportunity to blow off some steam," Katie assured, pressing her lips to Callie's forehead. "You should let your hair down. Run wild while you're still young. One of my biggest regrets in life is that I didn't have enough fun when I was your age, but I plan on rectifying that now."

"Don't be too hard on yourself," Callie offered. "It's hard to cut loose when you have a baby toddling around the house."

"True," Katie agreed, adding, "But I wouldn't change it for the world. One great advantage of having children when you're young means you get a second chance at fun when they've grown and flown."

"That's the spirit, Mamacita!" Callie said as their golf cart pulled to a stop on a grand cobblestone drive where several staff members gathered amid a pack of four large-breed dogs that sat on their haunches. The estate was decked out with multiple performance stages being constructed for entertainment, tall tables were wrapped with apple-green satin, and there was seating for over a hundred guests. A band shell glimmered in the sunlight with iridescent colors like the inside of an abalone shell, where a crew of workers was busy setting up equipment and running through sound checks.

"You made it!" Zoya descended the stairs like a regal queen greeting her subjects. Dressed in a long lilac-colored gown that hugged her curves, she brushed cheek kisses on the kids, Frankie, and Harry before sending them off to check out their bedroom suites in the estate. They were enamored with the property already, taking in the lush topiaries being strung with twinkling fairy lights and the flower chains florists wrapped around poles and pulled to the center to create an exquisite overhead canopy. The whole effect was jaw-droppingly gorgeous and magical all on its own.

Terrance rushed to Zoya's side. "My queen, the chef needs you for a tasting before he begins production."

"Will you excuse me?" Zoya asked.

"We should talk first," Yuli said.

"What is it?" Zoya's eyes narrowed.

"I'm concerned about the children finding out your real identity," Yuli explained. "This is dangerous. Having them all here together, it's risky."

"You worry too much," Zoya discounted Yuli's fears immediately.

"Loose lips sink ships," Yuli muttered. "And Francesca has a tendency to be the loosest, especially after a few cocktails."

"I'll have a talk with her," Zoya offered. "I can be very persuasive."

Katie chuckled. "Good luck with that."

"Is it a crime to want to get to know my great-great-great-grandchildren?" Zoya asked. Katie was still surprised by the glimmers of softness she was seeing from Zoya. Maybe this was her Spring Solstice growth?

She wanted to believe it, but Yuli was right. It was too early to tell.

"It's a tad selfish," Yuli insisted, "and puts us all in danger."

"Only if we're discovered," Zoya answered. "Can we agree to put a pin in it and cross that bridge when we get there?"

"Okay," Yuli reluctantly agreed.

"Good." Zoya then changed the subject with a smile. She glanced down at the ruby-studded watch on her wrist. "I must get back to the chef, but first there is something I want you to see." Katie was instantly intrigued. "I'd like you both to accompany me to the archives," Zoya said.

"Really?" Katie was excited at the prospect of seeing the family archives in person for the first time. Since learning the family memories were a living diorama contained inside ornate music boxes, she'd been curious about the collection. Several had been delivered to her doorstep already, and experiencing each one had shone such a bright light on her family's colorful history. They were completely immersive, giving the viewer the sensation of being a participant in the actual moment. Each encounter she had with the music boxes filled her with wonder, and she couldn't wait to see the collection in its entirety.

Yuli sighed, then shuddered at the memory. "The last time I was in that building, you ripped my heart out."

Her accusation made Zoya blanch, and she humbly

lowered her voice. "I was terrible to you, and I would like to offer an apology."

"Talk is cheap," Yuli muttered, cutting Zoya's olive branch down to the quick.

"But we've also got to start somewhere," Katie reasoned, hoping she could convince Yuli to soften her heart enough to allow for the possibility of change. She wrapped an arm around Yuli to offer her support.

"You have my word. This will be a much different experience," Zoya promised, trying to persuade her granddaughter.

"Fine." Yuli conceded, allowing herself to be led to the golf cart. She was a reluctant participant, unwilling to let Katie go with Zoya alone.

They pulled up to a tiny metal building covered with overgrown brush. Zoya produced a skeleton key from her pocket, twisted it in the lock, and beckoned them inside.

Once inside the dimly lit building, it opened up, defying all the rules of physics Katie had ever learned. The interior of the building stretched out as far as her eyes could see.

"Wow." Katie was shell-shocked when her eyes finally adjusted to the dim light. She was standing in front of a stone wall and had to squint her eyes to make out the words carved into it.

Women's history is rewritten by the men in power.
Here lives a collection of our important hours.

Painful days must be re-lived.
To prevent them from happening ever again.

Beautiful memories should only be felt.
If viewed more than once, the music box will
melt.
Our family history is nothing to fear.
But you must heed the lessons inside the boxes
here.

Zoya watched recognition register on Katie's face as she finished reading the poem. "It's all here. The good and the bad," Zoya said as she extended her palms and began to circle them, and golden sparks showered from her hands to the floor as the shelves shifted and rushed past. It created a breeze that made Katie's white hair blow back from her face. The shelves rushed by in a blur on the tracks until they shuddered to a stop. The marker carved into the side of the closest shelf said 1926. Zoya walked over to where a pink music box shaped like a teddy bear rested. The closer she got to the box, the brighter it began to glow.

Katie's eyes widened with delight at the sight of it, and when Zoya pulled it from the shelf, a gentle smile softened her features.

"Your first birthday," Zoya said, handing the box to a startled Yuli. "This is the box I should have shown you on your sixteenth, but I was bitter and hurt." She met Katie's eyes. "I've already been inside it once, years ago. I think it will open your eyes a bit, and hopefully your hearts. Wait until I take leave. It's much too precious to be destroyed. Remember, this is your only chance to experience the joy of it." She pointed to the engraved stone as a reminder. Yuli's usual skepticism was silenced as the box glowed brighter between her hands.

"I've got to head back to the main house for the tasting and make sure the glam squad is getting started with Lauren and Callie. Dresses were delivered a few days ago to the estate, and I can't wait to see which ones they choose." Stopping to give one last-minute instruction, she said, "When your journey is over, simply go outside and wait. My security eagles will alert Higgins, and he will take you back to the main house so you can get ready for the party."

"Security eagles?" Katie repeated, sure she'd heard wrong.

"Yes," Zoya confirmed. "They travel in pairs, and I rely on their eagle eyes to keep all my guests on their best behavior."

As she closed the door behind herself, Katie was still in shock. "She can communicate with birds, too?"

"Why is that so hard to believe? They are smarter than dogs."

Katie laughed. "I don't know why anything around here surprises me anymore."

Yuli nodded, still completely focused on the music box in her hands. Katie glanced over at Yuli in the darkened room.

"Are you ready?" Katie asked in a hushed tone that startled Yuli.

"I think so?" Yuli answered as Katie stepped closer and rested her hands on the bear for the first time. It began to hum, and the warmth surprised Katie. She brushed her finger along the bear's cheek, and the softness of the ceramic fur was a surprise.

"It's so soft," Katie remarked in awe. "I guess it makes sense. The ominous ones were sharp and painful to touch. This is like holding a hug." Noticing Yuli's confused expression and hesitation, she asked, "What are you afraid of?"

"The story I've told myself for decades is that Zoya is evil. I guess I'm afraid if I go inside this box, I'll discover I was wrong."

"No one is infallible," Katie consoled in a soft voice. "The box is a neutral third party, allowing us to view the memory without the bias that occurs with oral history."

Yuli nodded and exhaled a heavy sigh. "You're right. The truth is what's important. I think I'm ready now." She turned the little gold crank on the side of the bear's belly, and the first few notes of "You Are My Sunshine" played on a xylophone tinkled out of it. Her thumb found the groove, and she pulled the tiny door to open the box, and seconds later, they were whisked inside.

———

Katie and Yuli floated down, landing in a dirty alley, and it took a couple deep breaths for Katie to adapt to her surroundings. Model-Ts drove down the busy streets of downtown Chicago and, glancing around at the people walking on the sidewalks, Katie felt a nostalgic tug. She'd long loved the Golden Age of Hollywood and was obsessed with black and white movies. It seemed she was now living inside of one.

She people-watched for a few minutes, taking in the women dressed in lace flapper shifts and pearls, their hair coiffed into finger waves, strolling down the streets on the arms of dapper men in three-piece suits.

"What year is this?" Katie asked, swooning over the flood of people who passed them.

"1926," Yuli reminded her and closed her eyes.

"What are you doing?"

"Connecting to the source," she added, and a few minutes later, she grabbed Katie's hand and tugged her down the street as they blended in with the crowd. "Do you feel it?" Yuli whispered as their pace quickened.

"Yes!" Katie said, "It's magnetic. It feels like we're being propelled down this path."

"Because we are," Yuli confirmed knowingly. They flowed with the energy and picked their way across the street until they were standing in front of the rickety steps of a boarding house. On a hand-painted sign that flapped in the gentle breeze, it simply said, "Olena's."

Having only met the diminutive woman a few times, Katie was excited at the prospect of gathering more information about the supernatural women in her bloodline. She started up the stairs and, after a brief hesitation, Yuli followed.

Inside, scantily clad women were perched on the laps of drunken men. They were carousing and carrying on, and Katie's cheeks pinked up at the sight of meaty hands gliding up the tanned legs and heavy bosoms of the working girls.

"What is this place?" she whispered.

"A house of ill repute," Yuli answered as they took in the rowdy scene playing out in front of them. At one table, a beautiful topless woman poured shots of whiskey for the three men gathered around it. They pounded them on the table with a shout of glee before knocking them back. The woman hurried to refill their glasses and then was pulled onto the lap of one man whose rough hands kneaded her breasts like bread dough. It was such an outrageous, lusty act that Katie had to avert her eyes.

"This is no place for a child," Katie said.

"Beggars can't really be choosers. When the only power you have as a woman rests between your legs, you have to work with what you've got. Olena took us in when we arrived in Chicago." Katie nodded, remembering the tough road Zoya had been forced to walk down mere weeks after her beloved daughter, Nadia, died in childbirth.

A piano was pushed against the wall at one end of a huge bar, and a man seated at it strummed one hand down the keys rapidly to grab everyone's attention.

"It's time!" a younger Olena shouted out into the

madness. When the crowd didn't settle down, she climbed on top of one table and thrust both of her pinkies into her mouth, executing a piercing wolf whistle. "Gather round, you degenerates! It's time to celebrate the birthday of the Babi." She hopped off the table by way of the chair and disappeared through a swinging door.

Grumbling and tipsy, the crowd struggled to their feet, dragging heavy chairs across the wooden floor into the dining room. Katie and Yuli followed closely and hid in the shadows of the hall among them, lost in the darkness and the crowd.

"Is that you?" Katie asked in a hushed tone, pointing at the plump baby seated in a wooden high chair at the head of the table. A soft smile turned up the corners of Yuli's lips, and she nodded. Astonishment filled Katie, seeing Yuli so tiny. The man at the piano began to play the birthday song, and the crowd gathered around the baby began to sing.

"Happy birthday to you!" Olena sang as she walked a cake covered in pink icing and one tall candle over to the table. The warm glow from the candlelight lit her cheekbones from below and softened all the lines on her face. The closer she got to the high chair, the more animated Yuli became. She thrust her pudgy thighs out of the leg holes, rocking with excitement. Her mouth was wide open, smiling and drooling and exposing her four baby teeth. In front of her, Erina, who nursed Yuli back from the brink of starvation when she'd first arrived, sang the loudest. Erina clapped her hands and squealed with delight when little Yuli repeated the gesture and cooed as the cake made it to within reaching distance.

"Who is that?"

"Erina. She was one of Olena's working girls."

"She loved you," Katie stated, seeing a tear break free from the corner of Yuli's eye and zigzag down her lined face. Yuli was spellbound by the overwhelming evidence of the care and concern she'd received as a baby; it contradicted the story she'd told herself.

"I always felt so unwanted," she whispered to Katie.

Standing, Erina stepped behind Yuli's chair and grasped both of her chubby fists in her own to keep her from burning her fingers on the flame. Seeing Yuli so tiny pulled on Katie's heartstrings and took her back to the first birthday celebrations of her own kids. Katie looked at Yuli, completely engrossed in the events happening in front of her, with a soft smile on her face.

The last chorus ended, and Erina said, "One… two… three!" before she helped little Yuli blow out the candle. The breeze in her wispy dark hair made Yuli giggle with joy, and in the shadows, Katie wrapped her arm around her grandmother and squeezed. "You were so cute," she whispered.

"I was." Yuli grinned as she watched herself reach out to touch the thick icing that covered the cake, swiping a handful of cake and frosting in one palm and thrusting it into her open mouth. The women in the room cheered and clapped, and Yuli clapped her sugary fingers together, sending bits of frosting to her cheeks, which made the women clap even harder.

Over the next fifteen minutes, baby Yuli's hands returned to the cake again and again, ramming fistfuls of it into her mouth until she was completely covered in icing and blissed out on sugar. Olena brought a pitcher of water and a bowl to the table and spent the next several moments gently washing the icing and cake from between Yuli's sticky fingers. Then she dipped the washcloth into the water and swiped it across Yuli's cheeks. When she was clean, Olena shook out the cloth and placed it over her head.

"Where's my Babi?" Olena sang out and then snatched the cloth from her head. An action that made baby Yuli chortle with laughter. For the next several minutes, she repeated the gesture and Yuli dissolved into a fit of gut-busting giggles each time. Yuli eventually yawned, and Erina picked up the baby and wrestled her legs free from the highchair. She handed the child to Olena, who squeezed her tightly to her diminutive chest and covered the top of her head with kisses.

Tears glistened at the corners of Yuli's eyes from the shadows. "You were deeply loved," Katie whispered.

"I wish I could have remembered this moment," Yuli whispered back, never taking her eyes off the pudgy raven-haired baby. "As a child, all I remember feeling was lonely." Yuli turned her full attention back to the scene unfolding in front of them.

"She's so close to taking her first steps," Erina said to Olena as she welcomed Yuli back into her arms. She gently set the baby down on the ground, and Yuli grasped one of Erina's fingers inside each clenched fist, toddling around the table to prove it, leaving a trail of drool behind her.

Suddenly, the front door whipped open, and sailing in on the warm July breeze, a much younger Zoya walked into the room. Dressed to the nines, she expertly sidestepped the pawing of the men's hands. She was beautiful, hourglass-shaped, and poured into a black lace flapper gown. All eyes in the room slid over to her, the men's gazes feasted on her cleavage. The women's turned to daggers as jealousy made them shrink into shrews. Zoya didn't even register the energy shift in the room. She was oblivious to it.

Olena ignored the interruption and focused on Erina instead. "Show me."

"Why don't you take a few steps over there? Maybe she'll let go and take a step on her own if she sees a familiar face." Erina grinned into the baby's wide eyes, and Yuli clutched a handful of her curls and tugged. Untangling herself from Yuli's grasp, the good-natured wet nurse asked, "Are you ready to show them what you can do, Yuli?" She swooped her down into the air and right back up as a jubilant Yuli's laugh bubbled around them. She stood the child on her sturdy legs across from Olena who called out to her, smiling with her arms open wide.

"Come here, sweet girl," Olena begged, cheering her on. "You can do it." Yuli shoved her fist in her mouth, chomped down, and drooled. Olena adopted a singsong tone and clapped to get the baby's attention. "Come see Olena. Just three little steps."

Next to Olena, Zoya was not paying attention to her granddaughter's milestone moment. Instead, she was engrossed in conversation with a man, while helping herself to his valuables inside his jacket pocket, as Yuli toddled out her first step.

"That's it! Come to Olena!" she hollered out, and the women cheered her on. Yuli took another step and then two more before twisting and reaching out with both hands to grasp the fabric on Zoya's skirt. Surprisingly, Zoya bent down and swept the baby up in her arms, and for a moment, the perpetual frown disappeared from her face and her scowl softened. She burrowed her head into the child's soft neck as the rest of the room burst into applause at her accomplishment. When Zoya pulled her head back, Katie and Yuli both saw her cheeks were wet with tears.

"You ignore and neglect her, and she still prefers you," Olena said bitterly, opening up her shorter arms, knowing Zoya did not like to hold Yuli for long. Olena's unrelenting honesty broke the spell, and Zoya quickly turned on a heel. Katie saw her swipe a tear from her eyes as she crossed the room and let herself out. Erina rushed over to Olena and grinned, happily taking the baby into her arms like a proud surrogate mother would.

"You did it, my sweet. It doesn't matter who you walked to; the point is you did it!"

She nuzzled the chubby baby and, over her shoulder,

said to Olena, "I'm going to nurse her before I put her down for the night."

Olena nodded, and the brothel came to life again. "Chop, chop, girls! Shoulders back! Tits out!" Swanky jazz music started up again, and Katie and Yuli disappeared into the crowd heading to the bar. On instinct, Katie walked toward the door, pulling Yuli with her, down the rickety stairs and to the alleyway of the boarding house. Below them, at the bottom of a concrete stairwell, they could hear a woman sobbing a few feet away. Looking down at her from their perch, they discovered it was Zoya. She let out an angry scream into the dark night, clearly frustrated and in agony. The tears came faster as she struggled to catch her breath.

"Nadia, I can't believe it's been a year, an entire three-hundred and sixty-five days I have lived on this earth without you," Zoya cried. "I hate seeing life go on in your absence. You should be here. You should have been the person whose arms Yuli ran toward. You! Not me! Not Olena, and certainly not some trollop wet nurse at the boarding house. There isn't a day that goes by that I don't think about you and what you have lost."

Zoya tipped her chin to the sky, and Yuli and Katie pulled back from the railing and out of her line of sight. "Do we share the same heavens, my darling? The same sky? Do you see the brightest stars in the galaxy? The same moon that I see?" She let out another choked sob, staring at the night sky filled with stars.

"So much has changed, and yet so much has remained the same. You are not here, and I hate existing in a world without you in it. I curse the God who stole you from me and have begged the devil to put an end to my suffering, but neither has responded to my pleas."

Zoya swiped her tears away with a gloved hand. "I miss you. Today is not a day of celebration for me. It will forever be the one I dread most." Letting out one more anguished cry, she shook off the oppressive energy.

Yuli was riveted to Zoya's distressed pleas, and Katie saw a sadness flash across her features. Below them, Zoya let out a heavy exhale, wiped her face with the back of her hands, and brushed her palms down to smooth the front of her dress. Then she quickly rushed up the steps and down the sidewalk into the night. Gas street lamps turned on and spilled warm light onto the streets as she sped away, swallowed by the darkness.

Katie and Yuli hid in the shadows, pressing their bodies into the darkened bricks of the building. A second later, they were swept away like feathers on the breeze and transported back to the darkened archives.

Yuli was silent after the journey, deep in thought.

"You were such an adorable baby," Katie said, thinking it would be a soft opener in case Yuli wanted to talk about what they'd just witnessed. Yuli returned a gentle smile. "How do you feel after seeing the inside of this box?" Yuli clutched the pink bear in her hands that had stopped glowing. Katie reached out for it and discovered the porcelain had cooled to room temperature.

"I'm really torn," Yuli said. "Seeing the evidence of

her struggle and the pain she endured after losing my mother is opening my heart, especially after the revelations from the *Fioletovy Mahiya*," she admitted as she considered everything they'd learned from the recent lunar event.

"No matter what transpired between us afterward, I survived the days after my mother died because of Zoya. To be honest, I'm finding it hard to stay angry with her."

Katie felt hope well up and was in awe once again of her grandmother's resilience. "Your capacity for forgiveness is remarkable."

"It's easy to judge someone's actions from the outside, but you never really know what they were going through in the moment," Yuli said. "I've wasted so much energy being angry at her and holding grudges. I didn't want to give her any grace. Maybe I'm getting softer in my old age, but I am finally open enough to acknowledge the events that shaped Zoya into the woman she became. Yes, she made mistakes, but we all do, and it's got me thinking that maybe it's time for forgiveness." She was quiet for a long moment. "A new dawn is coming, and there isn't room for hatred or selfishness. It's a rebirth of hope, joy, and love. That is what I want for you and for all the powerful women in our lineage this Spring Equinox."

"Even Zoya?"

"Even Zoya."

TWELVE

The Spring Equinox Ball was in full swing by ten p.m. After their arduous journey into the music box, Yuli begged off for the rest of the night.

"I'm going to stay in. You go ahead and enjoy the celebration with everyone else," Yuli said as Katie tucked the old woman into bed after her shower, looking every bit her ninety-eight years. Yuli stifled a yawn with the back of her hand. "I'm exhausted." She was dressed in a flannel nightgown, and her brilliant white hair spilled down her shoulders and back as she rested against the fluffy pillows in the four-poster bed waiting for Terrance to bring her a dinner tray.

Katie adjusted the blanket around her grandmother, assessing her worn face. She brushed a kiss on her soft cheek and then said, "If you're sure?"

"I am. I'll get a bite to eat, then it's lights out for me."

"Okay." Katie let herself out and went back to her bedroom, where Arlo quivered with unrestrained joy at seeing his favorite human again. She knelt down and scratched under his chin, laughing when he flopped over onto his back, exposing his belly. Katie scratched his under carriage vigorously until he was reduced to a pile of grateful bliss.

"I figured you'd be down with the guests at the party already. What are you doing up here?" she asked.

"Waiting for you." He stood on his paws, his brown eyes boring into hers. "You know I'm a companion animal, and my loyalty is to you."

He jumped up on his hind legs, and she brushed her hands against his curly coat, starting at his neck and running down his torso to his flanks.

"You're a *needy* little companion animal," Katie teased, and he dropped down on all fours and took two steps away.

"Needy!" he huffed. "As if!"

"You are!" She walked into the lavish bathroom and, unwilling to be left behind, he followed closely, right on her heels.

The Carrera marble gleamed from floor to ceiling, an emerald green floor-length gown was hooked on a high hanger, and resting below it was a pair of gold pumps in her size. She reached up to pull off the note clipped to the hanger.

"For Katia." At the bottom of the card, a flourished Z confirmed who it was from. She pulled the hanger down and held it in front of her body, assessing her reflection in the mirror.

"Gotta give it to Zoya. The woman has great taste," she admitted as she bit back a yawn.

"She does," Arlo agreed. "And you'll be the belle of the ball in that dress."

Katie smiled at him. "I think my belle days are far behind me, but it will be fun to dress up for the special occasion." She yawned again into the back of her hand.

"Maybe a shower will wake me up." She glanced over at Arlo. "Do you mind?"

"What?" he asked, oblivious as he plopped down on the bathroom rug and began to lick himself.

"We are going to need to set some new ground rules. No more following me into the bathroom to watch me pee. It's weird."

"I suppose you're right. I only have four more months left on my sentence until I'm back inside my ordin body. I might as well adjust to human boundaries again." He stood, shook out his coat, and trotted out of the bathroom, jumping up on the bed to rest while his mistress got ready.

Katie quickly shut the door behind him and showered, grateful the hot water woke up her senses that had been dulled from the journey inside the music box. She quickly dried off, donned a terry-cloth robe, and wrapped a towel around her hair, then opened the door to see Arlo splayed out on his back on the bed napping. "Maybe Yuli had the right idea," she mused, sitting on the edge of the bed and gently tugging his velvety ears.

Her eyes walked back to the dress that had been picked out for her, and she reluctantly got up, shut the door for privacy, and pulled it over her head. It cascaded down her body like a smooth waterfall. The gorgeous green fabric encircled her waist, cinching in and then flaring out from her hips to the floor. The green was the same shade as her eyes, and her confidence soared when she caught the first glimpse of her reflection in the mirror. "Not too shabby!" She twisted in front of the full-length mirror, swiveling her hips back and forth and relishing the way the skirt billowed out when she spun. It was the dress of every little girl's dreams—perfect for twirling around a dance floor—and she couldn't resist testing it out.

Next, she curled her hair into long white waves, pulling up the sides and pinning them behind her shoulders. Finally, she added a coral-tinted blush to her cheeks and two coats of black mascara to her lashes. Satisfied with her reflection, she walked over to Arlo, who was snoozing on her pillow.

"Ta-Da!" she sang out with jazz hands.

Arlo sat up. "Ooh!" he howled, then added, "You are a vision, absolutely stunning."

"Thank you, sir." She grinned and held up a matching bowtie in her hands. "Zoya left this for you."

He wiggled with joy to be included and sat still as Katie bent down to clip it into place over his collar. Then he jumped down on the ground and followed her out of the suite and down the marble staircase. Her heels clicked on the stairs as she drifted down them, past other party guests in formal attire who were taking selfies in front of Zoya's impressive art collection.

When she got to the double doors, they were opened for her by gloved doormen. Outside in the evening breeze, fairy lights twinkled in tune with the stars in the navy sky above. She followed the path toward the sound of music, glancing around for a familiar face. The first one she recognized was Callie, flawless in a gold and black form-fitting sequined Prada gown with her jet-black hair flowing down her back in smooth waves. She was on the edge of the crowded dance floor, swaying to the music with a very attractive dark-haired man in a linen suit. Their bodies melted together in the sultry night, and it almost felt like an invasion of privacy to watch her daughter dancing with such wild abandon. She averted her eyes and made her way to a table where Beckett, Lauren, and Tom were gathered.

"Mom?" Lauren said, "You look… wow!"

Katie grinned and reached out to clasp Lauren's hands. "I can say the same about you!" Lauren was rocking a red latex body-conscious dress. Her hair was pulled into a high ponytail on the top of her head, and the effect was edgy punk rock glam.

"Not very many women can pull off red latex," Katie said. "But you sure can!"

Tom agreed. "I did a double-take when I saw her." He waggled his eyebrows and pulled Lauren in close by the waist. "I didn't even recognize you!" He kissed her cheek, and she shot him a thousand-megawatt smile. Their interaction made Katie's heart swell with happiness. As a mother, there was no greater joy than seeing your child choose a partner that brought out the best in them. Witnessing Lauren in love was a spectacular sight. She glowed from the inside out. Katie reached out one hand to squeeze Tom's shoulder, grateful for the man who lit her daughter up.

Then Katie turned to Beckett. "And you cut an impressive figure in that tuxedo! Talk about tall, dark, and handsome." She reached up to straighten his bowtie, and he kissed her on the cheek, then pointed over to where Callie was pressed against the pelvis of a different man, this one blond.

"Looks like Callie's taking your advice literally," he deadpanned as he sipped at a rum and Coke, watching Callie gyrate across the dance floor with a pained grimace. He was fiercely overprotective of his little sister. "Looks like we might want to keep an eye on her."

"It's not your job, honey," Katie reminded him. "She's an adult and can handle herself. Why don't *you* go find a dance partner and enjoy the night?" Beckett considered her suggestion for a long moment before finally nodding in agreement.

"You're right, as usual." He smirked. "By the way, you look sensational, Mom. Why don't you take your own advice and go find your next ex-husband?" From under the table, Arlo bared his teeth and grumbled a warning growl.

Katie grimaced painfully at the thought. "No way! I don't need a man. I'm much happier on my own."

"Well, *I* am not," he declared and slammed back the rest of his drink. As Beckett wandered off in search of his own fun, Katie watched him stroll away and disappear into the swaying crowd on the dance floor.

"Where's Yuli?" Lauren asked.

"This isn't really her scene," Katie offered. "She decided to call it an early night. Traveling tends to wear her out. She's so active for her age that people forget she's almost a centurion."

"It's hard to believe she's two years away from triple digits," Lauren remarked. "I swear, she has more energy than Grandma most days!"

Katie nodded, unwilling to add anything else to the conversation, afraid to rouse Lauren's suspicions. Luckily, the next musical act had just taken the stage and gave her daughter something else to focus on.

"Is that Adele?" Lauren was stunned to hear the first bars of "Easy on Me" drift through the speakers.

"I believe it is," Tom answered.

"If P!nk gets on stage next, I'll have died and gone to heaven," Lauren gushed.

"Well, get your wings ready," Zoya said, clearly within earshot of their conversation. "She's up tomorrow."

"No way!" Lauren was jumping up and down, her heels stabbing into the soft green lawn. "Are you my fairy godmother?"

"Possibly," Zoya boldly declared, her voice more playful as she sipped on her gimlet. "Is it okay if I steal your mother for a few minutes?"

"Of course," Tom answered for her. "I've been waiting for the chance to whip this gorgeous creature around the dance floor, anyway." They departed the table, and Zoya turned her eyes to Katie.

"I knew the Versace would fit you like a glove."

Katie grinned and cupped her hands on her hips. "You have a great eye."

"It's vintage. You can never go wrong with the classics." Zoya's voice quieted. "How did it go?"

"The music box had a definite impact on us both," Katie answered. "It was quite a journey. I never put together that Yuli's birthday was also the anniversary of Nadia's death." Katie's voice was laden with sincere empathy. "I'm sorry for your loss. It must have been difficult."

Zoya pressed her lips together and nodded. "I let the sorrow rob me of joy for years, and I let my anger fester and destroy any chance I had with Yuli." She glanced up at the full moon, reflecting on the previous one on the night of the *Fioletovy Mahiya*. Loosely translated in Ukrainian, it meant Purple Moon, and on that night, Nadia appeared and helped each woman in their mortal bloodline heal their heart in an attempt to empower the coven. Since the event, they were each grappling with the revelations and finding their way.

"Seeing Nadia again was a reset for me," Zoya admitted. "I realized I was holding on to rage in my heart with an iron fist and there wasn't room for anything else. Now that I've let go of some of it, I think there might be space for Yuli. Do you think she will ever be able to forgive me?" Zoya's voice was uncharacteristically wistful, almost childlike in its sincerity, and it caught Katie off guard. Her great-great grandmother was a study of contradictions.

"I don't want to put words in Yuli's mouth, but I know going inside the music box tonight helped *me* see you in a different light. I am certain it was the same experience for her. But change takes time, and you will have to prove you've changed your ways for good."

"I guess that's the best reaction I can hope for at this point." Zoya nodded her acceptance. On the main stage, applause thundered and then turned into catcalls and screams of excitement when "Rolling in the Deep" started. When the volume calmed down enough to carry on a conversation, Zoya said, "I went to the Adapt4Heroes Foundation."

"Whoa! You did?" Surprised yet desperate for an update, Katie tried to push away her initial annoyance.

"I hope I didn't overstep," Zoya added, uncharacteristically apologetic.

"While I appreciate the help, I would have preferred a heads up."

"Of course," Zoya said magnanimously. "Next time, I will inform you before I get involved."

"Did you get to meet Rox?"

"She wasn't in the office," Zoya paused, adding, "but I got to speak to Sam Williams."

"What was he like?" Katie asked. "Rox told me the story of how he saved her life when we had lunch a few weeks ago."

"Hmm." Zoya mulled it over. "He likes to drop that heroic little tidbit into conversation as frequently as possible as well. I'd say my first impression is that he's a typical alpha male, in love with the sound of his own voice." She took another sip of her drink. A server drifted over, and Katie plucked a flute of champagne and a stuffed mushroom on a silver napkin from the tray. She popped it into her mouth and chewed.

"I've agreed to accompany him to a black-tie event in a few weeks."

Katie sucked in too quickly and swallowed the rest of the appetizer without chewing. She coughed as it got lodged in her windpipe, washing it down with another swig of bubbly.

"That's ballsy."

"Don't worry, darling, I'm nothing more than a walking checkbook to him. I honed in on a few of his thoughts and it's purely business. He's got dollar signs in his eyes." She glanced into the crowd. "I guess it's not too much to ask to sacrifice one evening of my life to help you with your assignment from Karma."

"I appreciate it." Katie grimaced. "It feels like I'm floundering here."

"We'll figure it out together," Zoya reassured her. "Now, I can help gather intel, but Karma came to you. *You* are the chosen one to deliver the rebalance when it comes time. And for once, I promise not to get in the way."

Katie nodded, feeling the weight of it settle deeper on her shoulders. She was conflicted. On one hand, she wanted Zoya to butt out and give her the space to deliver the rebalance herself. On the other, she understood she was an inexperienced witch, and it would be smarter to lean on Zoya's experience than to blaze her own way.

"I'll see what I can learn at the fundraiser. I'm looking forward to meeting Rox. Sam said she's a tough one to nail down at the office. She clearly prefers to spend her time at the hospital and in the field in a fundraising capacity for the foundation."

"I'm not surprised at all." Katie perused her few memories of the woman. "She doesn't seem like a paper pusher."

"I would agree," Zoya said, bringing the conversation to a close. "Do have some fun tonight, dear. I know I plan on it." She winked at Katie and then sauntered over to a man Katie recognized from the tabloids. Within minutes, she had him eating out of the palm of her hand. Katie watched her interactions, wondering if it was a joy or a curse to have that kind of effect on men. She decided it was the latter and then called it a night and walked Arlo back to her suite. She'd take the steadfast love of a dog over a man any day.

Two days later, Katie boarded the aircraft to head home with her family. This time, they were all exhausted from the non-stop party atmosphere at the compound. Callie was visibly relaxed and in better spirits, and after hugs and promises to meet for dinner the following week, the beleaguered travelers deplaned and drove themselves home. Katie breathed a sigh of relief when she arrived home with her supernatural family secrets still intact. As she drifted to sleep that night, she felt at peace with the visit. She knew their time spent in the archives would someday prove to be a pivotal moment in healing the rift between Yuli and Zoya. Already, Katie couldn't deny the changes she was noticing firsthand in Zoya, and she was looking forward to the guidance she would soon provide in her rebalance for Rox.

THIRTEEN

After picking up Kristina, David, and Yuli, Katie drove toward the pin she'd been sent for their meeting on the beach with the clairvoyant and spiritual medium, Talulah LaRue. Katie had arranged a private reading to connect with Yuli's husband, Otto, as a Christmas gift, and it was finally the day of the reading. Her thoughts were preoccupied as she drove, trying to untangle the clues of her latest assignment from Karma, and she welcomed the distraction this detour would provide. Sometimes you just needed a break from a problem before the most elegant solution would present itself.

"Are you guys excited?" Katie asked, glancing in the rearview mirror into the back seat where Yuli had been silent on the drive. Katie knew it was because she dismissed most psychics as charlatans who preyed on the grief-stricken. Yuli had been around the block a time or two and had her guard up, but she didn't want to spoil her daughter's excitement at the prospect of reconnecting with her father.

"Oh, yes!" Kristina said with enough enthusiasm for them all. She was practically effervescent with anticipation. Though Otto had passed several years before Katie was born, his absence left a gaping hole in their lives. Yuli spoke about him with such sweetness. Through her stories, she'd learned he was the glue that held them all together, and his daughter, Kristina, had been the apple of his eye.

"I didn't sleep a wink all night," Kristina added, bouncing with energy in the seat next to her daughter. "I've been counting down the days since last Christmas!" There was a childlike wistfulness in her voice that tugged on Katie's heartstrings.

"Talulah LaRue's the original hippie chick," Kristina explained. "She lives in total seclusion off the grid in a treehouse surrounded by palm trees and palmetto bushes and only comes to the mainland for readings a few times each year. When a couple of videos from her readings went viral on Tik Tok three years ago, she exploded into the mainstream."

"Wait…" Katie was dumbfounded. "You're on TikTok?"

Kristina winced. "I can't help it. Those little videos are addictive."

Katie chuckled to herself as she checked their route to the pin on her phone. She couldn't imagine her seventy-three-year-old mother scrolling through the cesspool that was Tik Tok. "I gotta say, Mom, I love that you still have the ability to surprise me."

"She still surprises *me*, and I've been with her for the better part of fifty years," David chimed up in the back seat. Katie glanced at him in the rearview mirror. She adored the relationship her parents shared. One of her deepest regrets was she hadn't loved herself enough to make as great a choice for her partner. Though she'd finished beating herself up about it after her divorce, the occasional pinch of regret still reared its ugly head. Katie squashed it as quickly as it came, letting her mother's excitement about their appointment with Talulah LaRue infect her.

"Isn't she almost seventy?" Katie exclaimed.

"Hey, now," Yuli piped in from the back seat, taking offense and making Katie pink from embarrassment. "I've got a decade or two on her, and I'm not slowing down. Age is an issue of mind over matter. If you don't mind, it doesn't matter."

"Mark Twain?" David asked and was pleased when Yuli confirmed with a nod. "What a legend."

"Talulah must share his sentiment. Her Wikipedia page has her at sixty-seven," Kristina added.

"Wait… you're on Wikipedia, too?" Katie was stunned again and laughed at herself for confining her mother to a box she clearly wasn't willing to be contained in.

"What?" Kristina asked. "When you're retired, you have a lot of time on your hands." She was sorting through a handful of photographs in her hand.

"I didn't know which photo would give her the strongest connection, so I have five for her to choose from."

"Good thinking." Katie asked, "What personal items did you bring?"

"His bowler hat, one of his ties, and a cutting from the spider plant he gave us after we were married." Kristina grew clearly more excited the closer they got to their destination.

"Interesting choices." Katie made the final turn toward the pin. "I think this is it." She looked down at her phone that showed them on top of the pin as she pulled into a parking spot at Pass-a-Grille Beach. The view was spectacular, showcasing the sugary sand and turquoise water Florida was famous for. Approaching the twilight hour, it was even more breathtaking as the sun lowered and kissed the white caps of the waves rushing toward the shore.

"That's her!" Kristina said, pointing to a lone woman sitting at the edge of the water with long, violet-gray hair that flowed down her back to rest on the blanket she was sitting on. Next to her, a fluffy Samoyed sat on its haunches, its fur rippling in the sea breeze.

"How do you know?"

"The purple hair. It's her trademark. And the fluffy dog next to her is Chakra, her sweet pup."

Kristina flung off her shoes like a two-year-old, eager to get closer to the woman. Katie chuckled as she gathered them up and tucked them in a bag along with everyone else's but David's. He kept his trainers on to navigate the sloping terrain of the sand. She laced her arm through his and led him closer.

"This was a great gift, honey," David remarked as they walked. "I haven't seen your mother this excited since Callie was born."

Katie was touched by the praise. "For her sake, I hope we make contact with Grandpa tonight."

Just a few steps away from the woman and her dog, Katie watched Talulah rise from the blanket, stand to her full five-feet, and offer them a huge smile. When she grinned, her bright grey-blue eyes crinkled at the corners, and the gap between her front two teeth and wide smile made her appear years younger.

She was dressed in a long, flowing handkerchief dress in the soft blue hues of the sea. It had spaghetti straps, and her thin arms were tanned, liver-spotted, and exposed. Beaded bracelets walked up both of her forearms, and an amethyst, rose quartz, and tourmaline necklace encircled her throat. She was rail thin and seemingly floated over the sand. The dog stood and sniffed the new guests and, deciding they were not a threat, walked away to claim a corner of the blanket.

She pressed her palms together and bowed deeply toward them, her lips pressed to her fingertips. She extended both of her hands and wrapped Kristina's larger hand in her own. "I'm Talulah LaRue."

"Oh, gosh," Kristina gushed. "It's such an honor to meet you. I'm Kristina, and this is my husband David, my daughter Katie, and my mother, Yuli."

"It's great to meet all of you."

She closed her eyes for a moment and exhaled a long breath from between her teeth. Rolling her shoulders, she let out a long, loud sigh that made Katie shift uncomfortably. When her eyes popped back open, her voice was soothing. "Let's all try to relax. I can get a better reading if we remain calm and open." She pointed to the heavy blanket that was spread out on the sand. "Let's have a seat and form a circle, facing each other."

Kristina gingerly sat down next to Talulah, and Katie settled David across from her, knowing part of his enjoyment would come from watching his wife light up during the reading. On the other side, Katie took a seat next to Yuli, facing the medium.

"Who are you hoping to contact today?" Talulah asked.

"My father," Kristina answered for the group.

"Can I see the personal objects you've brought with you?"

Kristina opened a canvas bag and handed over the hat, tie, plant cutting, and a handful of photos. "I wasn't sure which one would work the best."

Talulah flashed her a wide, engaging smile. "Try to let go of the anxiety, honey," she coached with a smile. "Part of this experience requires us to tap into the ocean of energy within that is connected to the entire universe. We can't flow into this sea of consciousness when we white-knuckle the moments around us." Katie detected a hint of a southern twang to her sweet instructions.

Kristina nodded in agreement as Talulah held out

her hands to accept the objects. She rifled through the photos and chose one, handing the rest back to Kristina. "He looks like a real character," she said with a knowing smile. Yuli's wary eyes shot over to her, but she refused to verbally confirm this simple known fact as her skepticism won out.

"So, first, I will try to connect with him for a few minutes. I've been told my eyes change colors and brighten while I'm in this stage of the process." She explained, "Just a fair warning. It can be scary if you aren't ready for it. But there is nothin' to worry about." She then reached out. "Let's join our hands together to keep the flow of energy that will gather during the initial contact contained within our circuit."

She presented her palms to Kristina and David, and they all linked hands to complete the circle. Her forehead creased and then she began to sway and rock in tune with the wind. She emitted a low humming sound for the next several minutes.

Talulah shook her head no, and her eyes popped open and then narrowed on Katie and Yuli. She opened her mouth to say something and then shut it.

Her reaction made Katie panic. Could she feel their supernatural energy? Katie glanced over at Yuli, whose discerning gaze never left Talulah.

"Sorry. Let me begin again. I'm having trouble connecting. There seems to be conflicting energy."

Katie's eyes widened and darted over to Yuli's as she tried to let go, praying their supernatural abilities wouldn't be outed.

Talulah picked up the bowler hat and held it in her hands. She then gathered up the tie and started to mumble under her breath. Her lips moved as if she was having a conversation with someone. She set the two items in her lap and picked up the photograph that showed Otto laughing, his eyes twinkling behind his thick glasses. The longer she stared at it, her eyes began to glow, and Katie began to relax. Kristina's eyebrows shot up, and she leaned closer with hopeful anticipation.

"I'm connecting with a man. This is strange. He's showing me a recipe," Talulah said. Her lips continued to move, and then her nose wrinkled. "Sounds revolting. Peanut butter, bacon, and pickle sandwiches? Cut straight across. He says this is very important because his wife thought anything that wasn't diagonal was a crime."

Kristina's hand flew to her mouth. "Mom?"

Yuli was taken aback as Talulah continued, "He has a heaviness in his chest, around his heart maybe." She paused and concentrated again, her brow furrowing as she listened. "He says he didn't get to say goodbye." She laughed and nodded. "Says he was buried in his favorite hat and wishes you had chosen the second favorite instead. Such a waste. He's spitting on the ground."

Yuli cracked a smile that she hid with her hand and couldn't help but lean closer.

"This is strange. He also said he's proud of his... crabby crab? Does that mean anything to anyone?"

Yuli gasped. "That was his nickname for me when I

was getting on his case. My zodiac sign is Cancer—the crab." She shook her head in disbelief. "How are you...?" She cut herself off, rendered speechless by the irrefutable evidence of such specific details.

"The candy shop? Does that make any sense?"

"Kandied Karma!" Kristina cried out, thrilled he was coming through so clearly.

"He says he missed your second act and wishes he could have been your first taste tester." Talulah focused on Yuli. "He's telling me you started it after. He keeps saying after and rubbing his chest. Was it a heart attack?"

Yuli chuckled and nodded with tears in her eyes. "Yes. He was forty-seven." Stupefied, she listened in wonder. "We dreamt about it together for many years, but I only got the chance to make the dream come true after he passed."

Talulah laughed, and the sound was innocent, rippling joy bubbling from her and spreading outward. "He's a funny one. Always with the jokes." She turned to Yuli again. "He's saying something like, "Just his luck, he has a voracious sweet tooth, and you wait to open a candy shop until *after* he died."

A tender smile quirked up at the corners of Yuli's lips. Katie was in awe of the shift that she was witnessing in her grandmother with her own eyes.

"He's saying, 'Don't worry, I'm rocking the babies.'"

Hearing that, Yuli let out a choked cry, and Kristina

was stunned. Talulah turned to Yuli and asked, "Did that resonate?"

Yuli nodded. "We had two miscarriages before Kristina."

Then Talulah turned to Kristina. "He's calling you his little miracle."

"She is," Yuli confirmed as she wiped away a tear from the corner of her eye.

"He's been watching over you, Kristina, and regrets he never got to see you become a mother."

"Really?"

"He says you talk to him on his birthday." She stopped. "And he doesn't want you to feel guilty that you don't go to his grave anymore. He says, 'I'm not in the ground in Chicago, Krissy. I'm here. I'm all around you. I never left.'" She closed her eyes again, and her lips feverishly moved as she carried on a conversation. "He's showing me a copper coin."

"Oh my gosh! He put a penny in my shoe on my wedding day, and ever since he died, I've been finding them everywhere." Kristina melted and leaned toward her mother, putting her head on her shoulder.

"Check the jar?" Talulah said, her expression confused.

"There is a jar of them on my nightstand," Kristina said.

"He wants you to check the jar. He keeps pointing at it. Check the jar. In the jar."

Yuli reached out and clutched her daughter's hand as she brushed a tear away from the corner of her eye.

"This next message is for your mother." Kristina nodded and used a cotton handkerchief in her purse to wipe the tears from her cheeks.

"He didn't want to leave you, but he said if he hadn't, then you wouldn't have had the opportunity to shine so bright." Yuli pressed her lips together and moaned as a wave of bittersweet agony swept over her. "He's waving a wand. I don't understand... a magician?" Talulah was confused with the next message. She mumbled to herself, and her lips continued to move. "A conductor?"

"That doesn't make any sense," Yuli said, effectively shutting down the conversation. She pointedly stared Talulah down, and the woman quickly changed gears. She rocked from side to side and continued to hum.

"He wants you to know he's happy, and he is drawing an infinity symbol in the air with his finger. The love on the other side is infinite." A peaceful smile rested on Kristina's face.

Talulah turned back to Yuli, her forehead knit together in confusion. "He's handing me a Halloween mask. Does Halloween have any special significance?"

"Not particularly," Yuli said.

"He keeps lifting a mask up from his chin and handing it to me."

Katie racked her brain, trying to make sense of the revelation, but kept floundering.

Talulah's voice changed, taking on a harder edge. "A snake?"

Katie heard Yuli's voice in her ears. "Snakes are sacred beings." She glanced over at Yuli, who shrugged. They were both stumped. After a long pause, Talulah's tone softened, and she said, "He says, 'Don't worry about me, I'm surrounded by light. All light.'"

The medium opened her eyes, and the glow flickered, then diminished over the next few seconds before finally extinguishing completely. "He's gone," she whispered as she pulled her hands back and folded them in her lap. They sat spellbound for several long moments, each lost in thought over the soundtrack of the sea.

Finally breaking the silence, Kristina piped up, "That was incredible! You have such a gift."

Talulah thanked her, and her eyes pointedly sought out Yuli. "There is magic all around us. I just lack the ability to tune it out."

Yuli returned her gaze with a steadfastness that took Katie's breath away and made fear claw up her insides.

"There is magic in you two." Talulah pointed her long finger accusingly at Katie and Yuli and waved it between them.

On the verge of discovery, Katie deflected, "We've always been close," then quickly turned to Kristina to change the subject and asked, "How do you feel, Mom?" She knew they were flying too close to the sun, and she was grateful when the question broke the spell and Kristina refocused on the reading.

"Lighter, maybe?" she answered, dumbfounded by the experience that was hard to put into words. "To know he is up there, and we are still connected, it takes away some of the pain of missing him." She shook her head and hugged her arms to herself. "What about you, Mom?" She turned to Talulah and admitted, "She was skeptical. She only came along to humor me."

Yuli was just as transformed by the reading as well. "I have to admit, you're the real deal. You opened my mind."

"Thank you." Talulah nodded with a sweet smile. "I can't take the credit; I'm just the vessel. These are my favorite types of readings because they are so clear and heartwarming. Other readings are not so easy. Violent ends come with their own aura and overwhelming feelings of pain and loss. As an empath, I have to be very protective of my energy and balance the two so I can exist in this world. Otherwise, the darkness would consume me. I far prefer the quietude of my treehouse, falling asleep to the cries of the seagulls and the lullaby of the ocean."

Katie's eyes settled on the impish sea nymph with long flowing hair who personified peace and light. "That sounds heavenly."

"It is." Talulah grinned.

She got to her feet to signal the end of the meeting, and they said their goodbyes. Katie helped her dad navigate the stretch of sand to the car. Lost in thought, she noodled on their discoveries. Her view on the infinite possibilities of the universe was shifting again. The world she'd been living in before her awakening was but a speck in the vastness of the cosmos. Now, she was beginning to understand that souls were infinitely connected and mortal life was but one part of their journey together. It was a path that continued on forever, repeating the same lessons until they were learned, and the revelation was mind-blowing.

FOURTEEN

The night of Salute & Soiree, Zoya waited in her town car outside the opulent Palazzo Azure, a hotel perched on the edge of the bay and a hangout that she frequently enjoyed due to their well-endowed bartenders. But tonight, she couldn't partake in her usual dalliances. Tonight, she was on a mission. The ride from the airstrip had been blissfully silent. Zoya had politely declined Sam's offer to drive her to the event to keep her sanity. It would be draining enough to be stuck in a ballroom, forced to rub elbows with hundreds of sweaty do-gooder ordins.

She opened her sequined clutch and swiped a finger across the brown bottle of Verity Oil. She'd tucked it into the bag in case an opportunity presented itself to give her the chance to test its efficacy. The closer the oil was administered to the brain, the more potent it would become, but it was still five moons from full potency.

She knocked on the glass partition that separated her

from her driver, and a few moments later, Higgins opened the car door and she stepped out into the cooler night air in her red patent leather boots. She was dressed in a navy, lace ball gown, choosing to keep the bulk of her skin covered to avoid any wayward touches in case Sam was the kind of man that helped himself. On her hands, a pair of pristine white gloves would prevent her from accidental skin contact. Her white hair was gathered into a loose chignon at the base of her neck, and tender white ringlets framed her stunning face. Thanks to an extra few minutes in the glam chamber, she was glowing with vitality, and knowing men were visual creatures, she leaned on her assets, hoping it would give her an edge. Tucking her clutch close to her side, she strode toward the entrance of the grand hotel that was framed by several large palm trees swaying in the ocean breeze.

At the golden front door, she jumped when she felt an arm at her waist and whipped around to see Sam at her side, eager to enter the ballroom with her. She brushed the irritation at the unwanted physical contact aside and beamed up at him. "Oh! You frightened me!" She batted her eyelashes at him beguilingly, letting him feel powerful in the moment, knowing it was the secret to unlocking his desire. Deep down, all men wanted to feel powerful, which often led them to their own destruction. Her eyes assessed him in his dress uniform. His shoulders filled out the jacket in a not unattractive way. A colorful assortment of overseas service bars were meticulously aligned on the left side of his coat, as well as an assortment of medals. Zoya reached out to touch one of the gold medals dangling from the jacket in perfect alignment with five others.

"My, you've accomplished a great deal during your years of service. It's a wonder you can even stand up straight with all that extra hardware on your left side!"

Her praise had exactly the effect she'd hoped it would, transforming him into putty in her hands. He took a step closer and lowered his voice to a more intimate tone. "You're breathtaking. We'll definitely turn heads when we walk into the ballroom together." She turned away to swallow her irritation, facing him again when she had control over the emotions that liked to play peek-a-boo across her face. She loathed being reduced to arm candy like she didn't have a thought in her head that a man hadn't put there.

Playing right into his ego, she said, "When you're on the arm of such an accomplished war hero, you can't help but glow." The comment added fuel to his overconfident fire. Sam stood straighter as he clasped his hand over her gloved one and led her into the ballroom. As her eyes adjusted to the dim candlelight, she glanced around the room to get a lay of the land. A few moments later, the most obnoxious laugh startled her. "What in the world is that offensive noise?"

He grinned. "That's just Ricochet," he explained as he walked her closer to the harsh display of hilarity that grated on Zoya's nerves. "Come, I want you to meet the board."

"Do I have to?" she muttered under her breath,

fighting the draining thought of meeting more middle-aged men in uniform. "I was hoping to meet Rox Sullivan tonight."

He smiled. "Then you're in luck. Ricochet *is* Rox. She's the CEO at the Adapt4Heroes Foundation."

Finally making the connection, she brightened at the prospect. "It would be an honor to make her acquaintance."

Sam strutted like a peacock on full display as he escorted her over to Rox. As he cut through the crowd, Zoya heard the hushed whispers as she was recognized by onlookers who parted like the Red Sea to allow them passage. They joined a small circle of officers surrounding a woman who was dressed in a fitted navy coat and dress pants with golden buttons that glinted in the overhead spotlight. Her name badge read SULLIVAN, and a Purple Heart medal was dangling from her left side. Zoya noticed she was far less decorated than Sam. The rest of her ensemble was yawn-worthy and overtly masculine, including a pristine white shirt and a horrifically sensible pair of navy pumps with the smallest heel she'd ever seen on a shoe.

The woman burst into braying laughter again, and the obnoxious sound made Zoya jump.

"Sorry to startle you!" Rox apologized as she turned her bright inquisitive eyes to Zoya. "Sam, would you like to introduce us to your date?"

"This woman needs no introduction. Surely, you've heard of Ana Castanova?" Sam asked, and when Rox didn't recognize the name, her reaction intrigued Zoya. "Ana, I'd like you to meet Colonel Roxanne Sullivan."

Roxanne cupped one hand around her mouth and leaned toward Zoya. "My friends call me Rox."

Zoya cocked her head and studied the plain, unassuming woman in front of her with the easy smile and obnoxious laugh. Her mannerisms skewed more brash and confident, and Zoya appreciated the directness in her tone.

"Ana Castanova… from the *Castanova* Foundation?" Sam prodded when he didn't get the reaction he'd expected from Rox.

"Oh, shoot!" Rox said, snapping her fingers, finally putting the pieces together. "It's great to meet you. How did this knucklehead convince you to accompany him this evening?" she joked, ribbing Sam, and Zoya noticed his jaw tick, yet he pasted on a forced smile. The sight filled her with glee, and she turned toward Rox with a disarming grin.

"I'm a big fan of the work you do at the Adapt4Heroes Foundation on behalf of our valiant veterans and thought the best way to learn more about the cause was to come right to the source."

"I'm sure Sam can answer all your questions on his own," Rox said, picking up on the wing woman request vibe Sam telegraphed with his eyes. "He's been at the foundation the longest. In fact, he was the one who brought me on board when the CEO position opened up."

"A woman doesn't get to the C-Suite without her

own set of impressive qualifications," Zoya refuted. "Humility is overrated, darling."

Another short stilted, "HA!" shot out of Rox's mouth, and the group laughed in unison. Zoya recovered more quickly this time, and she brushed a hair from her cheek as Rox shot her a grin. "I like you!"

"The feeling is mutual," Zoya replied, and the next words spilled from her tongue like honey, "I'm always vetting deserving charities to become recipients of our resources at the Castanova Foundation."

"Well, say no more. We are *more* than happy to take those buckets of cash off your hands. Aren't we, gentlemen?" Rox beamed, and the group around her tittered in agreement. When they calmed down, Rox made introductions.

"Ms. Castanova, this is Staff Sergeant Matthew Alexander. He's been on the board for years, and served in Vietnam." Zoya reached out to shake the hand that was offered. "My administrative assistant, Sergeant Keith Landers, and his wife Alicia." Keith was in his dress blues and stood next to a frail woman in a cocktail dress who was very pale. Panic rolled off the man in waves. Zoya's curious gaze leveled on him, and the surrounding aura was a murky yellow indicating fear. She shook his hand, and he made brief eye contact before darting away.

Rox continued to introduce men gathered with their wives in the circle. Zoya tuned them out, shaking hands when they were offered, but she focused more on the woman making the introductions. She sized her up, looking for frayed edges, but there were none. At her side, Sam stood tall, his shoulders thrust back, and she noticed him glancing around the room, positioning himself as close to her as possible. Letting their body language tell an intimate story that was a lie.

"Are you the only female at the foundation?" Zoya couldn't stop herself from asking.

Rox thought it over and then admitted with an astonished snort, "Holy cow, I think I am." A wider smile spread across her face. "Looks like it's high time we diversified seats on the board. Are you interested?"

Zoya held up both her hands at the suggestion and took a step back in retreat.

Another sharp, "Ha!" darted out of Rox, and she leaned in. "It was worth a try! But if we can't get you on the board, we'd welcome your support with a donation. All kidding aside." She reached down and lifted her pant leg, and the metal of her prosthetic leg peeked out from the cuff. "Our wounded in action veterans deserve as many resources as we can wrangle, and I ain't too proud to beg." She shot out another halting chuckle, and Zoya was surprised when it crossed over from offensive to charming. She took a deep breath and listened to Rox and Sam recount the financial ramifications of needing a prosthetic limb for the rest of your life.

"It's not a one-and-done situation," Rox explained. "Most people are surprised to learn the life expectancy of a prosthetic leg is only three to five years. Especially during the first year when the limb is still healing and the tissues haven't settled into their permanent shape."

"What does a prosthetic leg cost?" Zoya asked.

"Low end is ten grand; the high end can be over a hundred," Rox disclosed.

"That's quite a range." Zoya's brows rose. "Does insurance cover it?"

Roxanne and the small circle of men surrounding her burst into laughter. "It's hard enough to get the VA to pay for the first one or two."

"Well, that is just unacceptable."

"I totally agree with you," Rox said somberly. "Being an amputee is something these soldiers have to learn to manage. First, there is the healing and rehabilitation phase, and phantom limb pain is no joke. When I was a new amputee, the VA recommended mirror therapy. Almost thirty years later, it's still the most effective tool to combat phantom limb pain."

"Mirror therapy?" Zoya was confused.

"I had to stare into a mirror reflecting my good leg for twenty minutes every day for several weeks. The therapy rewires the circuits in your brain into thinking your leg is still there to lessen the pain. You start to feel like you're going crazy, and you have no control over your own mind."

"I can't imagine." Zoya shuddered.

"It can take months to conquer this first battle. When I got back from Desert Storm, I vividly remember waking up soaked with sweat and my body wracked with pain from a leg that wasn't even there," Rox divulged. "Then you have to relearn how to walk with a prosthetic because your gait changes. To make matters worse, while you are battling your physical limitations, the emotional demons are lying in wait. Depression can set in and take hold when you realize all you've lost and that you will be managing your condition for the rest of your life." Rox offered her a small smile. "I intimately understand what these servicemen and women have lost. Since I'm further down the road they are just starting out on, I believe it is my duty to help them navigate their way."

Zoya nodded in agreement.

"When you restore mobility and give someone their autonomy back, it's a beautiful thing. It's a second chance."

The emcee walked to the podium at the front of the room and tapped on the microphone. "Ladies and gentlemen, if you could please take your seats. Our CEO, Rox Sullivan, is going to say a few words and offer the blessing. She did promise they would be few, right, Rox?"

Rox cupped her hands around her mouth and hollered, "Hooah!" and the room comprised of many retired and currently serving soldiers joined in. Once the crowd settled back down, the emcee continued, "Then dinner will be served. Following dinner, you're invited to dig deep into your wallet because tonight, ladies and gentlemen, with your help, we are going to smash the record we set last year for donations."

The crowd dispersed, and Rox strode confidently up to the podium. Sam turned to Zoya and offered her his arm. She took it and let him lead her to a linen-covered table at the front of the room. He pulled out the chair for her, and she offered him a thank you before settling down onto it, arranging her skirt around her.

Ten minutes later, the lights dimmed and slides cued up with music. For the next few moments, powerful photographs of the veterans the foundation supported, surrounded by their families, filled the screen, accompanied by photos of construction projects and wheelchair ramps. Zoya settled back and let the images wash over her, surprised by their effectiveness. She cleared her throat, felt the threat of tears prickling at her lashes, and internally applauded Rox's concentrated efforts.

At the podium, Rox clicked on a slide and leaned closer to the microphone. "This is Private First Class Travis Musselman. He lost his leg in Afghanistan. The Adapt4Heroes Foundation stepped up and was able to upgrade his prosthetic leg to allow him to compete in an Ironman Triathlon last year, where he earned a first-place medal in his division." The photo showed a grinning man standing in front of an inflatable finish line, sweaty from the effort it had taken to win. From a ribbon on his muscular neck, a bright gold medal dangled.

"This is Petty Officer Adam Bartholomew," Rox continued, flashing another photo on the screen. "He was brave enough to let me share his story with you."

She pressed play on a video, and a soft-spoken voice spooled out of a man seated next to his wife. "If it wasn't for the Adapt4Heroes Foundation, I wouldn't be alive today. At my lowest point, I remember cleaning my service weapon and thinking all of my problems would go away if I would just put the muzzle in my mouth and pull the trigger.

"When I got discharged from the hospital and went home, I was filled with anger. It was like a cancer eating away at me every day. My sister reached out to Rox at the Adapt4Heroes Foundation, and she immediately came over for an in-home visit. She listened. Really listened." His voice cracked with emotion. "Knowing she'd faced the darkness I was in and conquered it gave me hope. She immediately got me an appointment with her therapist and worked to qualify me for a PTSD clinical trial." Petty Officer Bartholomew reached out to squeeze his wife's hand.

He looked straight into the camera. "During our first meeting, I introduced her to our five-year-old daughter. I'll never forget what she told me." He choked up, and his wife squeezed his hand. A few seconds later, he was strong enough to continue. "She said, 'You are going to walk that sweet girl down the aisle one day. Isn't that moment worth living for?'" He wiped his eyes with his thumb and forefinger. "She didn't know it, but she saved my life that day."

Three more soldiers shared their stories, and when the house lights were brought back up, there wasn't a dry eye in the room.

Rox paused and added, "We owe our wounded veterans a viable path back to a fulfilling and productive life. It may not be the one they planned on, but more than anything, our brave men and women are resilient, and with your help, they will have the resources they need to build a brand new life.

"It is my hope tonight that you are inspired by their stories, and if you have the resources to do so, please dig deep. It tells our wounded service members, 'We did not forget you. We appreciate your sacrifice, and we will not rest until your quality of life has been restored.' Just like in battle, where our Army motto has always been 'No man left behind.'" Rox leaned closer to the microphone and added, "Or woman," and several low chuckles responded to her addition. After a pause, she continued, "We will not rest until we have fulfilled our promise to you. Thank you." After offering a short blessing, Rox stepped away from the podium, and the room broke out into thunderous applause. A second later, people began to get to their feet. Deeply touched, Rox looked out into the faces of the crowd giving her a standing ovation. Though this wasn't the way she'd imagined her life would unfold when she was a cadet at West Point, at that moment, she was awestruck by the imperfect perfection of her path and humbled by it. Shaking hands and waving to the sea of support, she finally made her way back to her seat when Sam put a bottle of beer in her hand. She took a long sip as dinner was served.

Zoya leaned in to congratulate Rox. "Not a dry eye in the house," she remarked. "I have to say, I've been to so many mind-numbing charity dinners. They all seem to blur together, but this was a special night."

"Thank you," Rox gushed. "I appreciate it."

After plates were cleared, under the table, Zoya felt Sam's hand land on her own and had to fight the urge to pull it away. Luckily, the DJ started to play music, and she had a reason to stand and put physical distance between them. Sam leaned over and grabbed her elbow, and she could smell the beer on his breath. "I'm heading to the bar. Can I grab you a drink?"

"Yes, please. Vodka Gimlet with extra lime?"

"Your wish is my command." Zoya had to fight the urge to yawn. Sam was proving to be a total bore. When he left, she shook her shoulders and closed her eyes, connecting with the energy in the room. The swell of thoughts started as a murmur and then increased in volume and frequency, as was usual during an event where there was a large crowd. She focused on Rox, who was making the rounds from table to table, and Zoya took a few steps closer to her casually, not to rouse suspicion. Her eyes bored into Rox's back, and she felt the first tremor.

We are so close to breaking records tonight. What a gift this life has been!

Wanting to fast-track her discoveries, and impatient with the lack of viable information she'd gathered, she sat down at the table. Hidden by the tablecloth, she opened her clutch and pulled out the small bottle of oil. She tugged off one of her gloves and dispersed a drop of oil to her finger tips, rubbing it in small circles. It wouldn't be at its full potency, but it still could be useful if it made contact with his skin. The closer to his brain stem, the better.

"There you are!" Sam said as he handed the beverage over to her. She pounced on her opportunity for skin-on-skin contact. Zoya brushed her thumb against his knuckles nonchalantly as she wrapped both of her hands around the gimlet. She took a sip, letting the oil seep into his skin, waiting for it to take effect.

A few moments later, Sam glanced over at Rox. "Look at Ricochet glad-handing over there. It's pathetic." His brow furrowed, and he took a step back, clearing his throat. "Wait. That's not what I meant." He tried to explain the slam away.

Zoya was stunned by how quickly the oil had seemingly taken effect. She hid her smile behind the crystal goblet in her hand. "Aren't you committed to the foundation?"

"It's merely a means to an end for me." He coughed, seeming to choke on the admission, and then said, "Gosh, I'm sorry." Sam quickly tried to backtrack. He pressed his fingers to his temple. Zoya held her breath as she watched in anticipation, hoping the oil would transfer from his knuckles to his head. It didn't, and she let out a defeated, heavy breath.

"I was thinking," he began, dangling a carrot in front of her. Her inquisitive eyes met his over the rim of her glass.

"Yes?"

"Maybe there is room for me at the Castanova Foundation? I think I've taken the Adapt4Heroes

Foundation as far as I can as the CFO. It's time for me to take the next step in my career."

Zoya was used to receiving pitches at charity events. It came with the territory, but this was bold. She resisted the urge to scoff at his suggestion and tried to evaluate it as an opportunity as he continued to make his case.

"I would be more than willing to take a look at your books and make sure you are implementing all the best tax minimization strategies to maximize your resources. I've found some very lucrative avenues for sustained growth that I would love to share. Perhaps I could be of assistance and prove my value to you?"

"Perhaps," she drawled, mulling over his request. "The decision is ultimately up to the board, but I would be happy to set up an interview." It was a board of one, but she didn't share that detail with him.

She wiggled her nose, and a second later, when his hand shot up to scratch an itch and briefly brushed his knuckles across the back of his neck, she rejoiced.

"That would make my day, beautiful," he crooned and leaned closer to whisper in her ear. "Might I also make myself available to you privately?" His breath brushed across her neck, making her next words flush with power.

"You must never dip your pen in the company ink, darling. I thought you were smarter than that." She relished breaking down his arrogance. It was infinitely more satisfying than the mediocre roll in the hay he'd just proposed.

"Again, my apologies. I don't know what has come

over me." He took a sip of his beer and cleared his throat.

Zoya threw him a bone to soften his fragile male ego. "I have no doubt your business acumen will prove very useful to the Castanova Foundation. I'll set up a formal interview after our next board meeting in a few weeks."

He grinned. "Can't wait."

FIFTEEN

A week later, Rox was sitting at her desk, tapping a pen between her fingers as she waited on hold with their lumber vendor. It was one of the last family-owned lumber yards in the south, and their military legacy went back generations. The current owner was in the National Guard and had served active duty in Desert Storm. His father went to Vietnam, and his grandfather spent most of World War II on a ship in the Navy.

"This is Tim." A gruff, authoritative voice came on the phone.

"Hey, Tim, I was hoping to catch you in a good mood." Rox infused warmth into her voice. "Because I need a favor."

"What kind of favor?" His voice was wary.

"With the way lumber prices have skyrocketed lately, I was hoping we could lock in a lower rate for the rest of the year since we do so much business with you."

He didn't object, so she soldiered on. "By my calculations, we've paid you almost eighty-four thousand dollars in the last two years alone. You know I'm not asking for myself. I'm merely trying to stretch our financial resources to help more veterans." Tim was silent on the other end of the phone. Rox knew he needed one more little nudge before he would give in. They had been working together for years and had developed a shorthand.

"We are united in this cause together since you're a veteran and you come from a long line of servicemen."

"We are, but Rox, we gotta eat, too," Tim said.

"That is understandable," Rox admitted. "How about we meet in the middle?"

"Give me a second to take a look." She could hear his fingers flying across the keys of his computer.

"Take all the time you need," she offered, waiting on the line.

A few minutes later, his voice shifted into confusion. "I think your math might be off."

"But I'm looking at the account right now," Rox said, just as confused as she cradled the phone into her shoulder with her chin while navigating the screens of the Adapt4Heroes account with the mouse. On the other end, she heard Tim typing.

"How much did you say you've spent on materials?" he asked.

Rox looked at the spreadsheet again, highlighting the line with the totals and then reading it aloud.

"Eighty-four thousand eight hundred dollars and some change."

"Hmm, That's interesting," Tim murmured. "I'm showing less than half of that."

"What?" Now, Rox was befuddled. "I've got all your itemized invoices right here."

"I'm looking at the same ones, and I am telling you, there's a huge discrepancy."

"How about we table our lumber negotiations until we sort this out?" Rox then asked, "Would you mind sending copies of all the invoices to Sam for the last two calendar years so we can look into it more closely?"

"You got it, Rox," Tim agreed. "Take a look, then we can talk. You know I'm not opposed to helping the Adapt4Heroes Foundation as much as I can."

"I appreciate it, Tim." She hung up the phone, more confused than ever. She walked over to Sam's office where all the financial records were archived, but when she tried to open the filing cabinets, she discovered they were all locked.

"That's weird." Rox returned to her office. A few minutes later, Sam waltzed through the door and into her office, humming and bringing her a fresh cup of coffee.

"My hero!" Rox said, taking a long sip. "Hey, I need your help."

"You got it."

"I gave Tim a call to see if he could cut us a better deal on lumber. My tactic was to try to guilt him into it by reminding him we've already done a substantial amount of business with him this year, and asking if he could split the difference on the increases coming this summer?"

"That's a good angle," Sam confirmed.

"I thought so, too, but when I gave him the total from our spreadsheet, he said we'd only paid him half that amount."

"What?" Sam's brow wrinkled in confusion. "That can't be right."

"Exactly! That's what I said, too." She added, "Then I went to find the original invoices in your office, and the filing cabinets are locked."

"Didn't Keith tell you?"

"Tell me what?"

"We changed protocol when an office down the street was burglarized a few weeks ago. It's better to keep all financials under lock and key," he explained. "I gave the key to Keith, and he said he put it in your desk." He shrugged. "Looks like I dropped the ball here and forgot to follow up. You've been out of the office doing so much fundraising lately, it completely slipped my mind. I'm sorry."

"Ah. That makes perfect sense." She nodded. "Keith's got a lot on his plate right now. I'm not surprised a few things are slipping through the cracks."

Distracted, he looked down at his watch. "Oh no!" Then he made direct eye contact and said, "This is an important conversation, but I totally forgot I scheduled a dentist appointment this afternoon." He offered her a warm, capable smile. "How about I gather all the necessary documents and we set up some time on your calendar tomorrow first thing to go through them page by page and get to the bottom of this? There's got to be some mistake."

"Perfect," she stated, and he stood. "Tim is sending you the invoices via email by the end of business today."

"Great." Then he looked deep into her eyes. "Don't worry, we'll resolve this and bring Tim around to our way of thinking!"

Rox smiled at his bold confidence. "Damn right, we will!"

"See you in the morning!" He offered a wave and departed her office. After he'd left, she pulled out the remaining beer from the refrigerator and popped the top off. She printed the spreadsheets from their accounting software and totaled them to prepare for their meeting in the morning.

She walked back into Sam's office to put copies of the paperwork she'd gathered on his desk, and her eyes locked on the framed shadowbox that was installed on the wall. On a bed of velvet, his Medal of Honor glinted in the last rays of sunlight that came through the window. Seeing it resting there destroyed her doubts. Her thoughts drifted back to the day she woke up stateside at Landstuhl Regional Medical Center.

The hospital air was sterile, and her throat was dry when she stirred and then opened her eyes, disoriented for several long moments, trying to get her bearings.

Her body felt heavy, and a dull ache in her leg surged and pulsed at the thigh.

Seated next to her bed, sitting in a chair, was Sam. He leaned closer and took her hand.

"Hey, Ricochet." His tone was warm. "It's about time you got up and faced the day."

"How long have you been here?"

"A while," he whispered.

Rox struggled into a sitting position, and her eyes registered that the lump where her legs should be looked misshapen. The first prickle of terror walked up her spine as she fought the weariness to tug her blanket away. Sam pressed his hand on hers, his eyes filling. "I think you should wait for the nurse," he whispered.

"No," she refused, then tugged the rest of the sheet away and gasped.

"I thought it was a nightmare," she mumbled quietly. Rox couldn't tear her eyes away from the span of white sheet where her leg should be. Her bandaged stump ended abruptly above the knee. She reached out to touch it, fighting the war of reality between her eyes and her mind. Scattered details of the event rushed to the surface, and she was desperate for answers.

"How's Monty?" she asked, bringing her eyes to meet Sam's concerned ones. Hearing her question, his shoulders sagged, and he shook his head no.

"What do you mean?" Rox's voice took on the edge of panic, and her heart rate monitor began to beep erratically.

"He cleared the way for us to make it to the caravan.

We were taking enemy fire from all around, and when transport finally showed up, we loaded you up and waited for him as long as we could."

Roxanne felt her heart clench in her chest and reached out to grip Sam's hand more tightly.

"We got orders to disengage and were forced to leave," Sam added quietly as Rox began to softly cry, her body trembling.

"Did they go back for search and rescue?"

"Yeah," Sam confirmed. "Their bodies were recovered a few days later, along with the other four."

"Oh my God," Rox cried. She wrapped her arms around herself and tried to focus, but it was impossible. Sam sat with her that entire night, never leaving her side. His own bullet wound in the shoulder was getting tended to, and he was persuasive enough to wrangle a room assignment in the bed next to hers.

Over the next week, reality set in, and Rox became despondent. She felt like she was floating away. Losing her leg meant all the career aspirations she'd had since she followed her father's footsteps into the military had been destroyed.

"I don't know who I am without the Army," Rox admitted late one night in the darkened room after they couldn't fall asleep. "I'm not cut out for civilian life."

From the bed next to her, Sam yawned, then answered. "You're an officer. You could transition to training and support."

"But I'll never see action again."

"True." Sam shifted in his bed. "The injury makes

you ineligible, but there are still plenty of ways you can serve in the States."

"I'm not sure I'm cut out for that, either."

"You'd still be leading soldiers, just giving them the tools they need to survive before they deploy."

"Maybe."

"Just think, less chaos without deployments. You might even be able to settle down and have a family."

She chuckled at the thought. "Are you telling me to wife up? That I'm useless as a soldier, so my only option now is to fall back on gender norms and enlist in the family plan?"

"You know what I mean."

"Would you say that to me if I were a man?" she questioned. "Of course you wouldn't. Are you saying now that I'm broken, my value is reduced to procreation? It's insulting."

"I'm just trying to find a silver lining," he explained, backpedaling. "You know. How everything works out for the best."

"You did *not* just call losing my leg a silver lining," Rox challenged him, anger crackling through each syllable.

"No, no, no," he backtracked. "I just mean that someday this setback will all make sense, even if it doesn't right now."

"We're going to have to agree to disagree on that," Rox groused. "Goodnight." She felt the bitterness growing in her soul. The reality was that Sam was going to be awarded a Medal of Honor for saving her life, and his career would fast-track after he recovered. He'd accomplish all the dreams she'd dreamed, and it would be hard to witness his rise in the ranks without the sting of jealousy.

The truth was, she didn't know where her life would lead her anymore. She'd painstakingly planned and plotted a course and had stuck to it her entire life. The injury hadn't just destroyed her leg; it destroyed her future. The idea of having no concrete future plan stirred up panic in her soul. Over the next few months, as she processed the end of her active duty career and segued into training, she felt like she was being forced to make more concessions when she'd made so many as a woman in the military already.

Over the next several years, Sam shot up the ranks as quickly as she knew he would. Roxanne received her Purple Heart the same day he was awarded his Medal of Honor and received a promotion. During the ceremony, she clapped for him until her hands were pink and stinging. The same painful sensation singed her heart. While she was happy for Sam, she was still munching on her own sour grapes. It would be years before she fully resolved her feelings of jealousy.

When Sam brought her on as CEO of the Adapt4Heroes Foundation, she felt vindicated. Though it was spiteful and she would never admit it, being the top executive had restored her sense of fairness in the world. Sam had spearheaded her selection, grateful to work under her. It had healed the crack in her heart she'd received from Desert Storm and dissolved the remaining bitterness that remained there.

That night, before she turned off the lights and left the office, she got an email invitation for their meeting set in the morning at 0800. She knew without a doubt they would get to the bottom of this together. Sam was always a man of his word.

———

Peacefully, Roxanne drove to her home in St. Petersburg, pulling into the garage, and closing the door behind her. After a dinner of leftover chili and a dried cornbread muffin that she washed down with a beer, she was relaxing on the recliner watching TV and almost drifted off to sleep.

At eight p.m., there was a harsh knock at the door that startled her upright, and she pushed the footrest down with her good leg in time to hear more pounding through the heavy metal. She quickened her pace, not even bothering to glance out the peephole in her haste to find out who was beating on her door.

"Yes?" She yanked open the door, confused by the presence of two police officers in full patrol gear standing on her front stoop. Their guns were in holsters at their hips. "Can I help you?"

"Roxanne Sullivan?" the stocky officer asked, his eyes hooded and boring into hers.

"Yeah. But you can call me Rox," she offered.

"You're under arrest for fraud and embezzlement at the Adapt4Heroes Foundation."

"What?" She was in shock. "Is this some kind of joke? Wait! Did Bert put you up to this? That cranky old goat!" She slapped her thigh and started laughing. "Where is the video camera?" She leaned out the door and looked around. "Bert!" she shouted through one cupped hand. "I am going to kill you!"

"No, ma'am, this isn't a joke," the officer countered. "Put your arms behind you and walk out slowly."

"What? Seriously?" Rox was taken aback, standing in shock as they read her Miranda rights. In a daze, she couldn't pull more than two thoughts together as her nosy neighbors watched her being led to a squad car and then her head pressed down to clear the door frame as she was put into the back seat. It was surreal, catching glimpses of the officers in the front of the car through the bars that separated them, knowing she was locked inside and the basic freedoms she'd fought for during her military service held no weight in this situation.

She sat in stunned silence while being driven to the station downtown. Her train of thought was constantly derailed by the radios on the officer's shoulders providing relentless chattering updates. When they pulled into the station to park, terror began to unfurl in her belly as the grim reality set in.

What in the sam hell just happened?

Sixteen

Katie was getting ready for bed at almost midnight when the phone at her bedside table started to vibrate and skitter across the wooden surface of her nightstand. Putting off answering it, she finished brushing her teeth, but then she heard the phone start to vibrate again. She picked it up and, seeing it was Lauren calling so late, quickly took the call.

"Hey, hon—" She was cut off by the sound of Lauren's choked sob in the background. "What is it?" she asked as panic surged adrenaline through her.

"It's Rox," she blurted, her tone high-pitched with disbelief. "She was arrested."

"Arrested?" Katie was in shock. "For what?"

"Embezzlement and Fraud at the Adapt4Heroes Foundation."

"No way," Katie gasped. "There must be some mistake."

"Tom rushed to the police station to try to get her

out on bail tonight, but he just sent me a text that she has to sit in there until her arraignment hearing in the morning. We're both in shock," Lauren cried. "What do we do? How do we help her?"

Katie commiserated, "If the news gets wind of this, there is bound to be backlash. She's been in the public eye, fundraising and being the face of the foundation for years. No one can resist a fall from grace. She is going to be bombarded the moment she's released on bail."

"God, I hate the media," Lauren lamented. "All the incredible work she's done over the years for so many military families will be wiped away by these unfounded accusations. Rox lives and breathes her work at the foundation. She's a good person, Mom. This is going to kill her."

Katie heaved a heavy sigh. "Sadly, people will pass judgment without knowing all the facts. The best thing we can do right now is rally around her. She's going to need our full support."

"I agree," Lauren said. "I'm worried about Tom, though. He's so close to his mom. I'm afraid he will get pulled into the crossfire." She let out a whimper. "I called Dad, but it just goes to voicemail."

"Did you try his clients only direct line?" Katie asked. Her ex-husband was a prominent defense attorney and partner in his downtown law firm, and was known to answer his phone twenty-four hours a day.

"No, but I will."

"In the meantime, Tom has valuable inside knowledge of legal proceedings, and he has a good head on his shoulders. Don't panic and let's focus on step one."

"You're right." Lauren sighed. "First, we need to get her out on bail."

"What if she stayed here with me at the beach house?" Katie intuitively knew she needed closer proximity to Rox to help Karma, and it seemed like the perfect solution.

"You'd do that?"

"Absolutely. There is no way she committed that crime, and she's going to need space to think and prepare a defense. What she *doesn't* need is the extra stress of being stalked by the media right now. Besides, I have plenty of room, and it's been too quiet around here since Marisa moved out. Aura Cove is the perfect place for her to hide in plain sight."

"I think it's a good option," Lauren agreed. "Let me run it by Tom. Thanks, Mom. Rox is important to Tom, and she's becoming important to me." Katie felt her heart twinge at Lauren's admission.

"There's no need to thank me," Katie said. "Let me know when she's going to be released. In the meantime, I'll get the guest room ready. Try to get some rest tonight and give Tom my love and support. We are going to get through this."

Lauren exhaled and Katie felt her tension relax between her shoulder blades. "I love you, sweetheart."

"Love you, too." Lauren's voice cracked at the end as she hung up the phone. Katie flung herself down on her bed as her mind churned through the conversation with Lauren.

Arlo hopped up, then circled and plopped down next to her. "What's got you so perplexed?" he asked, propping his chin on her upper thigh, a gesture that soothed Katie's jumpy heart.

She sat up and stroked the top of his velvety head while she explained, "That was Lauren. Roxanne was arrested, and when she gets out, I've offered to put her up here in the guest room."

"Arrested? What are the charges?"

"Fraud and Embezzlement."

Arlo tugged his chin back. "No way. I'll never believe it."

"Me neither." Katie shook her head. "Now, at least I know *why* she needs my help. I am hoping having her so close will help me unravel the how."

"She's a good person. I'd know if she was evil." Arlo spoke with complete conviction.

"How come dogs are such great judges of character?" Katie asked as he rolled onto his back, giving her full access to his belly. She rubbed down the length of it, lost in thought.

"We're intuitive creatures," he answered. "Most experts agree that most communication is non-verbal. Dogs don't get bogged down by believing lies we're told. We rely exclusively on actions as the barometer of good and evil and react to energy."

"Well, I *could* use your help," she added.

"Will this get me out of the doghouse?" Arlo asked,

thrilled at the prospect. He rolled back onto his belly and sat on the bed now, nose-to-nose with Katie. He'd been looking for a way back into her good graces since the eternal coven exposed his misdeeds at the *Fioletovy Mahiya.*

"Possibly." Katie said, "On one hand, I feel like I've punished you enough already, but on the other, I need you to understand you betrayed my trust."

"I *do* understand," he mumbled quietly, shame causing him to slide his eyes away from hers. He laid his chin on the bed and sulked.

"What if we set up some ground rules? I believe in second chances, but you won't get a third."

"Yes!" He lurched up on his hind legs, resting his paws on her shoulders, eager to agree. "Anything."

"No more secrets, and no more skulking around to secretly gather information for Zoya. I want to know what you plan on reporting to her from now on *before* you file your report."

"Deal," he agreed, holding up his paw to shake on it.

Katie smiled, took it in her hand, and wagged it up and down. Then she pulled him in for a cuddle and stroked his ears.

"I need you to be my eyes and ears when Rox gets here."

"You can count on me," he vowed.

SEVENTEEN

The next evening, the doorbell rang. Katie quickly crossed through the great room to open her front door where Tom, Lauren, and Roxanne stood waiting on the steps. A worn Army duffel was resting at Roxanne's feet. Katie stepped over the threshold to pick it up for her and dragged it into the house.

"Come on in," she said with a bright smile, trying to offset the somber mood casting a heavy pall over all of her visitors. Rox's eyes were weary, and the lines in her face were etched deeper. The last twenty-four hours had stifled her usual vibrance and left her looking like a caged animal; her eyes darted around the room, assessing her environment, looking for threats, and planning her escape route.

"Thank you for opening your home up to Mom." Tom was the first one to speak. "It's a media circus over at hers. God, I don't know how they find out so fast.

They are like cockroaches." Rox's arrest had also taken a toll on Tom, dampening his usually sunny and easygoing disposition under the immense weight of stress and worry.

"We understand that dynamic, don't we, Lauren?" Katie commiserated with him, remembering what her kids faced when she'd been a victim of a home invasion several months ago.

Lauren offered her mother a faint smile and nodded.

"Let's get you settled in the guest room," Katie suggested as she led Rox down the hall and up the stairs. She stopped at the door to the bathroom. "This one is all yours. Feel free to unpack and use the drawers to get organized. I cleared an entire shelf for you in the closet."

Rox nodded, but she still hadn't spoken at all.

Katie dragged the rucksack further down the hall and opened the door to the spacious guest room, feeling grateful it would be occupied again. She wasn't happy about the circumstances, but she was certain being in Rox's presence would bring forward the breakthroughs they needed to exonerate her.

Rox sat on the edge of the bed and palmed her face in exhaustion. She rubbed her eyes with a balled fist before yawning.

"Are you hungry?"

"I lost my appetite, but thank you."

"Well, I hope it returns tomorrow because I thawed out some gorgeous rib-eyes for us to grill."

"That sounds wonderful." Rox added, "I'm sorry to

be such a Debbie Downer right now. I don't think I've ever been so tired."

"You don't have to apologize to me. I bet after a good night's sleep and a shower, you'll feel like a new woman in the morning." Picking up on Rox's need for rest, Katie stood. "I'll leave you to it, but my door is open if you need me." She plumped up a pillow, started to leave, then turned to add, "Please help yourself to anything in the fridge or pantry. I want you to make yourself at home."

Katie pulled the door shut softly behind her to give Roxanne some privacy, and then she padded down the stairs and out to the kitchen where Tom and Lauren were seated at the island, sharing a glass of wine. Seeing her enter the room, Tom walked over to the wine rack and grabbed another glass to pour one for Katie.

"I've got her settled, but she's exhausted," Katie explained. "I'm so sorry this is happening. It can't possibly be true."

"We're all baffled," Tom said. "Sam Williams has offered to come by the day after tomorrow to see Mom and help us figure out our next steps. He's been swamped with the board and media circus."

"That's good. He will help keep her spirits up." Katie then asked, "What evidence do they have?"

"There is a discrepancy between the checks she signed and the actual invoices they were supposed to pay. The most damning though is a series of regular transfers from the foundation to an off-shore bank account." Tom's voice cracked, and Lauren rushed to his side and wrapped an arm around his shoulders. "There's no way she would do this. She gets a rush out of helping as many soldiers as she can. She would not be draining the fund for her own gain. She eats, sleeps, and breathes the Army's principles of honor, integrity, and service."

"I believe you," Katie said.

"Thank you." Tom's voice was grave, his expression a mixture of disbelief and shock. "I think we both need a little more time to process what happened, and then we can circle the wagons and mount a defense." He spread his arms out and leaned on the island, lost in thought. "If only I'd become a defense attorney instead of going into family law."

"Lauren, maybe you can ask your dad to help Tom with her defense?" Katie was thinking out loud. "Or, at the very least, bring him on board to strategize?"

"I already tried," Lauren admitted. "He said he doesn't have the capacity right now."

Katie had to pinch her lips together to withhold her criticism. Knowing it was destructive and would get nothing accomplished, she forced herself to let her frustration go.

She snapped her fingers when the next inspiration hit. "I have an idea!"

"What?" Tom asked, his eyes filling with hope.

"Davina Thorne might be able to advise us, or at least give us the name of her forensic accountant. He could do a thorough analysis of the financial records at the foundation. If anything is amiss, I guarantee he'd be able to suss it out." She didn't want to fill Lauren in on the ugliness and hidden assets that had been brought to light during the divorce. It would serve no purpose but to make her angry at her father, and Katie didn't want to cause a rift when she'd already moved on.

"That's a good idea, but Mom has limited resources, and forensic accountants are spendy. I already plan on arguing her case to keep her legal bills manageable," Tom insisted. "But if you could email me her contact info, I'd appreciate the option if we need to exercise it."

"Absolutely." Katie nodded, happy to have a small way to contribute.

"I've never seen Mom like this," Tom admitted. "She's always been tough as nails, capable, and positive in the face of adversity. Obviously, there was enough evidence to bring charges, but..." He trailed off, stuck in shock before guilt washed over his features and he admitted, "For about two seconds, I considered the possibility she was guilty." His weary eyes searched Katie's. "What kind of son does that make me?"

"I think that's a perfectly natural response," Katie said to soothe his obvious guilt. "Don't beat yourself up over it."

"It goes against everything she stands for. My entire childhood, I was force-fed the concept of integrity until it stuck. Mom almost gave her life fighting for this country, and there is no way she would betray it or the lives of wounded soldiers for any amount of money."

"I agree with you. She seems content to live a simple life," Katie remarked. "If she embezzled significant funds, then what did she do with the money?"

"Exactly. Mom is frugal to a fault. She's driving around a car that's almost twenty years old. She washes and reuses Ziplock storage bags for Christ's sake. Mom's not motivated by money at all. What would she do with an off-shore account?" He shook his head in disbelief. "If you had any idea how long it took me to show her how to set up online bill pay, you'd know she is not capable of this crime."

"The truth will come out," Katie said as she reached out to squeeze his shoulder. "You both look exhausted. Why don't you head home and try to get some rest? I've got Rox."

Tom rinsed out their empty wine glasses and set them in the sink.

"Come here, you two." Katie opened her arms and gave them a squeeze. "Everything will look better in the morning."

———

Roxanne stayed in her room the entire night, and when Katie woke up at six the next morning, the door was still closed. While she was brewing a cup of coffee, she heard the shower come on, and twenty minutes later, Rox walked into the kitchen. Her gray hair was still damp from the shower, and large black circles took up residence under both her eyes.

"Good morning," Katie said with a smile. "Can I get you some coffee?"

"Yes, please." Rox pulled out a stool and sat at the island.

"How did you sleep?" Katie asked.

Rox grimaced. "Not great," she admitted, "but not because of the bed or the hospitality."

Katie laughed. "Totally understandable. I bet you have a thing or two on your mind."

Rox let out an anguished sigh. "Honestly? I'm still in shock." She stirred a dollop of cream into her coffee and added a sugar cube from the plate Katie placed in front of her. "How the hell did I get here?" Rox wrapped her hands around the coffee mug and added, "Seeing Tommy's face when he got me out on bail? It crushed me. I've worked my entire life to make him proud and always tried to do the right thing. This accusation has cut my legs out from under me." She let out a jolted, "Ha! How's that for irony?"

It amazed Katie how Rox could still see the humor in the humorless situation as they chuckled. She reached out a tentative hand and placed it over Rox's.

A tingle passed between them as she concentrated, trying to flush out a reading. The colors of her vision intensified, and she saw Rox in her military dress uniform. On her chest, the Purple Heart was displayed proudly. In the next vision, a highly decorated white-haired general ripped the medal from her chest. She had to fight the gasp that was stuck in her throat. Seeing the vision cemented the seriousness of the situation.

"He *is* proud of you." Katie offered a pep talk to soothe Rox's biggest fear—losing the respect of her son. "Tom knows you are innocent, and he's going to exonerate you."

Rox nodded in response, still bereft and filled with sadness. Katie honed in on her fear. Listening, she felt herself drop into a more meditative state to hear Rox's line of thinking. At first, the words sped by in a torrent of spiked panic and tremendous anxiety. The tangle of thoughts overlapped each other and made it hard to discern anything coherent. Katie went deeper, and the train of thought slowed down.

What if he doesn't? I've served the United States Army my entire life. What if I'm asked to resign from the Adapt4Heroes Foundation? So many people trusted me and believed in the work we were doing, and now it's all destroyed. Who will fight for those soldiers now? How many servicemen and women will we lose to suicide without the resources needed to restore their wellbeing? I have failed them.

EIGHTEEN

The next day, after breakfast, Tom came by to check on Rox, who was sitting in the kitchen sipping on her last cup of coffee. As Katie watched Tom embrace his mother, she could feel the tension and anxiety rolling off both of them in waves, and their auras were murky and dark.

"I'm okay, Tommy," she assured him. "Stop your fussing." To prove her point, she waved one hand over to the wall of windows at the back of the house that had a breathtaking view of the ocean in the distance. "It's like a vacation here at Katie's, waking up to this view every day."

"Mom, you don't have to be Positive Patty for me," Tom whispered.

The admission cracked her thin veneer, and her shoulders sagged. The brave face was a mask she'd put on to make him feel more comfortable, and when he gave her permission to drop it, the mask shattered like it was made of glass. Sadness filled her eyes as the corners of her mouth tugged down into a despondent frown.

"For a second this morning, when I first opened my eyes, I thought it was all a nightmare. But the truth came rushing back when I realized the reason I was here instead of home. Normally, I'd be heading to the hospital to check on a patient, or on my way to a job site to make sure the deliveries arrived and the contractors had all the materials they needed. I hate sitting on my laurels and all this waiting. It's tearing me up inside." She wrung her hands together, but there were no tears. "What can I do? There must be something I can do to help prove my innocence."

Tom set his briefcase on the dining room table and tugged at the tie knotted at his throat to loosen it. "Now that you've had some rest, I was hoping we could get some details down." He took a seat next to her and, from his briefcase, pulled out a yellow legal pad and a fountain pen. "I need you to walk me through the day-to-day activities at the foundation."

Roxanne nodded, eager to have a task to complete. Katie jumped up to her feet, asking, "Did you want me to give you some privacy?"

"Heavens, no!" Rox denied. "I'm sure you have questions, and another set of ears might be beneficial."

"Happy to help." Katie turned to Tom. "Can I get you a coffee? Or warm up the quiche we had at breakfast?"

"No, thank you," he said. "But I appreciate the offer."

Katie tugged out a chair from the table and sat as Arlo ambled over and plopped down at her feet.

"It varies so much from day to day. Some weeks, I spend most of my days either on the telephone or at events, trying to drum up donations and support," Rox explained. "At the same time, there can also be entire weeks when I'm not in the office at all." Tom scribbled notes as she spoke. "No two days are alike, and that is why I love it so much. I also spend a fair amount of time visiting home sites to manage the projects we are funding, and work one-on-one with wounded servicemen and women at the hospital. When there is a mental health crisis, especially with an amputee, I'm often the first one the family calls."

"Isn't that outside the scope of your duties as the CEO?"

"Technically," she confirmed, "but I've never embraced the typical C-suite non-profit mentality, where my purpose is to sit on a board and collect a fat paycheck. I've always hated organizations who funnel donations into paying bloated administrative salaries."

"Me too," Katie agreed.

"It's such a waste of important resources that could be used to help more people. You know me, Tommy. I've always been a boots-on-the-ground type of leader. I can't do my best work for the foundation without seeing the impact it has directly, and being involved throughout the entire process reignites my passion for the work and gives me the stories I rely on to keep donations flowing in." As Katie watched Rox's internal flame burn brighter speaking about her work at the foundation, it was impossible to see her in a self-serving light.

"Can you run me through the paper trail and the financials at the foundation?"

"I can hit the highlights," she looked at her watch, "but the specifics would be better directed to Sam and Keith."

"Let's start with the basics then," Tom told her.

"Well, we work on a Net 30 schedule with most of our vendors. They send us an invoice at the end of the month, and after verifying the invoices, Sam prepares the checks for payment. At the end of the month, he brings them to me for signature, and then they are mailed."

"None of this is conducted electronically?"

"Not usually. We've experienced explosive growth, but our processes haven't exactly kept up. Growing pains, you know." The statement filled her with obvious pride. "In fact, we just received our largest single donation to date. We were going to help so many families with that money." She sighed as the disappointment of not seeing it through darkened her mood.

"The missing piece of this puzzle is the financial records. In light of the charges and ongoing investigation, you've been locked out of all systems at the foundation. But I filed a subpoena for the financial records going back five years."

"That's probably a good place to start," Rox agreed.

"We really need to speak with Sam," Tom said. "He could provide valuable insight into the investigation."

"Affirmative," Rox stated. "I talked to him last night, and he's just as flabbergasted as I am. He's coming by today."

"Good, we have a lot of questions he needs to answer," Tom said.

"He'll be here," Rox urged. "We can count on him."

"What about Keith?" Tom continued. "Did he have access to these invoices?"

"He worked closely with Sam at my request. To be honest, I delegated the basic bookkeeping to our accounting team and put Keith in charge as a liaison."

"Who had access to the bank accounts?"

Rox exhaled a hot breath between her teeth, considering the question before answering. "Several people. The accounting team, Keith, Sam, the board members."

"This is getting messy," Tom admitted.

"Isn't that a useful defense strategy?" Katie asked. "Plausible deniability?"

"It can be," Tom answered, seemingly unwilling to get too excited at the prospect.

"There was something strange that happened recently. I don't know if it's related, but…"

"Why don't you let me be the judge?" Tom leaned forward, his pen paused and ready.

"I was trying to strong-arm our lumber vendor into locking in a lower rate for the rest of the fiscal year, and when I was talking with Tim at the lumber yard, there was a discrepancy between our bookkeeping records and his."

"Hmm." Tom feverishly scribbled notes as she relayed the information.

"Sam and I were going to sit down and go over the account. We had a meeting scheduled, and then all hell broke loose."

The doorbell chimed, and Arlo stood and howled at it. "Excuse me," Katie whispered and crossed the room to open the door to a clean-cut middle-aged man in khakis and a navy blue blazer who offered her an amiable smile.

"Hello, ma'am. I'm not sure I have the correct address. I'm Sam Williams, here to speak with Rox Sullivan."

"You're in the right place," Katie said and waved him inside. "It's nice to meet you." Seeing her friend, Rox choked up. She rushed over to him and he gave her a hug. Worry for her was etched on his face as he led her back to the table. "How are you holding up, Ricochet?"

"Honestly? I feel like I'm in the Twilight Zone." Rox shook her head.

"Totally understandable. You could have knocked me over with a feather when I'd heard you'd been arrested," he said, shaking his head. "Sorry it's taken me so long to connect. Since the story broke, the foundation is an absolute nuthouse. The phone never stops ringing with media requests for interviews. Don't worry, I declined them all."

"I knew we could count on your discretion," Rox

said. "I'm sorry to put you in such a compromising situation."

"No need to apologize," he insisted. "I have no doubt you will be fully exonerated. I'm just waiting for the day when you come walking through the door and we can get back to work."

He reached out a hand toward Tom. "Nice to see you again. Wish the circumstances were different." His expression turned somber.

"Have a seat," Tom said, offering him the open chair across from Katie. "We're hoping you can help us fill in some of the finer financial details."

"Anything to help." He nodded with a winning smile, his deep voice infused with empathy as his gaze lingered on Rox. "I won't rest until we right this wrong."

Hearing him say those words, Roxanne visibly relaxed. Katie studied him from across the table. His confidence was obvious, and he exuded capable determination.

"Mom was telling me there was a discrepancy with a vendor recently. Can you tell me more about it?"

"I'm sure you can understand this situation puts me in a really difficult position," Sam said, wincing. "Technically, I'm not supposed to share specific financial details with you under the current circumstances." He leaned in to offer her a conspiring nod. "But off the record, and between you and me, Tim is a terrible bookkeeper. I looked for the invoices he was supposed to send over in preparation for the meeting we scheduled before…" His voice trailed off, unable to make himself finish the sentence. "But he didn't send them all. There were *seven* invoices missing that I can account for, and that was just in Q1."

Rox sighed. "Ugh. I had my suspicions."

"I've been back and forth with his bookkeeper since Tim just left on vacation. To be honest, she's borderline incompetent, but I guess that's what you get when you hire your niece."

Tom slid his eyes from the legal pad to meet Sam's, and Katie cataloged the slightest hint of doubt in his wary expression. He was walking a tightrope to keep the lines of communication open, and Katie felt his trepidation. She tried to tune in to Sam's inner dialogue, but between Roxanne's terror and Tom's frustration, the thoughts were bleeding together, making them an indecipherable chatterbox of emotion.

Sam leaned back in the chair, hooking his ankle on his knee, taking on a more relaxed stance. "Did the police shed any light on the evidence they have against Rox?" he asked.

"They were pretty tight-lipped," Tom admitted. "You know the boilerplate 'Can't comment too much on an ongoing investigation' jargon. But the gist of the case is that, during a routine audit, a series of withdrawals totaling almost four-hundred-and-fifty-thousand-dollars made to an untraceable off-shore account was uncovered."

Sam's eyebrows shot up in surprise, and he whistled at the unbelievable sum. "Almost half a mil. Wow."

"Did you even know we were being audited?" Rox asked.

"It's SOP when any charity organization hits a certain threshold and happens every two or three years. I didn't think to involve you since it's been my responsibility to lead the accounting team and see them through since we started. It's never been an issue before." He sighed and scrubbed his hand over his face in dismay. "Jesus, Rox, I'm so sorry. I bet you felt blindsided."

"Well, yeah," she said, stunned. "I always hated getting stuck in the minutiae and bureaucracy, and thought my time was better spent getting in front of donors." She shrugged. "It's my own fault. I probably should have tuned in more at the office."

"That's the understatement of the year," Tom mumbled under his breath, then immediately apologized. "I'm sorry, Mom." His frustration and fear were getting the best of him.

"Truth be told, I'm not supposed to be speaking to you at all," Sam admitted. "The board at the foundation called an emergency meeting and made that much clear, but I will not stand idly by and let them railroad you like this. Full transparency, I think you should know that they made me acting CEO for the time being."

Rox gasped in despair.

"Don't worry, I'm just there to keep your seat warm until you're back in it." Sam's voice was filled with conviction as he tried to calm her rising fears.

"What we really need is visibility into the financial records," Tom stated, getting right to the point.

Sam exhaled a hot breath between his teeth. "That's going to be tough under the current conditions." He pondered the request. "Can you make a motion for discovery and get your own copies of the records? Then I will be at your disposal to help comb through them. We'll figure this out together, I promise."

"Already done," Tom said. "When we get access, we'll definitely take you up on your offer."

"Absolutely. Publicly, I'm sure you understand I have to maintain my distance and steer clear for the sake of the foundation, but privately, I will do whatever I can to help." He glanced down at his watch. "Shoot! I've got to be going." He stood up and reached out to squeeze Rox's shoulder. "Keep me posted and stay strong."

Katie walked him back to the door to let him out, hoping for a moment of casual contact, but he maintained his distance and her heart fell.

"Ma'am," he said with a nod, and then stepped out into the sunshine and disappeared down the street to his car.

When Katie got back to the table, Rox was glum. "Well, that got us exactly nowhere."

"The wheels of justice turn slowly, Mom. You'll have to learn to be patient."

"I can't just sit here twiddling my thumbs," Rox argued. "Without my integrity and honor, I am nothing."

"That's not true," Tom said. "You're still my mother."

"I'm sorry," she whispered. "You're right." She reached up to brush one hand across Tom's cheek. "I need to know you believe I'm being truthful."

"I do," Tom told her, no trace of doubt in his voice.

"Then you have to let me do what I was born to do." When he looked at her in total confusion, she added, "I have to fight."

NINETEEN

A few days later, Katie turned on the lights at Kandied Karma and started the opening routine when the amulet at her throat began to hum. It jolted her out of her reverie and made Arlo howl.

"What is it, boy?" Katie asked when the back door opened and Yuli and Zoya rolled in the back door together. Eyeing them, she asked suspiciously, "What is going on here? Are you two hanging out now?"

"Heavens no, dear, it's just a coincidence," Yuli said as she set her handbag on its perch and untied the scarf from her neck. "How is Rox holding up?"

"The woman is unshakable." Katie admired Rox's inner strength. "I'm going to try to convince her to set up an appointment with Davina Thorne to retain her forensic accountant to do some digging into the off-shore account they are accusing her of utilizing."

"Off-shore account? How interesting," Zoya

weighed in as she braided her long white hair. When she pulled an apron from the pile of clean ones under the marble table, it made Yuli's eyebrows shoot to the ceiling. "What?" Zoya asked, amused by her reaction. "It's only fair you get to collect your winnings from our wager. I would have held you to it if I'd won."

"Hmm." Yuli remarked, "I thought I'd never live to see the day Zoya Castanova would be slinging truffles for ordins behind the counter at Kandied Karma."

"I'm a woman of my word," she said with a shrug.

Yuli burst into laughter. "Since when?"

"I might be *slightly* motivated by my desire to show the eternal coven I've changed," she admitted sheepishly. "But a bet's a bet and I lost."

"Well, look at you," Yuli remarked, still clearly stunned by the change in Zoya.

"Yes, darling, look at me." Zoya's tone was slightly mocking. She turned back to Katie. "You might be interested to know Sam threw his hat in the ring to join the Castanova Foundation."

"Why would he do that?"

"A golden parachute, perhaps? In light of the ugly allegations? Often, in times of turmoil, organizations will shake up their leadership to change the narrative," Yuli explained.

Zoya pursed her lips, considering Yuli's explanation. "Maybe. But I think he's more of an upwardly mobile overachiever who loves to bite off more than he can chew."

Yuli snorted. "Why? Has he already taken a bite off of you?"

"God, no! I find the man insufferable and a dreadful bore. I merely went to his event to gather information." She turned back to Katie. "He wouldn't shut up about his financial acumen and ability to utilize all the tax loopholes available to a charitable organization."

"What an opportunist!" Katie said. "That guy is a snake."

"No, no, no," Yuli said. "Snakes are sacred beings. He sounds more like a feral pig."

"Yes. That's much more accurate." Zoya nodded. "My guess is he's looking to distance himself from the Adapt4Heroes Foundation. Like it or not, as long as he is associated with a non-profit that's had significant funds misappropriated, his corporate value will decline." She turned to Katie. "With your permission, I will have him brought to the compound for an interview. One-on-one, I might be able to gather more useful information, but I don't want to step on your toes."

"That sounds like a good plan," Katie agreed, "as long as you are honest and share *everything* you learn. Good or bad."

"Ha!" Yuli chortled with laughter, enjoying Katie's wariness. "She's got your number!"

"Possibly." Zoya flicked an eye roll at Yuli before changing the subject, deciding to keep her test of the Verity Oil under wraps for now. "For the sake of argument, let's assume Rox is innocent."

"She is!" Katie exclaimed, easily frustrated and ready to defend her new friend.

"Your emotions are weakening your ability to reason and be objective," Zoya cut in, and even though she was right, Katie felt anger roar up in her center. She forced herself to tamp it down and listened as Zoya spoke, considering her next words. "Start with the basics. Who stands to gain? Who had access?" She straightened the apron and continued, "Typically, there's the board of directors to consider and rule out. It could simply be corporate espionage. Maybe they disagreed with the direction she was taking the organization?" Zoya wondered aloud. "Then you have to look at the C-suite. As the CFO, an embezzlement charge makes Sam look bad. He's going to want to rectify the situation as quickly as possible and save face."

"Or slink off to start a new career..." Yuli added, and Zoya nodded in agreement.

"At Salutes & Soiree, her administrative assistant, Keith, had a murky yellow aura," Zoya mused.

"Fear," Yuli said, decoding the color for Katie.

"Of what?" Zoya added, playing devil's advocate. "Of getting caught with his hand in the cookie jar? Was he checked out? Does he have a motive?"

"As Rox's administrative assistant, I would think he certainly had the opportunity." Yuli weighed in, being the voice of reason. "This feels like Occam's razor to me."

"The simplest explanation is usually correct," Katie remembered from her philosophy class during her freshman year in college. "If it's true, it's going to kill Rox." Katie sat down at the table as the possible reality weighed heavy on her heart. "She thinks of her staff like family." Katie glanced over at Zoya.

"Another reason why you should never get too close to the help," Zoya said, considering their next move.

"We can't just make this quietly go away. We have to exonerate her publicly and prove without a shadow of a doubt who is guilty by ordin law."

"This conversation is going to have to wait," Yuli said after consulting the watch face she opened from the lanyard on her neck. "We open in twenty minutes."

"You two suck the fun out of everything," Zoya muttered under her breath. She turned to Katie. "Well, let's get this over with. Show me what to do."

Katie led Zoya to the register as Yuli cackled with delight and took a seat at the table nearest the glass case so she could enjoy the view.

"Zoya Castanova engaged in menial labor? I never thought I'd live to see the day," Yuli exclaimed as she watched Zoya pull on rubber gloves and fill the glass case with truffles.

"You move like a turtle," Yuli said. "Chop, chop. Time is money."

"You're enjoying this too much." Zoya took the broom from Katie and began to sweep the floor of the showroom. Her next task was to pull the chairs off the tabletops and settle them underneath. When she'd finished, she wiped the sweat from her brow with the back of her forearm. The door jingled as the morning rush began, and their first customers flooded into the store.

"Can I help you?"

"Wait… Are you Ana Castanova?" a twenty-something asked Zoya, who was struggling to fold up a golden box before she could fill it with her order.

She huffed her frustration, "If I say yes, will you go away?"

"That's not how we speak to our beloved patrons, Ana!" Yuli admonished from her table.

"I knew it!" the twenty-something said, clearly happy with her ability to recognize a celebrity in a strange setting.

"She's sorry, aren't you, Ana?" Yuli urged with a delicious smirk, her eyes glittering with mischief.

Zoya grumbled under her breath.

"Use your words," Yuli prompted.

"I would like to extend my deepest apologies," Zoya muttered in frustration then turned to Yuli. "There, are you satisfied?"

"Very."

"Can we take a photo together?" the girl asked with stars in her eyes.

"Of course, allow me," Yuli answered before Zoya could, standing up and walking over with her hand out for the phone.

"Squeeze closer! Now, everyone smile," Yuli sang out with glee as she snapped three quick photos and handed the phone back to the girl.

"You be sure to post that to all your social media

accounts and make sure you tag Ana in it! This might be the first actual evidence ever discovered of Ana Castanova gainfully employed."

"There is nothing gainful about this place," Zoya grumbled, unable to stop herself. Katie witnessed their cat-and-mouse dynamic play out, acknowledging how far they'd come from when she'd first learned Zoya was her great-great grandmother. They'd developed an adversarial truce that was entertaining to watch. After the shop was closed and the case was clean, they were sipping on small crystal glasses of Horilka, a Ukrainian liquor Yuli kept in the chiller.

"I almost forgot!" Zoya exclaimed as she opened her handbag and fished around through the contents before pulling out a small airtight container containing a pitch-black truffle.

"What is it?" Katie was curious, and Yuli's inquisitive nature was also awakened as she regarded the container.

"You asked for help with your assignment from Karma, and I am here to provide it." Glancing up at the heavens, she bellowed, "I would like this effort noted, Olena, next time you gleefully decide to project my transgressions into the clouds for the entire coven to see." The shop's lights flickered, and a small smile curled Zoya's lips upward.

Zoya peeled open the container, and a putrid scent assaulted Katie's nostrils. She wrinkled her nose and her gag reflex engaged, making her stomach spasm as the offensive scent assaulted all of her senses. It was a macabre cacophony of rotting flesh and coppery blood. Drawn to it like a moth to a flame, Katie reached out to touch the black truffle, and Zoya's hand zinged out and slapped her hand away. Katie recoiled like she'd been stung and pressed her closed fist into her ribcage.

"You must not touch the Recurring Torment Rum Truffle with your bare hands."

Yuli gagged as she ground out her concern. "No! She can't ingest it! It's too powerful." She rushed over to the sink and emptied the contents of her stomach into it. Only taking a second to wipe the back of her mouth with her hand, she quickly placed herself between Katie and the offensive blood chocolate.

"She's not ready!" Yuli spat at Zoya.

"You cannot coddle her forever! Katia received this assignment, and I am certain she is strong enough to endure the magic required to carry out this rebalance. As her guides, we must give her access to the tools she needs." Hearing Zoya's confidence in her natural abilities gave Katie the extra boost she needed to address Yuli's fears.

"She's right," Katie whispered. "I know you want to protect me, but the only way I can step into the fullness of my power is to challenge myself and stand on my own two feet."

"You don't understand," Yuli argued, shaking her head and wringing her hands together, clearly distressed. "It's dangerous. We could lose you forever." Yuli began to pace.

Zoya ignored her warning and focused her full

attention on Katie. "It's true, we could." The truth sobered Katie instantly, and she forced herself to swallow the fear resting at the base of her throat.

Terrified at the prospect, Yuli rushed to Katie's side and implored her, "Do not, under any circumstances, attempt this spell without me." She reached out and squeezed Katie's forearms, her eyes locked on her granddaughter's. "Promise me."

"I promise," Katie said quickly, but her curiosity won out. "But what does it do?" she asked, in awe of the disgusting treat, wondering how she could possibly ingest it if touching it was off limits.

"It will allow you to enter into the darkest memory of a person for a limited time. You will live their bleakest hour as if it were happening to you."

"Whoa." Katie watched Zoya carefully shut the container. It lost its allure when the scent was sealed away, and Katie felt her attraction to it weaken. Zoya walked over to the back door and opened it wide to clear out the rest of the stench, and Katie felt its magnetic power rescind.

"It won't reach its full power until after your next birthday," Zoya explained. "Put it in the freezer, and when the moment is right, you will be inspired to eat it. But…" Zoya paused.

"But what?"

"It's not without its risks, Katia. Any time you enter the consciousness of another being, you are in jeopardy of being trapped there. Permanently."

Katie shivered. "How do I prevent that from happening?"

"Connect to the divine female blood within you. Work on calming your mind and connecting to the eternal coven. It will take practice to align with the stream of energy, but over time, you will be able to tap into it. You will be in a state of flow and goodness. It will align and direct you, nudging you to safety."

"Like meditation?"

"Precisely." Zoya nodded. "The unconscious mind is far superior to the conscious one. But most people—ordins and the supernatural alike—get distracted by the meat sack."

"Meat sack?"

"The external world and its motivations," Zoya answered. "In order to return to yourself, your motive must be pure. This is why I am unable to take this journey. You are the only witch in our mortal bloodline that is pure enough of heart to endure the journey."

"But what if something goes wrong?"

"Then you'll be trapped in that painful torment forever. Encapsulated in the agony and forced to repeat it endlessly like a horrific Groundhog Day." Zoya paused. "I wish I could go in your place. I've lived my lifetimes, but I am too selfish to go inside. Eating it would just make me physically sick. It would not open the portal."

"What about Yuli?" Katie asked, feeling fear pressing tightly against her chest and constricting her ability to breathe.

"I am too jaded," Yuli admitted bitterly. "To utilize the truffle in its most powerful state, it needs the clean and clear consciousness of a newly awakened supernatural heart."

Zoya and Yuli glanced at each other, the weight of their next words hanging heavy in both their hearts. In total agreement, their next sentence was uttered in unison, "The only one who can endure it is you."

TWENTY

Two weeks later, a very somber Tom appeared on Katie's doorstep. When she opened the door, she immediately sensed the shift in his demeanor. He was clutching Lauren's hand like his life depended on it.

"Is Mom here?" he asked as Katie invited them into her sunny kitchen.

"Yes. She never leaves the house. Honestly, I'm starting to get worried about her."

Tom let out a huge sigh. "Then this conversation is not going to be easy." Lauren closed her eyes for a long moment and nodded in agreement.

"Can you tell her I'm here?"

"Of course."

When Katie turned to leave, she caught a glimpse of Lauren leaning closer to wrap her arm protectively around Tom and whispering words of encouragement to him.

Katie disappeared upstairs, and a few moments later, Rox followed her into the kitchen. The physical change in the woman was alarming. Her skin was sallow, with deep black circles under her eyes. She tried to paste on a weary smile when her gaze landed on Tom, who'd always been her pride and joy, but it just fell flat. He hugged her tight and then guided her to a chair at the dining room table.

"Have a seat," he suggested, his expression grim.

"Who died?" she asked, desperately trying to summon a smile from her son.

Tom closed his eyes for a long moment, and Lauren leaned forward and laced her fingers together on the table.

"Spill it, you two," Rox demanded quietly. "You're scaring me."

"The board is calling for your permanent resignation," Tom said softly, averting his gaze, knowing this news would crush his mother. He couldn't look her in the eyes when he delivered the blow.

"Can't say I didn't see that coming," Rox muttered as she leaned forward, leaning on her elbows and propping her head up with her hands, rubbing her weary face with her fingers. "Is that all?"

"No. There's more," Tom ground out, his jaw clenched as he gritted his teeth. Katie's heart went out to him; he was obviously conflicted. He glanced away, and Katie studied the rise and fall of his chest as she synced her breath with his and focused on the center of his forehead.

God. This is going to kill her.

Alarmed, Katie braced for the worst.

Refusing to back down, Rox confronted the fear head-on, demanding him to speak, "Out with it." Tom pinched the bridge of his nose and closed his eyes to shore up his remaining resources as panic swelled in Katie's belly.

"A grassroots campaign on social media has been started to pass a new law that allows the revocation of a Purple Heart when a recipient is convicted of a crime against military members."

Outraged, Rox stood and banged her fist on the table, letting out a strangled cry of anguish and frustration.

"Don't worry, Mom, there is already a precedent set that a Purple Heart can only be revoked if it is determined it was fraudulently awarded. It's just a stupid publicity play."

Stunned, Rox staggered back to the table. All of the color drained from her cheeks, and she hid her face in her hands as she broke down in tears. It was the first time Katie witnessed the woman crack since she'd arrived, and it took Katie's breath away. Tom rushed to her side and tried to comfort his mother. She swiped her hands across her worn cheeks to brush away the hot tears washing down the lines of her face.

"How can everything I worked for my entire life be ripped away in an instant? I gave my life *and* my leg to the Army!"

"The burden of proof is on the Feds," Tom said, kneeling in front of her.

"But what about public opinion? I will never be able to continue my work at the Adapt4Heroes Foundation after this! There will be a black cloud hanging over me forever, regardless if I am found guilty or innocent." Surging with frantic energy she was desperate to dispel, she sidestepped Tom and paced the length of the dining room table with her arms folded tightly across her body.

Tom was taken aback by her reaction and eventually staggered to his feet. As he closed the distance between them, his astonishment was evident. "You'd *choose* to go back to work at the foundation? An organization that turned its back on you the second these ludicrous allegations came to light? I figured you'd find another way to occupy your time after all this is over."

"Those soldiers need me in their corner. They don't have anyone else! I can't bear the thought of losing more servicemen and women to suicide, or hearing about their families imploding because the stress of caring for a loved one with PTSD or a physical disability is too demanding."

"Mom, I appreciate your passion. I do, but right now, you have to look out for yourself."

"Tommy, you should know more than anyone that your mother is not built that way."

He threw up his hands in frustration. "But maybe it's time to be!"

"No!" Rox shouted. "I have done nothing wrong,

and I will not let these baseless accusations stop me from doing the work I was born to do!"

"Ahhh! Can you talk some sense into her?" Tom pleaded with Katie, clearly frustrated with his mother's allegiance to an organization that had betrayed her. The next several minutes ticked by while Rox paced and Tom huffed, leaning against the wall, eventually sliding down it to crouch at the bottom. Finally, Lauren broke their silence.

"Look. We're all on the same side here," she began. "Be frustrated, both of you, but we have to pull together right now. Rox's future is on the line."

"Don't you think I know that?" Tom said bitterly as he stood.

"Of course you do, babe," Lauren said. "Emotions are running high tonight. Maybe we should take a break?"

"No," Rox insisted, more determined than ever to spring into action. She hurried over to Tom's side. "I will not take a break, but I *do* need to apologize," she said to Tom. "I'm sorry if it sounds like I am taking out my anger on you. I know you are the strongest advocate in my corner, and you are doing everything you can to prove my innocence."

Tom nodded and quietly added, "I am."

Roxanne held out her hand and led her frustrated son back to the dining room table. After sitting him down, she filled a glass with water and set it in front of him before taking a seat. He drank the water in several long gulps, and it seemed to calm him down.

Katie was touched by their uncomplicated relationship. The goodness that exuded from Roxanne's every pore, even during one of the most stressful periods of her life, only strengthened her resolve to help. "What are our next steps?"

"We need a battle plan," Rox said as she leaned back in the chair and crossed her arms across her chest.

"We probably should start here." Tom picked his briefcase up from the floor and pulled out a thick manilla folder of documents. "I finally got the financial documents we requested from the organization. I'm not going to sugarcoat it for you. It's ugly."

"What do you mean?" Rox pulled the pair of reading glasses off the top of her head, settled them on the bridge of her nose, and began shuffling through the copies of statements and cleared checks. She spent the next several minutes organizing them into neat piles. "This doesn't make any sense," she muttered under her breath as she matched up the invoices with the statements. "These payments correlate with the documents."

"They do." Then he handed her another folder, this one filled with bank statements.

She went through the pile of invoices and cleared checks. "I don't understand. They are all accounted for. Everything is here."

He pulled out a monthly statement and pointed to a single line item buried in the middle of columns of figures. "Did you see this?" Tom asked. Rox pulled the paper closer. "There's a wire transfer each month, and since everything else at the foundation is paid by credit card or check, I find it unusual. The transfer is always just under the ten thousand dollar limit, so it's never gotten flagged in the system." He handed her several more monthly statements, pointing to the transfer each time.

"We need to talk to Sam," Rox said as she pulled out her phone and dialed his number. After a series of rings, it went to voicemail. "Sam, it's Rox. We got the discovery documents, and I need you to come through for me like you promised. Please call me."

"I wouldn't hold your breath," Tom muttered, his skepticism evident to everyone in the room.

"That's ridiculous." She pulled out her phone again and dialed Keith. It was another phone call that went straight to voicemail, and she hung up without leaving a message. Then she made four more phone calls to members of the board. She paced as they ignored her one by one. Katie could hear her frustration growing with every desperate voicemail she left.

"Charities hate to be in the news, Mom. It makes the donor pool dry up. Can't you see that everyone at the foundation is distancing themselves from you?"

"There's got to be an explanation."

"The Adapt4Heroes Foundation has one goal right now: cut you off at the pass and sweep these allegations under the rug so they can get the donations flowing back in. Public outrage has a short shelf life, but a trial would fan the flames and cripple the organization for years. It's in their best interests to make sure this case never goes to court, and they will push for a quick settlement."

"That's not right. I deserve my day in court." She palmed her face in irritation at a criminal justice system that didn't seem just at all. "Ugh!" Rox grunted in frustration as she slammed a fist hard on the table. "I have done nothing wrong."

"You know that and I know that," Tom said. "But it doesn't matter what we know; it matters what we can prove."

"I wouldn't even know *how* to set up an off-shore account in the first place," Rox admitted. "I haven't even downloaded the app from my personal bank. Where's the common sense?" On the table, the phone rang. Rox picked it up and, seeing Sam's name on it, held it up for Tom to see.

"See, Doubting Thomas? I knew he'd come through."

"Sam!" Rox answered the phone, her voice cheerier than it had been in weeks, and Katie heard her carry on a one-sided conversation, getting right to the point. "Definitely! The sooner the better." She ended the call and turned to her son triumphantly. "He's on his way."

Thirty minutes later, the doorbell rang, sending Arlo into a frenzy of loud barks. Katie let him in, surprised to see Sam carrying a stack of two banker's boxes.

"Good to see you again, ma'am," he said as she led him into the dining room where Rox and Tom were wading through a sea of documents.

Seeing her friend, Rox brightened, flashing him a

smile. After exchanging pleasantries and taking the beer he was offered, they got right down to business.

Rox pulled out the bank statements for the last six months, where she highlighted the wire transfers and passed the documents over to Sam.

"Every month, like clockwork, a transfer of around nine-thousand seven-hundred dollars was authorized from the account."

"What? That's impossible." He looked at the statements. "I would have noticed it." He took a swig from his bottle of beer and stood, pulling the cardboard lid off the documents he brought with him. It took a few minutes to find the corresponding statement. He pulled it out and ran down the list of transactions. The wire transfer line was missing. "It's not here," he said, shaking his head to clear the confusion. He handed the document to her. Rox stood and placed them side by side. Every line item was accounted for except for the wire transfer. "Pull the last five months of statements."

Sam rifled through the manilla folders, pulling the requested statements, and lined them up side by side with the documents that Tom received from the bank. They were identical in every way. Both versions had the logo of the bank in color and the same color ink. "What the…" Sam glanced from statement to statement.

"It's a forgery," Tom confirmed. "A very good one."

Stunned, Rox leaned back in the chair. She pulled off her reading glasses and absentmindedly chewed on one of the bows, turning over the discovery in her mind.

"All it takes is Photoshop and a little patience," Tom

added. "Bank statements are pretty basic and easy to replicate."

After a long pause, Sam pulled out the credit card statements. "There is something else I wanted to show you. On Keith Landers' credit card, there are what seems to be an excessive amount of charges to home improvement stores."

"No, those are legit." Rox dismissed his concern immediately. "I've authorized him to purchase them on several occasions when we were in a pinch and needed to get a project moving. The foundation earns extra points, so it's a win-win."

Sam pushed Keith's March statement over with two fingers. "To the tune of fifteen hundred dollars last month?" He pulled out another statement. "It's an amount that seems to be creeping up."

His accusation got Tom's full attention, and he leaned over his mother's shoulder to look at the statements that Sam laid out in front of them. Over the course of the last six months, starting at a few hundred dollars, it increased significantly month over month.

"Oh, Keith." Rox sighed, letting out a deep exhale. Clearly distressed, she leaned forward and scrubbed her hands over her face.

"He doesn't seem like the type." Sam then added, "I guess you never really can tell about people."

"There are extenuating circumstances." Rox explained, "He shared in confidence the medications his wife, Alicia, needs are nearing a thousand dollars a month."

"If he's capable of this…" Sam said.

"He's capable of anything," Tom finished, grateful for a break in the case.

"Whoa. Let's not rush to judgment. I want to talk to Keith first," Rox said.

"That is not advisable," Tom jumped in. "We need to share this discovery with the authorities and let them handle it."

"Ricochet, you have bigger fish to fry," Sam offered in agreement. "See if you can link him to the wire transfers. If you show your hand too quickly, he might disappear."

"Exactly," Tom confirmed as he nodded in appreciation of Sam's shrewd assessment.

Seizing her opportunity, Katie blurted, "Let's set up an appointment with Davina Thorne. Maybe her forensic accountant can help us figure out who opened that off-shore account."

Rox was clear-headed as she turned to Katie, resolute with her next steps. "Great idea."

"I don't know," Tom cautioned. "There is a reason why off-shore accounts exist in the first place. It's a way to evade capture, circumvent the rules of the US banking system, and avoid paying taxes. You need to prepare yourself for the fact this might lead us down a dead end, *and* it could be extremely costly."

"We have to try," Rox said. "I will not destroy a man's reputation based on a hunch. We have to have proof."

"Why? They tried to destroy yours! Why aren't you

jumping up and down with me for joy?" Tom asked his mother. "This is the break we've been waiting for!"

"Because it's not a joyful discovery, honey. If these allegations are true, they are the actions of a good man put in a desperate situation. If the tables were turned, I can't say I wouldn't have done the same." Lost in thought, she paged through the documents again, one by one.

Tom turned to Sam and extended his hand. "Even if Mom isn't on board, I want to thank you."

Sam pumped it up and down. "Happy to help!" Then he turned to Rox. "Won't be long until you're back in the office, Ricochet." His sentiment got Rox's attention. She stood and gave him a hug, then walked him to the door, watching him leave.

Back at the table, a much more cheerful Tom had popped the cork on a bottle of celebratory champagne and was pouring flutes for them all. Rox declined the drink and offered him a sad wave as she said goodnight. She just couldn't celebrate the painful truth they'd uncovered, so instead, walked upstairs to settle into her bedroom for the night.

TWENTY-ONE

Two days later, in the middle of May, Katie sat in the stadium as graduates from the University of South Florida filed in wearing their green robes and mortarboards to "Pomp and Circumstance." Her family filled an entire row of seats, and as she fanned herself with a program and glanced around the packed stadium, she briefly wondered if she'd set eyes on Jefferson. They'd shared their lives for decades, and she couldn't help but think of him when their children experienced milestones. Callie's graduation was the first one they'd arrived at since the divorce, and it was oddly bittersweet. Although Jefferson confirmed he'd be in attendance, he quickly refused her invitation for them to sit together, which was just as well.

Sitting in the seat next to her, Beckett elbowed her ribs. "There she is!" He pointed over at Callie, who shot them a triumphant smile when her eyes alighted on her family in the audience. She'd made it to graduation, and Katie was proud of her determination. School had never come as easy to Callie as it had for Lauren, and there was a lot of talk about dropping out her sophomore year. To see Callie walk across the stage for the diploma she fought for tooth and nail made Katie tear up.

A hot flash roared through her chest and neck, and Katie fanned the limp paper program in her hand in an effort to cool herself down. Her face reddened, and she tried to take a few breaths to calm her nervous system as the heat rushed through her body from torso to limbs. Beads of sweat trickled down her jawline.

The ceremony took the better part of two hours, and when Callie finally found her family members clustered together on the field in the sea of graduates, she let out a squeal and flung her tiny body into her mother's arms.

"It's over!" she declared, hugging Katie tight.

"You made it! I'm so proud of you."

"It feels amazing to know my days of organized education are behind me," she announced with obvious relief in her voice. "But now the actual work begins. I start my first animation gig in two weeks, but we both know it's just a stepping stone to greater things. Goodbye, USF. Hello, Pixar!" She grinned, surrounded by her family.

Callie was starting at the bottom in an entry-level position at a huge investment firm, animating customer service videos for their website and customer portals. But Callie's greatest aspiration was to work at Pixar, and she planned on using her extra time to create her online portfolio and demo reel.

"I am giving myself a year to create the best three minutes Pixar has ever seen. The day job will pay the bills for now, and help me keep my skills honed, but I am going to need to spend a serious amount of time on nights and weekends to create my portfolio in order to get a job at Pixar."

"I love seeing this side of you," Katie acknowledged, pulling back and cupping her daughter's heart-shaped face in her hands. "Dream big, sweetheart! This is the time to swing for the fences, before you are married and have children. It's much harder to take risks when you have others who depend on you."

"That's the plan." Callie nodded, then sighed. "Sheesh. I'm barely graduated and already overwhelmed." Callie was always her most anxious child.

"It will all come with time," Katie murmured soothingly. When Callie shared her dream with her initially, Katie researched animation and learned that getting a job at Pixar was the holy grail. It was the pinnacle career aspiration of any animation artist. "You'll get there. Work hard, but learn to rest, too. Burnout can set you back further than if you adopt a healthy work ethic."

"Quit hogging the graduate," Beckett teased his mother, who finally released her hold on her youngest. "Way to go, loser." He gave his baby sister a lopsided grin. "Welcome to the rest of your life." He pulled her in for a hug, and then she turned to accept congratulations from Kristina, David, Yuli, and Lauren.

Kristina reached into her purse and pulled out three envelopes, distributing them to Beckett, Lauren, and Callie. Her eyes danced with unbridled excitement. "Open them together," she instructed her grandchildren as she threaded her arm through David's, both of them alive with enthusiasm that lit up their features.

"What did you two do?" Katie asked as the kids tore into the paper. Callie's hand flew to her mouth. "Three thousand dollars?" Inside the other two envelopes was an identical check.

Confused, Katie cocked her head in her parents' direction.

"I checked the jar!" Kristina said, her eyes dancing with joy.

"What?" Yuli asked.

"Remember from our reading with Talulah?" Kristina enthused. "It took a while since there were so many pennies, but one by one we went through them. We cataloged each one and did our own research."

"Why didn't you just take the collection to a rare coin dealer?" Katie asked.

"We didn't want to become one of those swindler stories where someone gets taken advantage of because they don't know what they have," David explained. "You'll never guess what we found!"

"A 1982 small date Denver mint penny!" Kristina interrupted, unable to contain herself and clapping her hands with excitement.

"1982 was the last year pennies were made from copper." David added with a huge grin, "So I knew we had something special."

"Wow." Katie was swept up in the excitement, listening to her parents tell the story.

"We sold it to a dealer for ten thousand dollars!" David exclaimed. "Talk about a return on investment."

"You should have kept the windfall for yourselves," Lauren said.

"Oh, sweetie. We've lived our lives and have everything we need." Kristina looked at David. "We decided together it would be put to far better use by the grandkids." She grinned.

"That's so generous, Grandma and Grandpa," Beckett said as his sisters stepped closer and enveloped them in a group hug.

Katie observed their interactions with a sentimental smile spreading across her features when, at her throat, the purple amulet vibrated. She whipped around and saw a flash of long white hair. The purple amulet tingled and warmed to the touch in response to the close proximity of all three mortal members of the coven. Katie reached down to grasp it between her fingers, feeling the jewel come to life. She glanced over at Yuli, whose eyes were also scanning the crowd. Eventually, Yuli's gaze landed on Zoya, hidden in plain sight, and gave a barely perceptible nod, acknowledging her presence. A few minutes later, she disappeared into the sea of humanity rushing toward their cars.

Katie was pensive as she walked back to her Beetle.

Knowing she was always happiest surrounded by her family, she knew the day would eventually come when she would be alone. Due to their miraculous longevity, she would be forced to take on a new identity. Her heart clenched in her chest, unable to imagine a reality where she couldn't be surrounded by the people she loved most in the world.

Witnessing Zoya's participation on the fringes of their family during this special event, Katie knew she was seeing a glimpse of her future. One question needled her like a thorn stuck in her finger. How would she ever be able to endure the loneliness?

TWENTY-TWO

The following week, Zoya sent her private plane to fetch Sam Williams for his pseudo-interview at the Castanova Foundation. She had no intention of ever hiring him, but he would never know it.

The sun was rising in the sky, but the ocean breeze kept the air cool. Seated at a table near the garden maze, the hedges provided enough shade behind her yet preserved the sweeping shoreline view. Choppy waves lapped against the sugary white sand, leaving behind white foam and the occasional conch shell. It was the quiet before the approaching storm, and the silence was glorious.

She bit into a slice of hickory smoked bacon after dredging it through a puddle of warm maple syrup on her plate while she strategized her upcoming meeting.

At her feet, Terrance lingered, awaiting his next instructions. "Please tell Chef breakfast exceeded my expectations, and I would relish the opportunity to thank him properly in my suite this afternoon."

"Yes, my queen." He barked once and scampered off to fulfill her request. She leaned back in her espresso-stained all-weather wicker chair and savored her last cup of coffee. A few minutes later, her enjoyment was interrupted by Terrance walking down the stairs again, leading a perfectly pressed Sam Williams over to her table. With a heavy sigh, she got to her feet, smoothed a few strands of her brilliant white hair, and then pasted on a winning smile.

"Sam. It's great to see you again."

He flashed her an artificially whitened grin, pumping her hand up and down. She fought the urge to recoil when her palm brushed up against his moist one. Then she offered him the chair across from herself, eager to put a barrier between them. "Please, have a seat."

He was dressed to impress in a navy blue suit and shiny brown loafers. His hair was freshly shorn close to the back of his neck, and the silver strands laced through the dark blond glinted in the sunlight.

"Would you care for some coffee?" she asked.

"Yes, ma'am," he answered. She assessed him with a practiced eye. His perfect manners felt like a mask he was hiding behind. Zoya wondered if she pressed at his starched seams, if his authentic character would bleed through, and she was eager to get a glimpse.

She flipped the coffee cup upright on its saucer and stood to pour a cup of steaming Columbian roast into it.

Normally, she reserved this type of task for the servants, but she knew Sam would appreciate her willingness to serve him. It would put him at ease instantly because he was a traditional man's man. The kind of overtly masculine caricature the Army was famous for turning out since it was established.

"Thank you." He took a sip and set the cup back on the saucer. Sitting erect in his chair, he leaned forward and took in the surrounding view. "You have a magnificent home, and I appreciate you opening it up to me."

"My pleasure," she said. "If this interview goes well, you'll make it on the guest list for the upcoming Autumnal Equinox Ball." She winked at him. "That's the real coup."

"I have no doubt it will come to pass," he declared boldly, leaning closer to her. Zoya pulled her arm back, a defensive move in case he tried to make skin contact again, and wrapped her hands around her coffee cup.

"How are you handling all the current upheaval at the Adapt4Heroes Foundation? All this embezzlement business has definitely given your foundation a black eye."

His lips tightened into a more serious expression as he nodded in agreement. She took another sip and closed her eyes to tune in to the flow of information that swirled around him, trying to line up with his internal dialogue.

"It's been a very trying time, as I am sure you can imagine," he started in.

Be humble. It's all or nothing.

She cocked her head, amused by his internal pep talk.

"It *is* unfortunate," he continued, adding, "Especially when you are betrayed by one of your own."

"Are you saying Roxanne is guilty?"

"Anything is possible, but I'm not one to rush to judgment," he started magnanimously. Zoya had to glance away quickly to fight off an eye roll inspired by his overly gratuitous tone. "I don't believe she would have been arrested if they didn't have sufficient proof, but recently, some damning evidence against her administrative assistant was brought to light. As a result, he might become more of a focus of the investigation. It's hard to say," Sam offered with a shrug, leaning back in his chair, and crossing his ankle over his knee.

"I can't believe you're so forthcoming with information. Didn't you have to sign an NDA?"

His eyes flashed in irritation, and he held one hand up. "This is all off the record and needs to stay between you and me."

"Of course." Zoya nodded, waiting to see where this conversation would lead. Ordins always hung themselves when given the chance. Often, all one was required to do was wait.

He rushed away from the misstep and straight to the puffery. "I've been tasked with stepping in as interim CEO to lead the organization back to wholeness."

"So, you're not in the market for a new opportunity, after all?" Zoya questioned, just to see him squirm.

"Let's not be hasty. I wouldn't go that far," he corrected.

Easy. She's far too direct for her own good. Uppity women are the worst. Underneath it all, she's begging to be dominated, and I am just the man for the job.

The rambling thought was so ludicrous that Zoya choked on her coffee. It sent her into a coughing fit, and she gulped a glass of water to recover.

"Are you okay?" he asked, feigning concern, shuffling his chair back and getting to his feet. Zoya knew he'd use any excuse to initiate physical contact and swallowed the tickle in her throat to avoid it.

"Of course, darling. Please, continue." She waved him back to his chair.

"Adapt4Heroes was never meant to be the pinnacle of my career achievement. It was always meant to be a stepping stone," he admitted. "I believe my destiny is far more important than serving on the board of a Florida Veterans organization. My advanced skills would be far better utilized on an international level."

"Do you, now? Please, tell me more."

"Don't get me wrong; the work we do there is important, but the scale of it is so minuscule. I've cut my teeth and have evolved as far as I can at the Adapt4Heroes Foundation. I feel it might be time to tackle a new challenge."

"But to leave an organization when it is at its most vulnerable shows a lack of character."

His eyes narrowed, and a flash of rage worked its way across his face that he fought to conceal.

That bitch. Who is she to question my character?

His reactive thought warmed the cockles of Zoya's heart and, like a dog with a bone, she just couldn't stop herself.

"I'm curious, Mr. Williams. Why did you choose to enlist in the first place?"

"I believe military service is the highest calling. My father was enlisted and had high hopes I'd attend West Point and carry on the family tradition."

"I wasn't aware you were a West Point Graduate." Zoya had an investigator do the research, and this fact never appeared in the report.

His lips pursed. It was a slight that still stung. "I did not. I had the same admission qualifications as one of the minority candidates, but we all know how that turns out."

Getting caught cheating on my ACT exam didn't help.

Zoya cocked her head and heaped on the next statement with buckets of sarcasm. "There just are not enough opportunities for white men in America these days." She had to pinch her lips together to conceal the smirk that threatened to spread across her face at the absurd statement. "I bet that was a bitter pill to swallow, especially since Roxanne Sullivan graduated from West Point with honors and then went on to become your superior."

Sam's nostrils flared as he tried to contain another

flash of anger. His discomfort filled Zoya with glee. Busting the balls of powerful men was her aphrodisiac, and she felt a tingle between her legs. Making a mental note to have Higgins fetch the pair of twins whose tongues and fingers provided two days of blissful release at the Spring Equinox Ball. At the prospect of an evening of well-deserved debauchery, she leaned closer to him. A trickle of sweat raced down his jawline. She wasn't sure if it was from the increasing heat as the sun rose overhead or if it was the hot seat she'd sat him on. Either way, seeing him off balance in her presence filled her with power.

He cleared his throat and continued, "Ultimately, my years of service far eclipsed her meager service record after she lost her leg," he reminded Zoya. "The universe has a way of righting its wrongs." He leaned back, hugging his knee in an attempt to project relaxed confidence.

"It does," Zoya agreed. "The truth always comes to light."

Not always.

His admission was a whisper in her mind that made her eyes narrow. What was he hiding?

Sam met her intense gaze and said, "Yes. Yes, it does." He was able to lie with such practiced conviction, and Zoya was impressed. "Can we circle back to what I can bring to the Castanova Foundation?" He pasted on a disarming grin, shoveling on the charm, and Zoya realized she was being handled.

Eager to end the interaction, she said, "Absolutely."

"Understanding the nuances of complicated tax law is my specialty, and I have developed a unique skill set that has been underutilized in my current role." He locked his focus down on her. "Lucky for me, you need a Master's degree in accounting to understand the tax code, not to mention the financial literacy required to build a strategy that allows your resources to scale while protecting them from excessive taxation."

Zoya nodded in agreement. "Taxes *are* the bane of my existence."

"Says every CEO of a major corporation," he added with a knowing grin. "The right strategy can save you millions. Banking rules and regulations are not as stringent outside the United States."

Set the hook. She'll take the bait.

"I'm listening." She leaned closer, egging him on. "Are you suggesting an off-shore account? Isn't that illegal?"

"Technically, it's a gray area," he admitted. "But as with anything tax law related, there are loopholes."

"What about the legal consequences? Can't I be fined and then have to pay even more in taxes and penalties?"

"That's why we will preserve your anonymity and protect the foundation," he went on. "I can personally guarantee there won't even be a whisper of impropriety."

"How do you do that?"

Reel her in.

"I'll be more than happy to walk you through the

steps in their entirety when we've defined my role at the Castanova Foundation and I've seen a formal job offer."

Zoya smiled. Even with his outdated fish references, he was good at playing the game. She had to give him that. "Well," she stood to signal the end of the meeting and extended a hand once again, "you've certainly given me a lot to think about. The board votes on new officers in September, but I think you can count on an official offer at the end of the summer. We'll be in touch."

She watched him stroll away, happy with the performance he'd just given. Men like Sam Williams were a dime a dozen in finance. Constructed from the same overconfident cloth, they always believed they were the top dog. As he disappeared from sight, one thought surfaced. It might be time to neuter.

TWENTY-THREE

Memorial Day weekend, when Katie arrived to open the shop, she didn't notice Zoya's black town car pull up to the curb at Kandied Karma. She was filling the truffle case when Zoya strode through the door like she owned the place.

"Jesus. You startled me," Katie admitted, turning to lay eyes on Zoya, surprised to see her make an appearance in the early morning hours.

"Aren't you a timid little creature?" she teased. "Don't worry, darling, I'm simply trying to toughen you up." Dressed in olive green from head to toe, the simple flowing dress that covered most of her body was a departure from her usual fashion-conscious wardrobe.

"Good luck with that!" Katie said, laughing at herself as she walked back into the kitchen with Zoya right on her heels.

"Where's..." Zoya asked as her eyes swept the kitchen, looking for Yuli.

"She's not here yet."

"Ah, I remember sleeping in," Zoya reminisced fondly. "I do miss that sensation." She glanced at her watch. "She better enjoy it while she still can."

"Wait… you don't sleep?" Katie was astonished. "At all?"

"No," Zoya admitted. "At first, I chalked it up to insomnia induced by menopause. But I eventually discovered when you are the oldest matriarch of the mortal coven, you lose your dependency on sleep. Your powers strengthen to compensate for the energy loss, and sleep becomes obsolete."

"That sounds terrible." Katie winced, shaking her head in disbelief. "No rest for the wicked, huh?" she dared to add playfully, then cringed as she awaited Zoya's reaction, knowing she had a tendency to run hot and cold.

Zoya chuckled at the reference, and it set Katie back at ease. "Good one."

"I can't imagine being able to function without a solid eight hours."

"The meditation chamber provides some respite and peace, but the constant conscientious awareness does take some time to acclimate to."

"Wow." Katie said, "You must get so much done with all that extra time."

"Of course I do, darling." She offered a grin. "Speaking of getting things done, I wanted to fill you in on some tasty little tidbits I've recently acquired concerning your newest Karmic rebalance." Katie's attention snapped over to her like a rubber band as she nodded, marveling at the brilliant mind of her great-great grandmother. She wondered if she would measure up when her time as the coven's mortal matriarch came around.

"Fantastic! I've got some of my own to share."

"That Sam Williams is a smart devil," Zoya remarked. "He had his thoughts on lockdown during the interview, but I gleaned just enough to arouse my suspicions. He's hiding something."

Katie's curiosity was piqued. "I'm glad I'm not the only one who has had a hard time getting a read on him. He gives off an arrogant self-serving vibe, but so far has proven to be a man of his word and has been exceedingly helpful in going through the financial documents with us. He uncovered a series of ongoing credit card abuses by Rox's administrative assistant."

"Hmm." Zoya mulled it over. "He mentioned it to me as well, but I must say, the timing is a bit convenient."

"You think he had more nefarious intentions?"

"I do. He's riddled with jealousy and is a cheat. Sam's still holding on to grudges that go all the way back to his rejection at West Point."

"Really?" Katie tried to grapple with this version of the man she'd met. "In Rox's eyes, Sam can do no wrong."

Zoya shook her head. "She's blinded by her desire to see the best in people." She turned to Katie. "Someone else I know suffers from this same misguided belief."

Katie felt her cheeks pink up.

Zoya's voice lowered with deepened conviction, "Never take anything an arrogant man says at face value. Always dig deeper." Both women were silent for a long moment, lost in their own thoughts. Hitting a dead end and making a mental note to bring Zoya's suspicions up to Tom, Katie changed the subject.

"Can I ask you a question?"

"You may, though I might decline to answer it."

"Touché." Katie smirked at her response. At least Zoya was consistent.

"Why did you choose to live your second lifetime in the public eye?"

"A better question to ask is, why not?" she answered flippantly, shrugging her shoulders.

"It seems to get in the way."

"I respectfully disagree." She explained, "Celebrity is the hinge that swings open the door of opportunity."

"That's the only reason?" Katie questioned, her curiosity getting the best of her.

"Boredom, perhaps?" she offered. "I always wanted more. After my awakening, when I finally rose like a phoenix from the ashes, it was an experiment to see how far I could swing the pendulum the other way. I've come a long way from being banished to a simple cottage in America to becoming one of the richest women in the world. But it was never about the *money*, darling. It was about the *power* that accompanied it. It was about proving my worth as a woman."

Katie took the explanation in and let it settle in her

heart. She knew about undervaluing herself as a woman and found Zoya's words resonated more deeply than she ever thought they would. "Your story fascinates me. It's a riches to rags to riches tale that turns the paradigm on its head about what a person is capable of accomplishing in their one beautiful life."

"Mmm," Zoya mused, thinking over Katie's observation. "I never looked at it that way." She cocked her head and studied Katie as if seeing her for the first time.

"Did you do it?" Katie asked.

"Do what?"

"Prove your worth as a woman?"

"In some ways. In others, I failed," she admitted truthfully. "But I'm fighting generations of misogynistic programming. There's still a long way to go."

"Why give it all up? Why take a chance on reincarnation when the odds of your soul finding Salvatore's are five billion to one?"

Zoya bit the inside of her lip, carefully considering her response. "You do not have insight into your full destiny yet, so I am sure my decision is difficult, if not impossible, to understand." She paused and Katie waited, interested to learn what her response would be. "Having every material object your heart could ever desire is heady at first, and the accumulation of fine things takes away the sting of loneliness, but the joy of acquiring doesn't last." Zoya paused, then added, "I heard a quote once by a man named David Viscott." She hesitated briefly, then said, "To love and be loved is to feel the sun from both sides."

"Whoa! I just got goosebumps," Katie said, showing the evidence on her forearm to Zoya.

"It speaks to me, too." Zoya appreciated her reaction. "It also explains why I *must* go. Since Sally's death, I have been chilled to the bone by his absence. Once you've felt that warmth, the joy of both sides of the sun, you can never live happily without it again," Zoya admitted. "You will forever chase the feeling. It has a stronger pull than a junkie to a needle."

As Katie absorbed her sentiment, she felt a tingle of truth accompanied by a wave of sadness that she'd never felt both sides of the sun herself. Her life with Jefferson had been a one-sided journey where she poured into his cup constantly, but he never bothered to reciprocate. It was a grim contemplation that at fifty years old, she'd missed out on the kind of love Zoya had intimately known. The sobering realization left her speechless.

She was pulled out of her melancholy mood when a burst of warm air and bright light infiltrated the kitchen by Callie, who whipped open the back door. "Coffee. I need coffee," she muttered with a yawn. Her eyes widened when they settled on Zoya. "I'm sorry, Mom. I didn't know you'd have such an important visitor this early in the morning!"

Zoya offered her a warm smile. "No apologies necessary, darling! I popped in to order truffles for an event. We were just finishing up."

Katie brightened up immediately, seeing her youngest daughter. "What a nice surprise!" She pulled her in for a hug and then pulled back, still holding Callie's forearms. "You seem a little anxious." Katie had always been a barometer of human emotion, especially whenever her children were concerned.

"I was up all night working on my submission for an animation award. I'm hoping it might help open the door to Pixar."

"Ooh! Pixar, you say?" Zoya remarked, leaning in and inserting herself into the conversation. Katie was touched she was taking such an interest in her daughter.

"It's my dream job," Callie gushed, then sighed deeply with regret. "Making explainer videos for an investment firm is draining my will to live. There's no room for creativity or innovation at my current employer. It's a dead end."

"You have to pay your dues. Everyone starts somewhere," Katie reminded her.

"Do you, though?" Zoya chimed in without being asked. "Sure, you can play by their rules, and you might attain the outcome you desire, or you can shake up the board and make up your own."

Callie's chin swung over to her, intrigued. "What would you do, Ana, if you were in my shoes?"

"Shock and awe, darling," Zoya answered. "You have about twelve seconds to hook them and grab their attention with your project." She leaned in. "And then I'd find a way in and make that first meeting so memorable, your name lingers on their tongue forever."

"Ballsy," Callie whispered. "I like it." She accepted the espresso from Katie and said, "I better go. Thanks for the coffee." She raised the cup and then turned to Ana. "And the pep talk."

A shaft of warm light filled the kitchen when she opened the back door to return to her car. Callie let out a squeal of glee seeing Yuli and gave her a quick hug before heading out. Afterward, Yuli shuffled in and settled her medicine bag satchel on the back shelf, surprised to see Zoya again.

"What are you doing here? Is this a social call?" she asked as she pulled a clean apron from the folded batch on the shelf and knotted it around her waist.

"No, just checking in. Katia can fill you in." Glancing down at her wrist, Zoya added, "I need to get back to the compound, anyway." She turned to Katie. "Would you be a dear and put some of the caramel amaretto turtles into a box for me?"

"That will be $24.95," Yuli interjected.

Zoya's jaw dropped. "You're going to make me pay for them like a common ordin?"

"I'm running a business," Yuli offered in explanation. "And you can afford it."

"Technically, the recipe is protected intellectual property of the Castanova Foundation," Zoya returned, poking the bear and testing Yuli's resolve.

"The family recipe is as much mine as it is yours." Yuli stood firm.

"Fine." Zoya pulled a wallet out and produced a fifty-dollar bill that she promptly handed over to Katie.

"Keep the change." Turning on her heel, she pushed the swinging door open with one boot and stood fuming at the counter. Katie followed her out to the case and started filling the box.

"You two and your bickering," Katie said as she closed the box and added the decorative ribbon. "You're like oil and water."

"Old habits die hard," Zoya acknowledged, taking the box and leaving a few minutes later out the front door, stubbornly refusing to pass by Yuli who was holed up in the back. Katie watched the town car pull to the front of the shop, and a few minutes later, Zoya was tucked inside and speeding away. She washed her hands at the sink and went back into the kitchen.

"Was that really necessary?"

"No. But it was fun to watch her squirm, wasn't it?" Yuli quipped with a naughty grin that made Katie chuckle. "Besides, she has to earn her rebirth by proving to the coven she's a changed woman. All I am doing is providing an adequate training ground."

Yuli's practical way of looking at it won Katie over. "Do you think she'll be able to do it?"

"One thing is true. Zoya is capable of anything when she is properly motivated. Time will tell."

———

Later that evening, after a long day at Kandied Karma, Katie let herself in the door at her home to see her dining room table filled with visitors. Tom, Lauren, and

Rox were hard at work sifting through a sea of paperwork, and white bankers' boxes now lined the walls of her great room.

She brought in a gold-wrapped box from the shop filled with chocolate and caramels and set it on the table. "I brought a little sugar to keep the troops properly motivated," she said brightly, trying to inject positivity into a task that looked daunting.

Rox offered her a grateful smile and rubbed her hands together. "I can never say no to Kandied Karma!" she said, pulling out a cashew cluster and biting into the dark chocolate shell.

"How's it going here?' Katie asked, trying to figure out how to broach the topic of conversation that had been tickling her subconscious. "Anything else from Sam?"

"I'm sure he's been busy playing both sides. I don't blame him. He's probably under the microscope right now," Rox sympathized. "I'm sure after the heat settles down a bit, he'll reach out again." She continued to peruse the thick stack of papers in front of her, consumed by the task.

"Do you think he had anything to do with this?"

"Absolutely not. No way." Rox shut her down instantly.

"Let's not be so hasty, Mom." Tom tried to bridge the gap. "We can't afford not to look at him. He had unrestricted access. The real question is, what would be his motivation?"

"Money," Lauren interjected. "Power."

Roxanne discounted them immediately and jumped up to pace the length of the room. "I know Sam inside and out. He's not motivated by either of those things."

"How can you be sure?"

Katie was not surprised by her loyalty but wondered if it was her Achilles heel. She walked over to Rox and led her back to the table. Her fingers brushed Rox's skin, and she received a flash from the past. Retrocognition was the first of Katie's supernatural powers to surface, and this vision was especially vivid.

A glimpse of dark skin, a flurry of bullets from an automatic weapon as pounding heartbeats thundered in her ears. A man dressed in desert Army fatigues cradled a bloody and unconscious Roxanne to his chest. His path zigzagged through the sand and rocky terrain in an attempt to stay out of the line of fire. The grinding gears and roar of a fleet of Humvees closed in.

Katie blinked in rapid succession as the vision melted away and the saturated colors shifted back to normal. Karma kept taking her back to that moment of terror, and she needed to figure out why.

"Sam is the reason I am standing here today. He carried me out to the rendezvous point after taking a bullet to the shoulder. I would have died over there if he hadn't saved my life." Distressed, she stood and paced again.

"What do you remember about that mission?"

"Not much. With the blood loss and shock after I was hit, I lost consciousness for most of the evac," she said. "It's all bits and pieces." She shuddered at the fragmented memories. "Honestly, I'm grateful it never came back. Not sure I want to remember every moment of that day. Eight of us went in, but only two made it out alive. I owe Sam my life."

"Hmm," Katie considered as she remembered Zoya's observations. It was impossible to reconcile her version of Sam with the one Rox presented.

"What?" Lauren picked up on her mother's uncertainty immediately.

"Nothing, honey," Katie said as she mulled over the flashes. Unsure what the next move should be, she thought about the putrid truffle buried deep in her freezer and what price she'd have to pay to uncover the truth.

TWENTY-FOUR

A road trip was just what she needed, Rox thought as she drove the almost hour to the Florida National Cemetery. She cranked up a classic rock station and sang along to it, letting the music lift her mood as the miles spooled by. In the back seat, two wreaths of greenery and a bouquet of loose flowers rested inside craft paper. She parked the car in the lot and pulled them out of the back, noticing the subtle shift in the air as a sense of profound peace and reverence filled her on the cemetery grounds.

As she headed toward the grand administration building, the scent of freshly cut grass lingered in the air, mingling with the gentle bouquet of blooming roses that dotted the landscape. The hum of a breeze whispered through the Avenue of Flags, each flag's fabric rustling in the wind. It was a visual homage to honor and sacrifice that took her breath away. She stood still in front of the display for a long, reflective moment before saluting the American flag.

The sun hung low on the horizon, casting a warm, golden hue over the sprawling grounds of the cemetery and outlining each marker that stretched out as far as the eye could see. It was a sacred place where decades of brave warriors were laid to rest, providing a tranquil atmosphere that stilled Rox's wounded heart.

Continuing down the path, she glanced over to the Committal Shelter where a small group of mourners dressed in Army dress uniforms and black were gathered near a flag-draped casket. The crisp, clean scent of rain-washed earth mingled in the air as the final rays of sunlight filtered through the roof.

A woeful bugle cut through the trickling water of the fountain as "Taps" played evoking a poignant mix of sorrow and gratitude. Rox stopped in her tracks and stood at attention. It was a reflexive action of respect deeply ingrained in her during her military career. She felt tears prickle at her lower lashes as the music transported her back to the day they honored Monty and Peabody's sacrifices in the same shelter. She'd been numb from the loss of them and her leg. The painkillers took the edge off the physical pain but didn't even touch the emotional agony she'd felt.

Continuing down the path, she located their markers and reached into her pocket to pull out four quarters, taking the time to place one on each headstone of her commanding officer and the three fallen soldiers who'd led the caravan. It was a visible reminder that she'd visited and affirmed their sacrifice, a tradition traced all the way back to the Roman Empire when soldiers would insert a coin into the mouth of a fallen soldier to ensure they could cross into the afterlife. Now, leaving a quarter on a headstone acknowledged being with a service member when they were killed in action.

She added flowers to their urns, then continued with a heavy heart with the two wreaths ringed through her left arm. Rox passed rows upon rows of graves, each marker standing with quiet finality, and reverence filled her heart with introspection. She walked further into the quietude and came to the section where they had laid Monty and Peabody to rest, side by side. She carefully stepped onto the vibrant green grass and looped a wreath over each marker. Bending over, she swept away the dust and traced the black lettering on their headstones with her finger. Corporal Michael Montgomery and Specialist Alfred Pinnick. Standing there, the profound sense of loss filled her heart again, just as it had the first day. The grief and the guilt never got easier to bear. She simply adapted and learned to live with it.

From her pocket, she pulled two remaining quarters and placed one on each headstone.

"It's been a while, boys," she whispered as she stood looking down at their polished white marble markers.

"Not a day goes by that I don't wonder if I could have done more to bring you home safely. When the mission went south, I was foolish enough to think I was qualified to step up as your CO. My inexperience got you killed. I was responsible for your lives, and I failed you."

Sadness, anger, and regret washed over her as she took a knee in front of their graves. Tears welled up in her eyes, and she fought to hold them back. Normally, Rox preferred to maintain her composure but, surrounded by the silent sacrifice of all the heroes surrounding Monty and Peabody, she let herself fall apart. Tears fell freely, and she didn't even bother to swipe them away.

"You made the ultimate sacrifice for your country and upheld all the ideals of the United States Army. You both have made me so proud." She stood to salute each of their gravestones. Her movements were deliberate and respectful.

"Now I need your guidance. The enemy is triumphing against me. I'm being wrongfully accused of crimes I didn't commit, and I don't know how to combat the charges. If you two could put in a good word for me with the Big Guy, I'd appreciate it." Another wave of warm tears broke free and fell down her cheeks, and she swiped it away. "I think about you knuckleheads every day." She pressed her lips together to contain the raw cry that threatened to escape. "You are supposed to be here with me."

She closed her eyes and felt the impact of the loss shudder through her. "Your memory has lived on and fueled my fire to do important work at the Adapt4Heroes Foundation. When we laid you to rest, I vowed to honor you by carrying your sacrifice and bravery into every day of my life." Her voice cracked. "It was a legacy I carried out in your name, and now that it's been jeopardized, I don't know how to deal with this anger and guilt that remains."

A gentle breeze picked up, and the flags beside their graves fluttered in the wind.

"Help me find my way," she whispered. "Help me restore my honor so I can get back to the foundation and continue to build your legacy."

The wind swirled, and the flags waved up and down as if nodding. Rox let out a strangled laugh and smiled in relief. "I promise I won't go as long between visits." She reached out to gently touch the quarter atop each headstone once more before turning and walking down the path back to her car. For the first time since she'd been arrested, she felt a tender peace fill her soul. Now that she'd reconnected with her purpose, she was resolved to figure out a way to prove her innocence.

TWENTY-FIVE

A few days later, Katie was driving Rox to an appointment at Davina Thorne's office. "Finally, today we should get some answers," Rox said from the passenger seat.

"You might want to adjust your expectations. Davina is not one to sugarcoat her findings."

"Ahh! A woman after my own heart." Rox smiled a disarming grin, clapping her hands together. "I wouldn't have it any other way." She was upbeat, far from the deflated version of herself that had occupied the guest room at Katie's house. Though Katie was grateful to see her bouncing back to her typical buoyant personality, she was afraid Davina's answers could send her spiraling down again.

They settled in the reception area next to Tom, who had already arrived. Katie darted a nervous glance over at him, startled by the changes in his physical appearance. He'd been on edge for the last two months, engaged in the battle of his life to prove his mother's innocence, and the stress was taking a toll.

Tom was thinner and his skin more pale. During a recent phone call, Lauren confided he'd been forgoing his religious gym practices because he was totally consumed with the case. While they waited, he hunched forward, his jaw clenched, and his fingers steepled together. Katie felt his anxiety climbing.

"You okay?" she asked, concern wrinkling her forehead.

"Yeah," he gritted, biting the inside of his cheek.

Finally, Davina's assistant showed them into her office and, after turning down her offer for coffee, they all waited on pins and needles for the lawyer to make her appearance. A few minutes later, Davina strode in and offered them a curt nod before opening her briefcase and pulling out a thick stack of paperwork carefully organized in manilla folders. She handed them over to Tom, who started to page through the documents.

"My guy did some digging. Now, none of this will be admissible in court. But he did uncover an account in the Bahamas that was receiving regular monthly deposits from the Adapt4Heroes Foundation. The deposits started over two years ago, and the agent of record is MP Holdings. "

"How did you get this?" Tom asked.

"I think it's better for everyone if you don't know how the sausage was made." She leaned forward on her forearms, making direct eye contact. "My advice would be to start with the deposits. Make a list of the dates they were made. Maybe you'll get lucky and it will line up with a day when Rox was out of the office, on vacation, or had taken a sick day." Tom nodded in agreement as he continued to flip through the thick report.

"Do you have any insight into who opened the account?"

"That's a harder nut to crack," Davina admitted. "As far as we can tell, it's a shell corporation. Part of the issue of origination stems from the fact that an anonymous shell was created in one jurisdiction that controls an anonymous trust in a completely different country. This trust also controls a bank account in a third country," Davina recounted.

"Setting up an off-shore account sounds really complicated," Rox mumbled, astonished at the level of difficulty. "I barely understood what you just said." She glanced over at Tom, hopeful the complexity would help prove her innocence.

Davina shot it down immediately. "Actually, it's simpler than you'd think. Setting up a shell corporation turns out to be something any average person can do in just a little more time than it takes to open an email account."

"What? Really?" Katie was shocked.

"Not to mention, there are law firms and financial advisors all over the world who specialize in setting up this kind of corporate structure," Davina answered.

"Isn't setting up an off-shore account against the law?"

"Opening the account is perfectly legal. Failing to report your assets in it or crossing the line into money laundering or tax evasion is where it becomes illegal." Her lips curled down in a frown. "With the Bahamian laws providing anonymity and the fact interlocking shell companies were utilized to set it up in the first place, it will be difficult, if not impossible, to trace ownership back to a single individual. The Bahamian government knows it's in their best interests to be discreet and keep the money flowing into their country. I'm afraid we might have reached a dead end."

"Do you think Keith is capable of this?" Rox asked, unable to wrap her head around it. "He denied it when we spoke on the phone. He was sobbing and begging for my forgiveness."

"Mom! You agreed to let the authorities handle it." Tom palmed his face in frustration. "If you won't listen to my professional advice, I am going to have to bring on another attorney."

Katie watched Rox grimace. "I can't afford that."

"I know," Tom muttered as he turned toward Davina, bringing the meeting to a close. "We appreciate your time and effort. Please forward the invoice for your services to me." He pulled a business card from the pocket of his suit coat and handed it to her.

"No way," Rox said, her steely gaze meeting Tom's as she pulled the card out of Davina's hand. "This is my mess. I'll be the one to pay."

"Mom, you're being ridiculous." The tips of Tom's ears turned beet red as he stood and pulled a combatant Rox to her feet. "Let's talk about this privately." Katie quickly fished her keys out of her purse and handed them off to Rox as she passed, still arguing with Tom over who would pay the bill.

"I'll meet you at the car."

When the room was cleared, she addressed Davina. "Thank you for your help with this."

"I'm afraid I didn't do much. It's a pretty murky situation and will be hard to navigate."

"Information is power, and Tom is a brilliant attorney. If it can be used to help Rox clear her name, he will figure out what to do with it." Katie made a snap decision. "But, despite their bickering, I would like to pay the legal fees. Tom and Lauren are dating, and I have a feeling he's going to be my son-in-law someday soon. I don't want them to have to shoulder the financial burden."

"Congratulations! *Now* I understand why you've been so involved." Then Davina winced. "Are you sure? The billable hours were unusually high because of the complexities of the case."

"Absolutely sure." She cupped one hand around her mouth and lowered her voice to a conspiring tone, "I can afford it because my divorce attorney helped me win a kick-ass settlement not too long ago."

Davina shot her a confident smile, still flabbergasted by the way the case ended. Jefferson's desire to settle out of the blue and the generous division of assets left

Katie living more than comfortably. "I still can't take all the credit for that one."

"You should," Katie declared, even though she knew Zoya had done the heavy lifting. "I'm considering this a pay-it-forward moment to help another deserving woman."

"That's very generous of you."

Katie stood to leave and offered Davina a hand. When her palm connected, she felt a tingle, and the colors in her view saturated. Her eyes closed, and a small flash of bright light popped into her consciousness. Concerned, her intuition made her ask, "How have you been otherwise?"

Davina's expression soured. "I sure could use some of the magic of your divorce settlement right now."

"What do you mean?"

She sighed. "Oh, nothing."

Pretty pathetic. Mother always said a woman needs female friends, and I never believed her. Now look at me, fifty-five years old and drastically close to oversharing with a previous client. Get it together, woman.

Davina's thoughts saddened Katie. She couldn't help herself from offering, "If you ever need someone to talk to, I am available. It's got to be very difficult to find the time to invest in friendships when your practice is so busy."

Davina was taken aback. Katie watched her chew on her bottom lip, considering her statement.

"You probably don't know who you can even trust,"

Katie continued, trying her best to open a door of communication.

"I've always been sort of a lone she-wolf," Davina admitted with an awkward laugh. "I prefer it that way because I don't have to pretend to be something I'm not."

"I get it, but if you ever change your mind..." Katie left it open-ended.

"...I know where to find you," Davina finished.

Katie offered her a warm smile and then started walking to the door. When she got to it, she paused and glanced back over her shoulder. Davina was already engrossed in her phone, tapping feverishly into it with her thumbs. Something was definitely on her mind, but she was determined to go it alone. Katie left feeling sorry for the powerful attorney. For the first time, she could see it was lonely at the top. Shattering glass ceilings was an often thankless endeavor. It left her feeling at peace and grateful for her big, messy life and all the people who inhabited it.

TWENTY-SIX

"Fifty-one looks great on you," Arlo said. He was resting at Katie's feet, watching her get ready for the annual family birthday dinner to celebrate both her and Yuli's birthdays. Working quickly, she swiped a creamy blush stick up her cheekbones, blended it with her fingers, and brushed two coats of coal black mascara onto her lashes. Now that she was rocking a full head of white hair, the contrast made her green eyes even more striking.

"Thanks, buddy."

She twirled back and forth in the full-length mirror and, satisfied with her reflection, walked out to the kitchen as Arlo trotted behind her.

"This is it! Tonight is the night I've been waiting for since Zoya banished me into this dog body."

Katie chewed the inside of her lip.

"What is it?" Arlo asked, jumping up on his hind

legs and pressing his paws on her torso. "You're anxious. I can feel it."

"It will be strange not coming home to a dog anymore," she explained. "You're the one creature who is always ridiculously happy to see me." She reached down, tangling her fingers in his soft caramel-colored fur. "Don't get me wrong; I am happy for you. I am. I guess I'm apprehensive about being alone."

"Alone? I was hoping to still be a significant part of your life."

"How?" she wondered out loud. "The kids will be suspicious of any man hanging around me."

Arlo whined, a forlorn cry that stirred something deep in Katie. "I guess I never really thought that far ahead. I was so focused on my release."

"Where will you go? What will you do?" These questions weighed on her mind. "What happens if she changes you back and you don't even know who I am anymore?"

"That's impossible," he said. "You've imprinted on my soul."

"The truth is, we don't know what's next. The physical transformation might wipe your memory clean."

"That's true. We don't know for sure, but I believe we're soulmates, deeply connected by much more than the physical realm."

Katie arranged her skirt around herself carefully so she could sit back on her heels. She ran the palms of her hands down his flanks. "You've been my best friend for the last four years. What am I going to do without you?" She felt tears gathering at her lash line, threatening to spill down her cheeks.

"You're my best friend, too. But I believe in my heart of hearts, this isn't goodbye but see you later." He licked her hot tears away, and she chuckled, feeling the sandpaper sensation of his tongue for the last time. He whispered, "I *will* come back for you."

"How can you be so certain? How would I even know it's you?"

"You'll just *know*," he tried to convince her. "I've watched you grow and develop over the last year, and your intuition has increased by leaps and bounds. Now you just need to lean in and trust it," he explained. "You'll know when warmth floods your heart and it feels like déjà vu."

Katie nodded and stroked down the fur on his back as he continued, "The greatest lesson I learned inside this canine body is the concept of unconditional love. In my previous life, I was shallow and selfish, but experiencing life through the lens of a canine has taught me to go deeper than the physical. To love someone purely because they exist, not for what they can do for you. For a dog, love is simple. Humans, on the other hand, find endless ways to screw it up, discount, and doubt it."

"How did you get to be so wise?"

Arlo's tongue hung out of his mouth, and for a minute, it looked like he was grinning. He chomped on the air. "As much as I hated my sentence, it brought me to you, and I would never want to change that for anything. I love you, Katie."

"I love you, too," she whispered through her tears.

The doorbell rang, silencing the rest of Katie's fears. She stood and swallowed her despair, wiped the tears from her eyes, and walked across the room to the foyer to open it.

"Happy Birthday!" Frankie and Harry cheered with two bottles of bubbly cradled in their arms.

Yuli, Kristina, and David were right behind them. Katie hugged each one, her heart so tender from the impending loss of Arlo that it made her squeeze them even tighter. When she pulled away, Kristina pressed a cool palm to Katie's forehead. "Are you okay, honey? You look pale."

"I'm fine. Birthdays make me sentimental is all. Frankie's inside with the bubbly."

She hugged Yuli next, clinging to her grandmother and whispering in her ear, "Arlo is leaving. He's served his time, and Zoya will be changing him back tonight."

"Don't despair." Yuli pulled back to cradle her granddaughter's face in her weathered hands. "He was never meant to be your dog forever."

"I'm happy for him. I know he's been eager to resume the life he gave up, but I'm sad for me. He's been my confidant and best friend for years. It's hard to imagine my life without him."

"Dogs are the best of us," Yuli said. "Perhaps when you're ready, you'll find room in your heart for another."

Katie grimaced. "I don't know if I should if it hurts this much to lose him."

"Your heart will heal."

Katie laughed and wiped her tears away. "Can't you fast-track the healing? Send some of your golden sparks direct to my chambers?" she asked with a teary grin while tapping on her chest.

"If only it were that easy," Yuli answered with a knowing smile. "Overwhelming grief is the price you pay for great love." She leaned forward and touched her forehead to Katie's, a sweet gesture that cracked Katie's heart open even wider. "If you don't open your heart, then no one can ever break it."

"I couldn't keep it closed if I tried," Katie whispered.

"And that is your superpower and also your greatest weakness." Yuli pulled her in for one more hug. Over her shoulder, Katie smiled, seeing Beckett, Callie, Lauren, and Tom waiting at the landing.

"Already in tears? This might be a new record, even for you," Beckett teased as he wrapped his arms around his mother.

Katie laughed at herself as her children encircled her. She felt her heart swell with love and understood Yuli was exactly right. She laced her arm through Beckett's and let him lead her into the kitchen, where Frankie was busy pouring flutes of champagne. Tom pulled Lauren close and kissed her forehead, a gesture that melted Katie. There was nothing better than seeing her oldest find a man who lived to cherish and protect her, even during the most stressful days of his life. When push came to shove and a person was tested, that was when you really saw what they were made of, and Katie now knew Rox and Tom were made of the same resilient stock.

Tom led Lauren closer to Rox, who was holding a glass of champagne aloft. Her face broke into a huge grin when her gaze settled on the face of her only child. It chased away the dark shadows that had taken up residence there.

Katie lifted her glass. "What a year my fiftieth circle around the sun has been!" Her eyes drank in everyone gathered in a circle, toasting her. "I feel like I've started a whole new life, and I can't wait to see what fifty-one brings. Here's to all of you, my nearest and dearest. I love you."

They chimed their glasses together and broke into small groups, chatting among themselves. Katie flitted from group to group for the next hour as they enjoyed drinks and charcuterie.

"We better head over to the restaurant," Katie instructed. "Our reservation is at seven-thirty. Can you guys go on ahead? I've got to run an errand on the way home, so I'll meet you there." Amid chattering and grumbles, everyone departed and the house finally fell silent.

"I have to say one last goodbye." Katie sat down on the sofa and patted her lap like she had for years, encouraging Arlo to jump up onto it. She hugged him tight and buried her face in his soft fur. "I sure am going to miss you, boy," she whispered into his neck as she burst into tears. A high-pitched whine was emitted from deep inside his throat.

"And I, you."

"I hope you find goodness and love and that the next part of your life is the happiest it could ever be, regardless if I am a part of it or not."

Arlo cried and whined, popping both his paws onto her shoulder, snuggling into her, totally distressed. "Loving you has changed me," he whimpered. "You taught me how to love."

"I like to think we taught each other," Katie responded, tears coursing down her face.

"Don't doubt yourself anymore," Arlo begged. "Promise me you will trust your instincts and pour all that love you gave to me inward."

Katie nodded, brushing the tears from her cheeks.

"I'll never forget you." She exhaled a heavy sigh for both of them.

"I'm coming back for you someday."

"I hope so." She kissed the tip of his wet nose for the last time. Katie stood and headed to the door, hearing Arlo's tags jingling right behind her. She turned once more, shot him a sweet smile, and then ducked out the door. Arlo watched her pull out of the driveway, and Katie stole one last glance at him through the sidelight of her front door. He jumped up, pressing his paws and nose to the glass, then fell down on his front legs and howled as she drove away.

After a long dinner, Katie drove aimlessly down the streets of Aura Cove, not wanting to go home. Rox left the birthday dinner celebration early with Tom. She was due at the FBI Tampa Field Office the next afternoon for questioning, and from her quiet demeanor and Tom's tight expression and clenched jaw, Katie knew a lot was riding on the interview. They both refused drinks most of the night and left early together after many apologies. Their minds were obviously elsewhere, but so was Katie's.

Finally, around midnight, she pulled into the garage and sat in her car for a long moment. She glanced at the console and, seeing the time reading 12:04 a.m., knew the house would be silent, so she braced herself for the shock. Reluctantly, she gathered her purse and climbed the steps to the door. She turned the knob and shut the door quietly, not wanting to awaken Rox. Reaching for the bank of switches, she turned on the lights in the hallway when the most familiar jingling sound made her heart leap in her chest.

She heard his claws scraping on the travertine and laughed at her mind playing tricks on her. Seconds later, when a furry form came barreling into her, Katie gasped with joy and dropped to her knees, welcoming the warm dog into her arms. She squeezed him tight against her body and felt him tremble and shake.

"What happened?" she asked as she released her grip on him. "I thought you'd be long gone by now."

"Your great-great grandmother is a liar," he spat out angrily. "I knew I couldn't trust that woman as far as I could throw her." Arlo paced the length of the room, cagey with angry energy as he fumed. He growled and bared his teeth as he stalked up and down the hallway. Katie held a finger to her lips to shush him and led him into her bedroom, shutting the door behind them.

"I'm sorry, Arlo. Maybe I can talk some sense into her."

"Ha! Good luck with that."

"At least we're still together," Katie offered optimistically.

"That's the only silver lining of this entire mess." He plopped down on the ground with a huff. "I'm done."

"Everything will look better in the morning." Katie pulled out a pair of pajamas, and after washing her face, she sat on the edge of the bed, patting it. Without needing another invitation, Arlo jumped up onto the bed and circled himself next to Katie's warm body. She tugged on his ears slowly, then swiped her fingers under his chin and began rubbing small circles on his curly chest, a massage move she knew he loved. She kissed the tip of his damp nose. "It will. Trust me."

TWENTY-SEVEN

The next morning, Rox was pale and silent in the car as Tom drove to the FBI Tampa Field Office, barking out last-minute commands as his nerves chewed at him.

"Say as little as possible," he directed, turning toward his mother. His tone was unrelenting. "Seriously."

"I have nothing to hide. I'm going to answer their questions, Tommy, to the best of my ability."

"Mom." He exhaled with a heavy sigh. "That is a terrible idea. You have to trust me. Right now, I'm not your son. I'm your *lawyer*, and I'm advising you to plead the Fifth whenever appropriate." His eyes darted over to her and back at the road as he white-knuckled the wheel. "Our mission today is to figure out what evidence they have against you. This isn't the time to speculate or offer explanations. We need to know what they have so we can prepare a stronger defense."

"Okay, okay," she relented.

"Remember to pause. If you have any doubt whether or not you should answer the question, look over at me. Err on the side of caution. They can use anything and everything you say against you in court, so it is important to use as few words as possible."

"God, I hate this," Rox cried as they sped through traffic.

"I do, too," Tom said, chewing the inside of his cheek, a habit he developed in middle school. It was a nervous tic Rox immediately picked up on.

"You're worried." Rox reached out, placing her hand on his arm to comfort him. "No matter what happens today, I am grateful to have your brilliant legal mind in my corner."

He blanched at the word brilliant.

"It was meant to be a compliment," Rox said, then softened her tone. "Don't put so much pressure on yourself."

"How can I not?"

"It's a pressure cooker situation, that's for sure, but one secret I learned at West Point was the art of emotional detachment. When you get in your own head, that is where mistakes are made. It's the hesitation and fear that can get you killed. Now, I'm certain no one is going to die in this battle this afternoon, so relax."

"That's easy for you to say," Tom muttered, his eyes focused straight ahead. "I'm more concerned about the war."

"We can only fight one battle at a time, sweetheart."

She squeezed his forearm, tensed by his fingers gripping the wheel. "I love you."

"Now you're really scaring me," he said, trying to keep it light.

"Ha!" Rox rewarded him with a sharp, stilted chuckle. "That's the guy I know and love."

Tom pulled into an empty spot in front of the limestone building, and a few minutes later, they were shown to a nondescript beige and gray room. Concrete walls were painted an institutional gray, and a two-way mirror was installed on one wall. Rox and Tom took seats at the table and were made to wait for fifteen minutes before the metal door buzzed, opening to reveal a stocky man in a suit, his hair buzzed short, entering the room carrying a thick file folder.

"Thank you for coming in voluntarily today," he greeted, taking the seat in front of them before reading her Miranda rights. "This interview is being recorded and can be used against you. Do you understand?"

"Yes." Rox sat on the edge of her seat. She laced her fingers together in her lap to keep them from shaking.

"I'm Alan Ripple from the Department of Homeland Security, conducting an interview of Roxanne Sullivan." He spoke clearly and with a quiet confidence, giving the date and time.

"Are you aware of the Bank Secrecy Act?"

"No," she answered and pressed her lips shut to stop the flow of any additional words. Desperately, she tried to keep Tom's advice in the forefront of her mind.

"It requires taxpayers to report certain foreign

financial accounts. This law requires annual reporting every year of bank accounts, brokerage accounts, and mutual funds outside the States to the United States Treasury Department."

"But I don't have any foreign accounts," she tried to explain.

"That's an interesting statement." He opened the folder and pulled out a sheath of papers. "Interesting, indeed, since we've been able to trace regular deposits made from your office to this account number in the Bahamas."

Rox's eyes flicked over to the paper he was pushing in front of her. She gulped as her good leg jiggled up and down nervously.

"We've been able to prove the transactions originated from your computer at the foundation."

"What?" Utter shock and outrage registered on Rox's face. Unable to quell her frustration, she hopped to her feet and paced behind the chairs. "There's no way. I didn't do this."

"All digital transactions leave footprints," he stated, pointing to an IP address on the paper. "We can track it down and isolate it at the device level. I bet you weren't aware of that capability."

"That's not possible." She glanced over at her son, feeling warmth flush up her chest.

"Transfers have been made on a pretty consistent monthly schedule for the last two years. At first, they were small amounts that wouldn't attract attention. Well under the ten thousand dollar daily limit."

"I'm telling you, it wasn't me."

"Then how do you explain the fact that the deposits stopped after your arrest?" He leaned in. "Are you telling me this is a coincidence?"

She shook her head, feeling the weight of it settle on her chest. Panic rushed in, and she clenched her hands tighter together. His voice wavered in her head as if she was listening to him speak underwater.

"You were doing so well, flying under the radar for years, but a large transaction in March actually got our attention and triggered a major audit. What happened? Did you get greedy?"

"No?" she muttered. Her breaths were quick and left her feeling light-headed.

"It was inevitable," he continued. "With that six-figure payday getting deposited in March, we were closing in on your scheme. Your fundraising success at the Adapt4Heroes Foundation meant a bigger piggy bank that must have been impossible to resist. I mean, how long could you be content to skim paltry sums when a big payday could set you up for life?"

"Is there a question in there, Officer?" Tom asked. Rox glanced over at him, feeling her heartbeat thrum in her chest.

"Look, Ms. Sullivan, cut a deal. Confess to the crime and we can recommend restitution and community service."

"But I'm innocent."

"Man, if I had a dollar for every time I've heard that

statement in this room, I'd be set for life. Just like you almost were."

Rox gasped at the offensive accusation.

He leaned in to intimidate her. "News flash, people who declare they are innocent rarely are."

"I'd like to remind you that my client is innocent until proven guilty. Your intimidation tactics will not work on us."

"I want my day in court." Rox stared him down. "The Adapt4Heroes Foundation was my purpose for living. I would have never stolen money and used it for my own gain."

Alan leaned back in his chair, holding up his hands with a chuckle. "You might want to rethink that strategy." He closed the folder and laced his fingers behind his head.

"Willful failure to file a Foreign Bank Account Report can lead to criminal penalties of up to $250,000, five years in jail, or both." He let that sink in for a long moment. Rox's eyes bugged out, and she cast a glance at Tom. Under the table, he reached out to squeeze her hand for support.

"That doesn't even take into account the fraud charges for the gift card scheme you and your administrative assistant were running."

"What?" Rox was stunned. "I have no idea what you're talking about! I had nothing to do with that either!"

"C'mon, Ms. Sullivan, you keep shoveling the shit

and I'm just supposed to swallow it?" His eyes drilled into hers before flicking over to Tom.

"Has Keith Landers been brought in for questioning?" Tom asked.

"He's been interviewed, but I cannot discuss the specifics."

Tom's eyes bugged, and a vein in his forehead bulged. "That bastard," he mumbled as Rox felt the bottom drop out from under her. Overwhelmed, Rox squeezed her hands into fists under the table, feeling her fingernails dig half-moons into her palms. She focused on the discomfort to ground the litany of thoughts rushing through her mind.

"I plan on sending this evidence to the DOJ, and I would expect formal charges to be forthcoming." He turned to Rox. "But before I do, I want to give you one last chance, Ms. Sullivan. After this folder leaves my desk, my hands are tied. I won't be able to make any recommendations to the Attorney General."

"I didn't do this, and I will not let you strong-arm me into admitting to something I didn't do," she reiterated.

"This meeting is over," Tom announced, standing up. His face was drawn and his expression pinched.

"Very well," Alan said. "Have it your way."

Tom ushered Rox out of the room and straight into the car before saying a word. Once inside the vehicle, the usually unflappable Rox burst into tears. "I won't confess to a crime I never committed," she cried. "I didn't do this."

"Keith cut a deal and threw you under the bus!" Tom hit the steering wheel with his fist. "It's our word against his. Dammit!" Grasping at straws, he said, "Did he have unrestricted access to your login credentials? Or know where they were located?"

Stunned, Rox nodded slowly as bile rose in her throat. "Yes."

The idea he'd been secretly siphoning off funds earmarked for veterans who desperately needed them was sickening. Even worse was the reality Keith betrayed her when she'd always tried to help him. The truth stung and was accompanied by a sensation of free-fall that left her terrified.

"I assume you use a password app to protect your login credentials?"

She blanched, and her tear-stained face turned white. "Not exactly." Unable to look at Tom, she closed her eyes and felt the weight of the world pressing down on her. Huffing a sigh between her clenched teeth, she finally admitted, "I'm old school. I kept all my logins and passwords inside a password journal locked inside my desk drawer."

"On paper?" Tom croaked immediately, understanding the ramifications of this new piece of information coming to light. "Jesus, Mom." He scrubbed his face with his hands in frustration.

"Keith and I had an understanding. He handled the paper, and I handled the people."

"That understanding is going to send you to prison," Tom grumbled.

"It's bad, isn't it?" Rox dared to ask.

"Yeah, it's bad."

TWENTY-EIGHT

Katie was washing dishes at the sink when Rox shuffled in, her face a sickly gray and her expression grim. Knowing she'd just reported to the FBI field office, Katie dared to ask the question she already knew the answer to. "How did it go?"

Rox just shook her head and sighed as she sat down on a stool at the island, the weight of the world on her shoulders. She palmed her face, and Katie noticed her eyes glistening with tears.

There was a long pause before Rox finally answered. "There is a very good chance I could go to prison for a crime I did not commit."

Katie turned off the water and wiped her hands on a dishtowel. "Do you want to talk about it?"

"There isn't much to say. The FBI traced withdrawals from my computer to an off-shore bank account. It was the smoking gun they were looking for.

It's over. They offered me a deal if I was willing to make a full confession."

Katie sat down next to her. "Could Keith have…"

Rox ground out a stilted, "Ha! Seems he beat me to the punch. He pled out and incriminated me."

It's time.

The message was a whisper so clear in Katie's head, like it was carved into a stone tablet. It sent a shiver of trepidation down her spine as she heard the faint ring from a tuning fork intensify in her ears.

Next to her, Rox folded her hands together on the marble and stared down at them. "Everything I worked for… it's all gone." A lone tear spilled from Rox's eye and cascaded down her cheek. "I always believed that, if you were a good person and did your best to help people, things would work out in the end," she said bitterly as she brought her deepest fears into focus. "Turns out the world doesn't work like that at all. It's a cesspool of ugliness and war where good doesn't always triumph over evil."

"I'm so sorry." Katie reached out her hand to comfort the woman, who swiped the tears from her cheeks before clutching it. The physical contact, combined with the warm tears, opened a flow of consciousness that swept Katie up in its turbulent path. Her breath quickened in her chest and a heavy weight settled on her ribcage as she connected with Rox's energy.

"Tommy thinks it might be better to take a deal," She stated, bewildered at the idea. "How can I set aside my integrity when I am being asked to lie about my involvement?" She heaved a heavy sigh. "I know it might be difficult to understand, but when I took my Oath of Office, I meant every word I said. The Army's values of honor, integrity, and selfless service are the guideposts I rely on to live my life. Without them, I am nothing."

Katie just listened. She could find no words to console the distraught woman. Instead, she sat with her in the pain and felt the wave of it crest then threaten to knock them both over in its intensity.

I'd rather die.

Katie heard Rox's distressed thought and panicked.

I'd rather go out on my own terms, knowing my honor and dignity were intact, than accept the blame for destroying an organization I loved.

Katie's eyes widened, and she gulped as terror knotted in her throat. Next to her, Rox clawed at her neck. "I feel a noose tightening around my throat, and I don't know what to do to stop the stool from being kicked out from under me."

"I know it is hard when things seem so dark, but you must keep the faith."

Rox snorted in disbelief. "That's easy for you to say."

"You're right," Katie said. "But the truth always comes to light, even when it is up against formidable enemies desperate to keep it hidden." Searching for the right words to bring calm to a situation that was spiraling out of control, she added. "You are the strongest woman I know. You cannot let this setback defeat you. How many soldiers have you counseled on the brink of suicide, inspiring them to dig deeper, stay in the game, and play one more inning? You only fail if you give up."

It's time.

The tuning fork intensified, and she couldn't ignore the call any longer. After convincing Tom and Lauren to stay overnight at the house to keep an eye on Rox, Katie sped over to Yuli's house. Arlo sat in the passenger seat, and the black truffle Zoya had given her was tucked into her bag. "What is that stench?" he asked, his nose twitching.

"It's the nuclear option," she explained as she parked and quickly got out of her Beetle. Yuli was waiting at the door for her and opened it before she could even knock. She'd already set up a circle of candles around the perimeter of her home, and the flames flickered when Katie entered and walked to the center of the room. Picking up on the shift in energy, Arlo whined at her side and jumped up on his hind legs.

"It's too risky," he howled. "I'm begging you. Don't go through with this."

Yuli nodded in agreement. "I agree with the dog."

"I have to." Katie stood firm, knowing it was the right move, but wished she felt more confident in her decision. "I've been practicing the meditations, and I received clear direction from Karma. She said, 'It's time.' No matter how terrified I am, I have to go."

Yuli took her granddaughter's hands in her own. "Katia, I am afraid for you. Please reconsider."

"I can't. And if you're honest with yourself, you could not ignore the calling either," Katie said.

"I wish I could take this journey for you."

"But you can't. You and Zoya both agreed I am the only one with a pure enough heart to endure it. You said, 'To utilize the truffle in its most powerful state, it needs the clean and clear consciousness of a newly awakened supernatural heart.' "

"That is true." Yuli blew out a hot breath between her teeth and asked one more time, "If you're sure?"

"I am." Katie nodded.

"Then come, let me get you settled inside the sacred circle." She walked Katie into the intersected points of the pentagram that were carved into her wooden floors. Points of the star jutted to the edges of the house, each tip connected to an altar of one of the five elements. Katie sat down in the center of it and felt a surge of strength and resolve settle deep into her soul. She pulled open the lid to the container, and her eyes widened as she felt a lusty pull toward it. Although repulsed by the overpowering aroma of rotting carcasses and coppery blood, she was oddly drawn to consume the black truffle despite her disgust.

"Don't touch it with your bare skin!" Yuli shouted, and quickly pulled out a pair of pure silver tweezers and handed them to Katie.

Before she could change her mind, Katie grasped the truffle in the tweezers and bit into it. On her tongue, it seared the skin instantly, and her face wrinkled up in aversion as she fought to swallow the vile candy. Bile surged up from her belly and, panicked, she glanced over at Yuli who offered instructions, "Still your breathing and swallow it. You need to ingest it all."

Katie nodded, popped the rest of it into her mouth, chewed quickly, and swallowed. A surge of vomit welled up, and she gulped the hot acid back. It burned down the length of her esophagus. She heard Arlo growl and bark as she convulsed onto her back in the center of the pentagram and writhed around as the truffle made its way into her bloodstream. The last sound her body emitted was a piercing scream as a wave of pain and terror crashed over her.

She was zinging through all space and time. The movement was dizzying as she rocketed through the cosmos. Eventually, she skidded to a stop, landing hard inside a pit of fear. Katie heard a skittering of automatic gunfire. Loud explosions rocketed around her, and she blinked as she tried to get her bearings. She was surrounded by three men in desert Army fatigues. Looking down at herself, she saw was dressed the same and carrying an automatic weapon.

"LT!" Monty shouted at her over the pockets of gunfire. "We're taking sustained fire!"

"Take cover." She heard the shout in Rox's voice, coming from the body she currently resided in, over the hellish din. They dodged behind a cropping of rocks and tried to catch their breath. "On my command," she said. "We need to clear each quadrant." She looked over at

Peabody. "Slow and easy. That's how we get out of here alive." She pulled out a canteen and chugged a long gulp of lukewarm water. Then she wiped the gritty sweat off her forehead and cheeks with the back of her sleeve.

"Peabody, we gotta move. Cover us."

He pulled out a hand grenade and yanked the pin before launching it into the sand dune, where the pack of enemy combatants was hunkered down.

"Move, move, move!" Rox shouted, and they fanned out. Bullets zipped past, and Rox's adrenaline kicked into high gear. Rushing to the next cropping of rocks, she glanced over and heard the audible click. Katie felt the body she inhabited swell with fright and then explode into pieces as shrapnel sliced through her like razors and lodged into her soft tissue. Katie's senses heightened with Rox's heartbeat thundering in her ears. Katie heard her scream and cry out. She reached a hand over to where Peabody lay still. He was already gone. Awash in shock, Rox detached, and Katie studied the destruction in front of her.

An ebony face hovered over hers. Katie glanced to the right where his last name was emblazoned on his shirt. Montgomery. She gritted her teeth, choking on the pain. "Radio the base. Retreat and get back to the rendezvous point," she heard Rox demand. Her voice was losing its strength as agony settled in.

"We're not leaving here without you," he shot back, his jaw set in a firm line.

"It's a direct order," she said, coughing as acrid smoke filled her lungs.

"Williams, carry LT out. I'll cover you." A much younger Sam gathered her up in his arms and started to run. Shots rang out as he rushed through the burning sand. He hunkered down, dropping Rox's bloody body to the sandy earth, then hid between rocks while waiting for Monty to join them.

Her body was trembling, her hands sticky with blood. Katie felt fire where her leg should have been. Sam bent down and cinched up the tourniquet that was pinching off the blood flow to her leg while he waited. Rox drifted off, her body limp, while Katie lingered in her consciousness.

"Jesus Christ, you're heavy," she heard Sam say as he kicked her still body with his boot. A volley of bullets zinged overhead, and Katie watched him poke his head up, scanning the smoke and debris for Monty. Seeing the insurgents advancing, he reached down to drag her by her protective vest into a cave dwelling that was built into the stone.

A few minutes later, Monty rushed over and joined them. Catching his breath for a long moment, he assessed the approaching danger. "Pick her up. We gotta run!"

"She's too far gone," Sam argued. "We have to leave her here."

"But we're only a quarter mile from the rendezvous point!"

"They're closing in. We're outnumbered and

surrounded. Carrying her will only slow us down. We already lost Peabody today. I am not going to get myself killed."

"Pick her up!" Monty commanded "Now! Or God help me, I will drag both your asses out of here."

Sam stood his ground and refused. "It's too late. She's dead weight." Rox's blood was everywhere, coating the sticky sand.

Monty roared in anger and lurched forward to gather Rox in his arms. He struggled to his feet, running on adrenaline, and rushed toward the rendezvous point. The hum of engines from the caravan of approaching Humvees cut through the terror, but they couldn't see the support vehicles yet.

Rox's head lolled back, and Katie gasped in horror as she laid eyes on Sam running close behind. When Monty stopped to adjust the weight of Rox in his arms, Sam put the muzzle of his gun to the back of Monty's head. Dread filled Katie's consciousness as time slowed to a crawl and he pulled the trigger, his eyes wild. The single gunshot rocketed them forward. Monty dropped to the ground instantly, his eyes unseeing. Pink bits of brain matter landed on the sand around them, and then a pool of burgundy sand grew underneath his still form. Katie felt Rox's body drop to the ground to land next to Monty's now lifeless one, and Sam's brow narrowed like he was trying to make a decision.

He kicked her with the toe of his boot, nudging her. "You awake, LT?" Rox didn't even stir. Her skin was pale and clammy, coated in a sheen of gritty sweat.

Seizing an opportunity that had the potential to change the trajectory of his military career, he changed his mind. "Fuck it. You'll be more useful to me alive," Sam growled as he bent down to gather Rox's bloody body in his arms.

He ran the rest of the way to the rendezvous point, relieved when he heard the approaching caravan. It skidded to a stop, and he squinted his eyes as he rushed toward it. Two soldiers jumped out of the vehicles and helped carry Rox back to the Humvees. Another soldier offered Sam a hand and yanked him inside the vehicle.

"Monty? Peabody? Where's the rest of the squad?"

"All confirmed casualties. We're all that's left," Sam said, letting his body fall down into the seat behind him.

"Let's go," the soldier said, and Katie felt the Humvee rev up and race away while the medics attended to Rox's body in the backseat. Sam sat still as a statue, his face filthy and haggard as they rushed back to the base. He didn't utter another word as a full canteen of cold water was pressed into his bloody hands. Katie studied him. His eyes were hollow, his expression blank. He didn't even shed a tear.

TWENTY-NINE

Yuli watched in horror as Katie convulsed and shrieked for an hour, and then her body stilled and all the candles blew out. Afraid, Yuli rushed to her side and shook Katie.

"Katia!" Yuli cried, "Wake up." She continued to shake her granddaughter, and when her amulet dimmed, terror unfurled in her belly. She got to her feet and pressed the purple stone between her thumb and forefinger, begging for the energy to return. Feeling it dissipate more by the second. She rushed back to Katie and swept her hands up into the air, building the intensity of her healing energy over Katie's stilled form. Chanting and humming, she circled her palms as golden sparks surged from her palms to Katie's body.

Katie convulsed on the wooden floor again as if under the control of a Grand Mal seizure. Yuli's heart shattered and tears washed down her cheeks.

"Katia!" she shouted, trying to rouse her awake as terror flooded in. She was watching her greatest nightmare come true.

THIRTY

Rocketed back into the nightmare and burning in the desert sun, Katie gasped, choking on the air filled with smoke and gunpowder. Glancing around to get her bearings, she realized she was right back in Rox's body. She heard Rox shout out orders and braced for the impact from the shrapnel and the force of the blast that would blow her leg to bits.

Terrified and trapped, she repeated the agonizing event several more times in relentless succession. She felt a shattering in her soul when she realized she was stuck in the memory and would be forced to relive it until she could find an escape route. She was a prisoner trapped inside Rox's body, whose muscular legs carried her into the battlefield just seconds before she would lose one. As the gruesome events repeated, she realized she was being numbed to the atrocities of war surrounding her. Smaller details from the scene emerged and captivated her attention.

She felt wetness land on Rox's cheek, and when she looked down, crimson drops of blood and white chips of bone fragments landed in a clump on the tip of her boot.

Her body jerked sideways from a swift kick from Sam's boot, where Rox's body lay heavy behind the rocky rubble. She took notice of the bulging green vein that emerged in his forehead while he argued to convince Monty to leave her behind.

She saw Monty's haggard expression and the raw grit and determination evidenced as he gathered up Rox's unconscious body and carried her to the approaching caravan. The callous sneer on Sam's face was terrifying as he leveled the muzzle of the weapon on the back of Monty's skull. Spine-chilling horror surged through Katie at his lack of hesitation before pulling the trigger.

She heard the heavy thump as Monty's lifeless body dropped to the sand next to Rox's. His blood-shot eyes were open yet unseeing.

Nothing prepared Katie for the trauma of it, for the brutality of war. She was stuck there on repeat, with only a few minutes of blissful silence and peace when they were safely loaded onto the Humvee after the rescue, heading back to base, before the nightmare cranked up again.

What was even harder to grasp was her slow desensitization to the heinous acts of war. Each time she was subjected to the carnage, the shock diminished slightly, and the outrage softened. Her consciousness was shell-shocked into numbness, and a cold detachment chilled her soul.

Unable to stomach round after round, she summoned every ounce of her energy to call on the coven, on Yuli and Zoya, desperate for them to bring her back from the abyss. Unable to fathom a reality where she was stuck in this event for an eternity, her soul cried out for release. She scrambled to remember the instructions Zoya and Yuli had given her. Finding it impossible to concentrate with the hell storm around her, her panic rose to new heights. Then she heard a faint voice. An instruction being given from so far away, she had to focus all her energy on it to suss it out.

Katia! Connect to the divine female blood within you.

It was Yuli's voice she heard trying to guide her through the depths of her tormented journey. Straining through the sporadic bangs of gunfire, she focused on it and tried to align with the goodness within her. Outside of her mind, the war raged on, and she found it an impossible task to disengage with the repeating reality playing out in her mind.

I can't do it, she cried in response after several failed attempts.

You must. Keep trying. Do not give up.

THIRTY-ONE

Warned by the amulet burning at her throat, Zoya raced from the hangar to Yuli's house. When she arrived, a beleaguered Yuli opened the door and led her into the center of her home where Katie's body was lying in the middle of the pentagram. Unconscious, Katie's lips twitched. Every few seconds, her limbs would contort and tremble. As Zoya stepped closer, all of their amulets collectively brightened and began to hum.

"How long?" she asked as she knelt down at Katie's side. Her full skirt puddled around her as she gently shook Katie's shoulder.

"Katia!" Her voice was stern, and she gently slapped her cheek, hoping to get a response but receiving none.

Across the room, Yuli was clearly frozen in shock and struggled to answer. "How long?!" Zoya shouted as she assessed the dire situation.

"Three hours, give or take," Yuli finally muttered.

"I've been trying to wake her up, and she's been unresponsive."

Zoya felt a spike of fear crush her heart as Yuli's anger found a place for blame.

"She wasn't ready," Yuli muttered. "It was too risky."

"I informed her of all the risks, and she ultimately made the decision," Zoya reminded her. "It was an act of free will."

"What if she never wakes up?"

"That is indeed a possibility," Zoya admitted, glancing down at Katie's pinched expression. She pulled off her gloves.

"Not if I have anything to say about it," Yuli said boldly, making a decision. She walked to the side wall of her home and turned on a switch. A mechanical whirring sound hummed as the skylight overhead opened up and a rush of cool night air filtered in. In the starry sky above, clouds raced by the nearly full moon in double time, and a crackle of lightning flashed in the distance.

Then she rushed to her garage and rolled in the kiddie pool she kept on hand for her annual equinox rituals. Not wasting another second, she dragged a hose to the sink, filled the shallow pool with water, and dumped an entire box of salt into it.

"What are you doing?" Zoya asked, confused by the sudden flurry of activity.

"The salt water will conduct the electricity we

generate. We need to focus our energy to shock her out of the past."

Zoya exhaled a heavy breath between her gritted teeth. "Talk about risky. She could have a heart attack and die."

"Do you have a better idea?"

"No," Zoya admitted.

"Then help me," Yuli begged as her eyes filled with fear. She wedged her hands under Katie's arms, and Zoya leaped up and grabbed her feet. In the span of a few minutes, Katie was submersed in the shallow pool. Her white hair floated on the surface, and for a moment, her face relaxed and Yuli felt her heart unclench. Then she thrashed around wildly, covering them both in frigid water.

"Hold her head steady. Don't let her swallow the water." Zoya pressed her fingertips to Katie's temples and held her head still while her body writhed and bucked. Finally, after one more thrash backward, she stopped moving. Yuli glanced at the clock on the wall. "We have ten minutes until the next round of thrashing begins. Grab a hand and a leg."

Zoya nodded and grabbed the limbs, and across from her, Yuli did the same. Yuli closed her eyes and chanted a verse, and Zoya joined in when she repeated it. A golden spark tingled from Yuli's hand to Katie's and then another. The current surged down from her shoulder and then to her leg. Yuli chanted louder, concentrating, and a more powerful discharge ran from her hand to Katie's and down her leg. Zoya chanted with her, and a green spark met the golden one and raced from the opposite leg up the torso and down her other hand that was squeezed into Zoya's.

The energy in the room flickered and intensified as all three women connected and electricity surged through them, causing them to glow. Yuli's hair stood on end, and her chants elevated into shrieks as the amulet at her throat smoked and seared her skin. Zoya felt the same sensation as the amulet scorched her ivory skin. Determined to endure it, she clenched her jaw and held still. Louder and louder, their voices swirled together until they became one. Through the opening in the roof, there was a rumble of thunder, and then a lightning bolt shot from the sky down to the women. It zinged through them on their closed circuit of hands and legs, jolting them backward and ripping them apart, sending Yuli and Zoya skittering to the sidewalls of the home. In a gush of frigid water, the pool cracked and emptied. Dazed, Zoya blinked in confusion and glanced over at Yuli, who staggered to her feet.

In the center of the pentagram, Katie shot up to a seated position as if electrified and gasped for air. Her green eyes glowed neon and her hair was drenched. After the powerful surge of energy dispelled, she collapsed back onto the floor into a trembling heap as Yuli and Zoya rushed to her. Sobbing with relief, Katie rolled over to her side, coughing and choking for several long moments. Shivering, she finally pushed herself to a seated position.

"Katia!" Yuli exclaimed, gathering her up in her

arms. "Get her a blanket!" she shouted to Zoya, who ran over to Yuli's recliner, pulled off a chenille throw, and wrapped it around Katie's shoulders.

"I thought I'd never see you again!" Yuli said as she cradled Katie's sorrowful face in her hands. Tears spilled down both their cheeks. Katie's breaths were ragged as she attempted to contain the swell of emotion that surged through her. She hyperventilated for several long moments, searching for words that seemed just out of her reach.

Yuli looked her over. "Are you hurt?" Katie nodded, revealing her wrists where Yuli and Zoya had grasped them minutes earlier. A network of red branching wounds from burst capillaries traced down her forearms and up her shoulders in a treelike pattern. Katie stared at them in awe, stunned by the transformation on her skin. Yuli traced one finger down the wounds that lightened up considerably as they came in contact with her healing touch.

Katie clung to her grandmother, sobbing with relief she'd been freed from the prison she'd been entombed in. "Sam," she croaked out when she finally spoke, her voice hoarse. "He's not the hero everyone thinks he is. Remember the mask? Talulah was right, she was trying to warn us." She let out a forlorn cry, her body wracked with grief then whimpered. "He killed Monty."

"Who's Monty?" Yuli asked.

"A soldier who was killed in action in the battle where Rox lost her leg. Sam was awarded a Medal of

Honor for saving her life, when, in reality, he wanted to leave her there to die."

Stunned by the revelation, neither woman spoke. "I witnessed him murder Monty over and over," Katie sobbed. "I can't get it out of my mind." She trembled with fear. "We can't let him get away with this." She rocked herself from side to side, clearly traumatized by the horrific loop she'd been stuck in. Inconsolable, tears streamed down Katie's face.

"You need rest," Zoya said, and Yuli nodded in agreement. They gathered on either side of her to shore up her resources and help her stand.

"Lean on us," Zoya instructed as they led her to Yuli's bed.

Terrified, Katie looked down at her feet. "My legs… they feel weird."

"Don't worry," Yuli said. "Their strength will return. The Recurring Torment Rum Truffle suppresses your nervous system. It's a sedative of sorts and takes time to metabolize. After a good night's rest, you will feel much better."

Zoya pulled back the blanket and tucked her in while Katie shook uncontrollably. Sitting on the edge of the bed, she brushed her fingers across Katie's forehead to smooth her stray hairs away.

"You're safe now," Zoya whispered, feeling her heart rip into shreds from Katie's whimpering. Trying to comfort her, she tugged the blanket higher.

"He's a murderer," Katie whispered over and over in the darkness as she writhed on the mattress, clearly conflicted. "I have to tell Rox." She tried to pull away the blanket, and Zoya squeezed her hand.

"You're not in any condition to carry out retribution right now," Zoya said. "But I can." Katie breathed a sigh of relief. "With your permission, of course."

"Yes," Katie whispered and settled back down into the nest of pillows, completely depleted.

Yuli brought in a tray with a mug of warm tea on it. "Drink this, Katia. It will help you rest and recover."

Zoya helped her sit up in bed as Katie pulled the mug to her lips with trembling hands. Downing the bitter liquid in one long guzzle, she let out a long sigh.

"You were very brave," Zoya praised. "Now rest, darling. Trust me. All will be right in the morning."

Katie nodded and then drifted right to sleep. Yuli bent down to press her lips to Katie's forehead, tucked the blanket around her, and then followed Zoya out to the kitchen.

"You keep an eye on our girl," Zoya directed. "Let me handle Sam Williams."

Yuli nodded. "What are you going to do?"

"Katia did the heavy lifting. Now, it's time to let Karma do the rest."

THIRTY-TWO

The next evening, after her sapped energy had been replenished in the glam chamber, Zoya sat in the chair holding the golden gift-wrapped box she'd picked up at Kandied Karma in her hands. The Adapt4Heroes Foundation office was emptied, as she'd requested when she set up the appointment with Sam over the phone. While she waited, she looked over the stack of documents outlining her very generous job offer. Tucked inside her handbag, the amber bottle of Verity Oil had reached its full potency, and she couldn't wait to deploy it.

A few minutes later, Sam strode out to reception and flashed her a smile. "Ana! What a pleasure!" He brushed air kisses on both of her cheeks, then led her to his office.

She held up the box of perfectly wrapped chocolates Yuli had specially prepared. "I come bearing gifts... *and* an offer of employment."

His eyes glittered at the prospect.

"Is that Kandied Karma?" he asked as he rubbed his hands together in eager anticipation.

"Why, yes it is!" She tugged on the enormous fuchsia bow to open the box and offered it to him. With glee, he reached in, pulled out a sleek green candy, and popped it into his mouth. "White chocolate and matcha! It's divine!" Chewing quickly, he swallowed it and returned for another.

"I skipped lunch," he confided.

"Then feel free to binge the rest of the box, sweetheart," she said, handing it over to him. "You're in such great shape, you don't have to worry about the extra calories at all!" She reached out to squeeze his impressive bicep. "Besides, you've been working far too hard and deserve a treat." Then she waited for the candy to deliver its unique painful punch.

"Ooh!" His brow crinkled as she tightened her hands together like a vise.

"What is it?" she asked, already knowing the answer as she pinched her fingers tighter in masochistic delight.

"I'm getting another tension headache. Without Rox around, my workload has doubled. We are searching for a new CEO, but it will likely take several months before they find the right candidate."

"Well, hopefully, that won't be your problem for much longer." She offered a warm smile, handing off the official job contract. He eagerly accepted it and started to rifle through it at his desk when he let out an anguished groan.

"It's quickly veering into migraine territory, I'm afraid."

"Oof! I'm sorry to hear that, darling," Zoya cooed. "Did you want to go over the details of the offer of employment now?" She watched his brow furrow again as he fought the twinge of pain escalating at the back of his neck. He reached up to pinch it with one hand while his eyes scanned the document she'd given him. A smug grin slid over his features.

"I'll need some time to look this over," he responded.

"Playing hard to get, are we, darling?" Zoya teased with a well-timed wink as her fingers tightened again, and he yelped in pain. She cooed, projecting practiced warmth into her voice, "Do you have any more appointments today?"

"No, I was just going to spend the next couple of hours drowning in paperwork." He pinched at the skin between his eyebrows as the pain delivered from the truffle intensified. "But if this keeps up, I might need to call it a day."

"You poor thing," she murmured, stepping closer to where he was seated. Resting her hands on his shoulders, she rubbed her thumbs in circles on his back for a moment, letting them linger. The contact had exactly the effect she'd been hoping it would have. He dropped his guard and softened under her touch.

"Lucky for you, I have just the remedy." She reached into her handbag and pulled out the tiny brown glass bottle of Verity Oil. Smiling widely, she waved it in front of him. "A masseuse has formally trained me on migraine protocol. If you give me fifteen minutes, I'm certain I can fix you right up."

"Are you buttering me up so I will accept your proposal?"

She laughed. "Oh, you're good! I didn't realize I was that transparent."

He offered her a smirky grin.

"I just can't bear the thought of our new CFO at the Castanova Foundation suffering when there is something I can do to fix it."

"Well then, count me in!" He walked over to the front door, locked it, and turned out the lights.

"Perfect," Zoya said, pulling off her gloves. She pulled out the eyedropper and squeezed ten drops of the infused oil into her hands, then rubbed them together to warm it up.

"Shirt off, Sergeant Major."

He grinned and unbuttoned it, taking a moment to hang it on a hanger, then returned to his desk chair. His chest was thick and muscled from a lifetime of pull-ups and burpees. Zoya enjoyed the view for a moment. The idea of letting him pleasure her first before she destroyed him briefly flitted through her head, but she pushed it away. The eternal coven wouldn't find it half as entertaining as she would.

Zoya started at the base of his neck, rubbing circles over the tight muscles clenched there with her strong thumbs to dislodge the knots. Hearing him sigh with pleasure was the first sign. The warm oil dissolved into the base of his neck, close to his brain stem, and the successful delivery to its most potent location filled her with joy. Then she moved her fingers to his temples, digging in and pressing down on the crown of his head where she knew the pressure points were. She scratched her fingernails through his crew cut and then circled around the base of his skull again for several long moments.

"I'm getting goosebumps," he finally said, clearly enjoying the sensation as his eyes rolled back in his head.

"Just relax, dear." She pushed harder against the base of his neck and down into his shoulders.

"Your touch is magic," he moaned, delighting in the rub down.

"It is," she admitted. "Magic, indeed!" In seconds, the first truths would emerge, thanks to the Verity Oil. She grinned and licked her lips in wicked anticipation.

"Now that my neck is feeling better, why don't you move those magic fingers south of the border?" He took her hand and tugged it toward the growing bulge in his pants. "Wait…" His eyes snapped open and filled with panic.

"Sorry, darling, I have to draw the line at happy endings," Zoya remarked, taking a step back to observe him without being subjected to further sexual advances. "It might make things awkward around the office when you're our next CFO." She laughed, and he joined in, blissfully unaware he would never earn that designation.

"Ana, you'd be gorgeous if you got rid of that white

old lady hair." Stunned by his own words again, Zoya saw him clamp his lips together. "It ages you, but your tits are still perky. Guess I'll have to tell you I'm into bondage. You might need to blindfold me so I can maintain an erection."

Zoya's lips curled up at the criticisms. The oil was working beautifully. "If you're just going to insult me, then I will take my leave, along with my offer of employment."

"I'm sorry," he barked out, trying to regain control of his words, but the oil only made his honesty more brutal. "No. I'm not sorry at all. I'm the best thing that will ever happen to the Castanova Foundation. You need me."

"Possibly," Zoya lied, standing up to signal the end of the meeting. She'd had her fill of his toxic masculinity. "Why don't you look it over when you feel better and we'll reconvene next week?" Zoya strode out, eager to breathe clean air. Once settled into the town car and headed back to the private airstrip, she placed a phone call on a burner phone to the FBI Tampa Field Office Tip line.

"I have some important information about the Roxanne Sullivan Case." She waited while the call was transferred.

"Financial Crimes, this is Officer Alan Ripple. Who am I speaking with?"

"I'd like to remain anonymous, but I have a tip for you," Zoya said. "I recently attended a military function and spent some time speaking with Samuel Williams.

He was bragging about dodging taxation using foreign banks and international trusts. It seemed pretty shady. Isn't he on the board at the Adapt4Heroes Foundation where Roxanne Sullivan was accused of embezzlement? I think there is a connection there worth investigating. Maybe you could bring him in for questioning? He's at the foundation as we speak."

"Interesting," the man on the other end of the phone said.

"I believe you'll get all the answers you're looking for directly from the horse's ass—I mean mouth. Good day." She hung up the phone, pleased with herself.

"And now we wait," she said to Higgins.

THIRTY-THREE

Sam had the world on a string. After Ana left, he paged through the employment contract for the Castanova Foundation, feeling gratified. It was a huge coup and came with a fifty percent pay raise and a generous bonus structure. The fringe benefits, private-label healthcare, and retirement plan added another six figures to the deal. It was the bold career move he'd been waiting for, and seeing the concrete evidence of his hard work in black and white only further stoked the fire in his belly.

"This is the kind of deal I deserve," he said aloud in the empty office, pleased the tension headache vanished with Ana. Without hesitation, he pulled out his fountain pen from the desk drawer and scrawled his signature on the bottom of the contract, making a mental note to return it to her in the morning.

Sam was soaring, and the feeling of exhilaration was intoxicating. He sat at his desk, drumming his fingers, as he let the sensation wash over him. It was a heady feeling arriving at the pinnacle of his career. Thinking he deserved a treat, he tucked the paperwork into his satchel and prepared to leave the office early.

He gathered his keys and leaned forward to shut off his monitor. A few seconds later, Sam was jolted out of his joyous reverie when he heard the doorbell chime, indicating a visitor was waiting in reception. Annoyed at the last-minute interruption, he rose to his feet and walked out to the reception area to greet them, and an older man strode toward him with a plain woman in tow.

"Samuel Williams?"

"Yes?" he answered, confused. "Did we have an appointment?" He searched his memory bank but came up blank.

"Not exactly." Officer Ripple pulled out his wallet to display his FBI identification card. Sam's eyes drifted to his hip, where his badge was clipped, and to the bulge at his waist that did a terrible job concealing his firearm.

"What is this in reference to?" he asked, deciding to play dumb.

"I'm from the FBI Tampa Field Office, the fraud and financial crimes division. We need you to come to the station to answer a few questions."

"Regarding?" he asked, wondering how long he could keep up this charade.

"We recently learned deposits were authorized from Roxanne Sullivan's computer here at the foundation to an off-shore account in the Bahamas. And this evening, we received an anonymous tip from someone who met you at a charity event where you were bragging about dodging taxation using foreign banks and international trusts. I'm no financial wunderkind, but that doesn't seem like a coincidence to me."

Annoyed, Sam couldn't stop himself from blurting, "That's because it isn't."

"Can you elaborate?"

"Well, I set up an off-shore account through a series of shell corporations, and I've been funneling money from the Adapt4Heroes Foundation into it for the better part of two years."

And just like that, the soaring sensation came to a screeching halt and sent him into a panicking free fall. He bit his lips together and swallowed hard. What the hell was happening? He let out a choked laugh, hoping to distract the officer from the truth with humor.

"What did you say?" Officer Ripple's eyes narrowed, and he took a step closer.

"I *said* it was *me*, not Rox, who embezzled the money. Honestly? I considered it payment for services rendered. I am the only one with the financial acumen and resources at their disposal to be able to pull it off. Rox!?" He made a *pfft!* Sound, blowing hot air over his lips. "She isn't even smart enough to enable two-factor authentication on her accounts! It was too easy!"

"Holy shit," Ripple cursed under his breath, staring the man down, unable to believe his ears. "We want you to come with us to the field office."

"No. That will not end well for me," Sam admitted

as he turned to grab his keys and leave, eager to walk away from his urge to answer their questions.

"We're not asking." Officer Ripple turned to the woman. "Read him his rights and hook him up."

Panic welled up in Sam's throat. It was as if every thought he had came rushing right out of his mouth. Instead of thinking through the appropriate response and manipulating the person in front of him to gain the desired outcome, he blurted the unvarnished truth. It was as if the usual gatekeeper stationed at his lips was off duty. His stomach dropped as his mind spun on what he'd already said. He hadn't been read his rights, so the things he'd confessed were technically inadmissible. Any competent attorney would be able to refute them in court. Feeling a trickle of relief, he decided to cooperate with the officer and placed his hands behind his back.

When she said, "You have the right to remain silent," he focused on that sentence.

Remain silent.

Remain silent.

Remain silent.

He repeated the two words inside his head as he rode down to the station until they lost their meaning. While they drove, Sam focused on damage control, looking for ways to spin the few damning revelations he'd already made. Could he play them off as a joke? He studied the officers in front of him, listening to their banter for clues on how to handle them. He noticed Officer Ripple's staid demeanor, honed by years of interrogating suspects who often lied to save themselves. The humor angle was going to be a hard sell.

Think! His internal dialogue screamed inside his own head. *You've been here before. Find his lever and use it to open him up.*

The car eased into a parking spot at the rear entrance of the federal building, and a few minutes later, the back door was opened and he was pulled to his feet. At the door, the female officer swiped her security card, and the door buzzed to let them in. He was led down a long linoleum hallway and put inside a windowless room.

"Can I get you anything to eat or drink?" the female officer asked.

"So, you're the good cop?" he heard himself say. "And old Ripple over here is the bad one?"

Officer Ripple chuckled at the insult. "You're mighty perceptive."

"I'll have a coffee, black." He ignored the sarcasm as both officers left the room. Ripple returned alone an hour later, with a manilla file folder and a cup of black coffee.

"Took you long enough," Sam spat at the officer. His statement was more harsh than he intended so he quickly added, "Sorry."

"No apology necessary." Ripple pushed the coffee over, and Sam took a sip, holding the liquid in his mouth. His strategy was simple. If his mouth was full, he couldn't speak.

Officer Ripple started speaking in a loud authoritative tone. "This interview is being recorded. I am Officer Alan Ripple with the FBI Tampa Field Office. Please state your name for the record."

Against his will, he swallowed the lukewarm liquid and answered the question. "Samuel Williams."

"Let's start with Roxanne Sullivan," he began. "Can you fill me in on your history?"

"I'm not sure you're ready for that yet. It's a pretty twisted tale," Sam admitted.

"Please enlighten me," Ripple prodded without pause.

Sam's eyes widened as he heard himself speak as if under coercion. The words left his lips without effort, subconsciously, and he could not stop the flow. "We were deployed together to the Gulf War, and at first, things were peachy. She fit in pretty well and was as tough as any of the other men. About six months into our deployment, we were tapped for an intelligence mission. Things went south, and when a car bomb took out our commanding officer, Rox became the Officer in Charge by default. It was a promotion she got to enjoy for a record-breaking ten minutes." His sardonic delivery of the last line was especially riveting.

"What do you mean?"

"That stupid bitch walked right into a landmine following that idiot Peabody. What a dumb rookie mistake! It blew him to smithereens, and she lost her leg. But God! It was so deliciously Darwinian! You know, survival of the fittest and all. Neither of them was destined for greatness, not like I was."

Officer Ripple sat in stunned silence for a moment.

His eyes popped wide open as he scribbled notes on a pad. Sam paused, then took another long sip of the coffee as his mind raced. His words were a runaway train on the tracks, speeding faster and never slowing down.

"I bet that stung! A powerful man like you? Being forced to take orders from a woman?" Ripple asked.

"That dolt lorded her West Point acceptance over me as often as possible. God, I got so sick of hearing her brag about it! The only reason she got into West Point in the first place was because she has a vagina! The opportunities are just not the same for white men anymore in America. It's bullshit."

Ripple's face registered the astonishment that Sam's candid response deserved. To stop the flow of information, Sam reached up to clamp his hand over his mouth when Ripple asked the next question.

"You must not have hated her too much. Says here you were awarded a Medal of Honor for saving her life?"

Sam chuckled. "Joke's on her. I left her there to die. I mean, the medevac was coming, but we were taking enemy fire and I had to save myself. Right? It's like when a plane loses oxygen and you have to put your mask on first."

"Yeah," Ripple replied in a deadpan voice. "It's exactly like that."

"I wasn't going to die at nineteen in the sandbox. I had a greater destiny to fulfill!"

"What happened?"

"Well, if I tell you, I'll incriminate myself," he admitted, then giggled like a psychopath.

"We have already read you your Miranda rights, and legally, you are not required to answer any of my questions. But, again, I would like to remind you that anything you say, can and will be used against you in the court of law," Ripple confirmed.

"Oh, I know," Sam said.

His chatterbox cockiness inspired Ripple to continue his interrogation. "What do you mean, you left her there to die?"

"With all the combat gear, Rox was heavy and bleeding out. I figured I'd have a better chance at survival if I cut the dead weight and trucked it back to the rendezvous point," Sam explained, taking a sip of the coffee to stop himself from speaking. When he put the cup down, the words continued to flow out of his mouth against his will. "But fucking Monty, man. Had to be the hero!"

"What did Monty do?"

"He picked her up himself when I wouldn't, and ran to the rendezvous point. I have to admit, it was pretty impressive. That bastard zigzagged through a sea of enemy fire to carry out his rescue mission."

"I'm confused. Then why did *you* receive the Medal of Honor?"

Sam grinned, his eyes flashing and wild, and his words sped up as if he couldn't get them out of his mouth fast enough. "I couldn't let him usurp my authority and get all the glory! I had to do damage control."

"What do you mean?"

He shrugged like the next words out of his mouth would be insignificant, but they were far from it. "I shot him in the back of the head. LT was unconscious anyway, and they both dropped to the ground."

"You killed him?"

"I had to!" he tried to explain. "If the truth came out, my career, my life, would have been over!"

"Then what did you do?"

"When I heard the Humvees approaching, I pulled Rox into my arms and raced to the caravan. Then it was just a matter of letting the chips fall where they may and taking the credit when it was given," he said, plain as day, without a shred of remorse. "It worked out great for me, but not so great for Monty." He giggled and his eyes bugged out of his head.

"That is quite a tale," Ripple said, astonished by it. "This case just went from fraud and embezzlement to murder."

Sam's heart dropped. "Wait. Let me explain." His mind worked overtime, trying to piece together a plausible explanation and falling far flat. There wasn't one. There never would be.

"I'd love to hear more about your involvement in the fraud allegations. Can we circle back to the off-shore account?"

Sam nodded like he was thrilled to participate in the interrogation. "It was genius. Bringing Rox onto the board at Adapt4Heroes was my idea. I knew she felt like she owed me and would trust me implicitly. She did the lion's share of the work at the foundation, freeing me up for other pursuits. God, that woman is a master at jumping through hoops and pandering to donors! It allowed me to focus on the financials."

"Tell me more about the paper trail."

"There were a couple of tactics I leaned on pretty heavily. First, I created inflated invoices from our vendors. Then I'd have Rox sign the checks for the full amount plus twenty percent. I destroyed her original check, and then I would forge a lesser check to the vendor and skim the difference to the off-shore account. The key was to only add twenty percent. If it were more than that, it would arouse suspicion."

"You said a couple of tactics?"

"I discovered the real cash cow when I created a few fake companies and assigned vendor numbers to them, then submitted invoices for work they never performed. That allowed me to skim more money more rapidly."

"How long have you been doing this?"

"Over two years."

"But aren't your books at the foundation audited by a third party?"

"We passed a few simple audits with flying colors and flew under the threshold for years, but with the large single donation from Officer Mendoza, I knew it would flag us for an ongoing semi-annual audit. So, I made the last transfer count. It was two hundred thou, alone!"

"How did you plan to escape detection?"

"I set up Rox's assistant, Keith, to take the fall once I figured out the gift card scam he was running. Then I found a golden parachute and was working on my exit strategy."

"What did that entail?'

"A job offer at the Castanova Foundation."

"Impressive," Officer Ripple praised him.

"It was, wasn't it?" Sam said, patting himself on the back.

"It's also a much bigger pool to skim," Officer Ripple said.

"Exactly." He nodded in agreement. "I figured I'd rack up as much as I could there, then move to a country with no extradition treaty to the United States. I was already looking at real estate abroad."

"Where are the login credentials for your off-shore account?"

"Inside a leather wallet in my bedside table at home, you'll find the seed codes and online access information."

"How much is in there?"

"Last I checked, it was over half a million."

"Where do you keep the financial records for the foundation?"

"The real invoices and false ledger I keep locked in my desk at the foundation. The separate ledger and bank statements for the off-shore account are at my home," he muttered. His face twisted up in anger, but he still could not refuse to answer a question he was asked.

"Holy shit," Ripple whispered to himself, blowing

hot air out between his teeth. "This is, by far, the easiest interrogation I've ever taken part in." His mind was spinning, shocked at Sam's willingness to confess. Usually, it took a lot longer to break a man down. "I can't believe you're being so forthcoming with the truth. Guilty conscience?"

"I don't have one of those," Sam said and leaned back in the chair, lacing his fingers behind his head.

"Is there anything else you want to get off your chest?" Ripple asked offhandedly as a joke and was stunned when Sam opened his mouth again.

"Do you have any idea how intelligent you have to be to pull off this kind of scheme? I don't think you are giving me all the credit I deserve."

Ripple laughed at his audacity. "Well, how about this? I'm going to type up my report with all the information you shared. *Then* you'll get the credit you deserve." He stood and walked out of the interrogation room.

Sam let out a distressed cry, got to his feet, and paced the room. He balled a fist and struck the two-way window. Then pulled the chair from under the table and threw it across the room, howling with rage. Once the energy left his body, he crumpled and slid down the wall. Furious with himself, his mind circled and circled. He balled his fists and punched his head repeatedly until he tasted the copper of blood in his mouth.

"Stupid! Stupid! Stupid!" he shouted.

He had detonated a bomb in his life and had no explanation as to why he'd confessed in the first place.

The realization that his life was over hit him like a ton of bricks. Mentally exhausted, he tipped his head against the wall, and tears spilled down his cheeks.

An hour later, Ripple re-entered the interrogation room with his typed report. "I need your signature here." He offered Sam a pen that he refused to take.

"No," Sam said. "I'm not an idiot. I will not sign a document that will send me to jail for the rest of my life."

"That is well within your rights to refuse to sign, but we have your confession in your own words... on video," Ripple said, pointing to the camera in the corner of the room. "I have a feeling that, even without your signature, it will still be riveting testimony to any judge and jury." Undeterred, he asked, "Why did you do it?"

"Money makes the world go round," Sam said with an offhanded shrug. "Non-profits are just ripe for the picking. Combined with their fear of losing donors, even if you are discovered, there are typically few repercussions. I guess I was willing to risk a slap on the wrist in order to afford the kind of retirement I deserve."

"You deserve?" Ripple's outrage was evident in every syllable.

He scoffed at the officer's reaction. "I served our country for decades. I sacrificed!"

"Sacrificed?" Ripple's anger was rising. "You murdered a hero for your own selfish gain and then went on to treat an organization that provided resources for wounded veterans as your personal piggy bank. I don't think the United States of America needs or wants your service any longer."

Sam folded his arms across his chest. It was useless to fight anymore.

"With the video confession and the evidence I am certain we are going to find when we search your home and office, the only thing you're going to serve from now on is a jail sentence."

Thirty-Four

The next evening at Katie's beach house, they were gathered in the kitchen when Tom excused himself to take an urgent phone call. Lauren was busy chopping romaine hearts for a salad while Rox set the table for dinner. Katie was still exhausted from her hellish loop in the past and sat at the island stifling a yawn.

"What's that on your arms?" Lauren asked, noticing the network of pale branches stemming from her wrists. They had lightened up but were still visible.

"Some burst capillaries is all, hon. Nothing to worry about. The doctor said they should lighten over time."

From the study, they heard Tom murmuring on the phone. A few minutes later, he practically skipped back to the dining room table, capturing their collective attention.

"What?" Rox asked, picking up on the one-hundred-and-eighty-degree shift in his demeanor. He beamed, shooting her the same grin she remembered seeing when he'd finally learned how to ride his bike after two solid weeks of skinned elbows and knees.

"You should sit down," he cautioned.

"Just give it to me straight, Tommy," she insisted, hanging on his every word.

"That was Officer Ripple."

Hearing the name of the FBI officer, Rox felt anxiety well up in her chest. "And?"

"Sam just confessed."

The admission made Rox stagger back, and she took her seat. "Maybe I do need to sit down for this," she admitted under her breath. Her eyes searched her son's. "Sam confessed? What the hell happened?"

"There was a search warrant executed at the foundation and his residence, and it turned up falsified invoices and a register of forged checks." Tom was in shock as he recounted the information he'd been given. "He also handed over the seed codes and login credentials for the off-shore account."

"Whoa," Katie gasped. Zoya worked quickly. Knowing there was far more evil he'd been responsible for, she waited for Tom to continue.

"I don't believe it," Rox said, stunned by the admission.

"It's the FBI, Mom. I'm pretty sure they got it right." He reached out a hand and squeezed his mother's trembling one. "There was something else."

Katie's heart broke for what was coming next.

Taken aback, Rox's head popped up, and she

searched Tom's eyes. "What else could there possibly be?"

"He confessed to killing Monty."

Roxanne gasped, and her hand flew to her mouth. Then she leaned back in the chair, closed her eyes, and shook her head, unable to accept the information she was being given.

"And…" Tom stopped, unable to continue, knowing the next part would cut his mother to the core. Finally, he whispered, "Sam left you there to die."

"No!" she said as she walked back through her memories of that grim day. "He carried me out. He saved my life."

"But you've always said you were unconscious and didn't remember the details of the rescue until you woke up at the hospital," Tom offered in explanation, eager for Rox to see the truth.

"Then who? How?"

"Monty. Monty refused to leave you behind, and when Sam figured out his act of deserting his commanding officer would destroy his military career, he killed him and took the credit for the rescue himself." Katie felt despair form a pit in her stomach.

"I think I'm going to be sick," Rox said and rushed away to the bathroom. Several minutes later, she emerged white as a sheet, and Tom led her back to the table where a tall glass of ice water rested on a coaster.

"I don't know what to say," Rox admitted after downing the water in one long guzzle. "What happens now?"

"The case will be dismissed, though you might be called as a witness at Sam's trial."

"Will they reinstate me at the Adapt4Heroes Foundation?"

"They better or I'll file a lawsuit so fast it will make their head spin."

"What about Keith?"

"He was the patsy," Tom explained. "Sam used him to keep the heat off himself."

"We have to help him," Rox said. "He still broke the law, but maybe we can help him get a reduced sentence or a plea deal?"

Katie smiled. Rox was barely cleared herself and already looking to help someone else. It was admirable.

"Let's be happy for *you* today," Tom suggested. "Tomorrow, I'll see what we can do for Keith."

Rox sat at the table, still clearly dumbfounded by the turn of events. She rubbed her beleaguered face with her palms. "How could I have been so wrong about Sam for so long? Gosh, I feel like an idiot."

"You're not an idiot, Mom. You just trusted the wrong man. He fooled me, too." Tom reached out and squeezed her hand. "But justice prevailed."

"You have to be overwhelmed right now," Katie said. "And I'm sure these recent developments come with many feelings you will have to process, but the truth is finally out."

"Karma got him," Rox said, finally letting herself feel the relief flood in.

Katie nodded. She did not know how right she was.

THIRTY-FIVE

The next day at Kandied Karma, Katie was getting ready to open the store when a warm burst of air caught her off guard. Zoya breezed in the back door, pulling off her enormous sunglasses.

"The Verity Oil worked!" Katie exclaimed. "Though it seems a little low-key for Zoya Castanova."

"Yes, it did." Zoya laughed with a twinkle in her eyes. "Not every situation dictates unleashing Armageddon. Sometimes a little finesse trips the ordins up far better than bringing the hell storm."

Yuli's jaw jutted back in astonishment. "You? The voice of reason?"

Zoya grinned. "I don't discount *all* of your philosophies. While they lack the usual panache of mine, they are sometimes the right decision."

"Sometimes?" Yuli chuckled as she tied on an apron, then walked to the chiller to pull out trays of truffles to stock the case.

"I think I'm finally feeling like myself again," Katie admitted. "Last night was the first night I didn't have the nightmare."

"Good," Zoya added as she walked over to assess the skin on Katie's forearms. The pink branching scars were barely there. "It looks like you're healing nicely." She turned to Yuli. "Good work."

The compliment made the corners of Yuli's lips quirk up in a smile.

"I am proud of both of you. You worked together to bring me back," Katie reminded them. "I think that's a first. The eternal coven will be pleased."

"That's not why I did it," Zoya stated, and Yuli's interested gaze rested on her. The amulets at their throats began to vibrate and glow even more brightly. "We're stronger together." She looked down before admitting sheepishly, "And I might be starting to see the importance of not going it alone."

"What?' Yuli teased her, her voice twisted up in mock outrage. "Zoya Castanova isn't hellbent on being a one-woman show anymore?"

Zoya shook her head and rolled her eyes. "You'll never let me admit I was wrong without busting my balls, will you?"

"Is that what you're doing? Admitting you were wrong?" Yuli rushed to her side and leaned her chin on her hand to listen intently. As if the next words to come out of Zoya's mouth were the most important words she'd ever utter, she encouraged her grandmother with a waggle of her brows.

Zoya had to laugh at her antics. "Fine. I was wrong. Are you happy now?"

"Ecstatic," Yuli said with glee, making joyful laughter bubble up from Katie. Zoya rolled her eyes, but Katie could sense her amusement. "There's an apron over there if you want to take on another shift at Kandied Karma."

"Now you're pushing your luck!" She chuckled as she settled the enormous glasses on the bridge of her delicate nose and turned to leave. At the door, she stopped and called over her shoulder, "I expect to see all of you and yours at the Autumnal Equinox Ball. No excuses. We have so much to celebrate!"

THIRTY-SIX

Katie and her kids gathered at the landing strip on the morning of the Autumnal Equinox Ball. Engrossed in their phones now that the novelty of flying private had worn off, they didn't pay her much attention. Katie was just getting into the book she'd downloaded on her e-reader when Callie squealed and started to jump up and down, waving her cell phone in the air.

"What is it?" Katie asked.

"Pixar saw my short reel."

"The one you did about Arlo?" Katie asked.

"Yes!" Callie was beaming. "They want me to come in for an interview!"

"No way!"

"Holy shit!" Beckett was beaming almost as much as Callie.

"Really?" Lauren was thrilled for her sister.

Callie cradled the phone to her chest and swung

around in a circle, emitting gleeful noises. It took Katie back to the time when Callie was six and missing her two front teeth, and a trip to the ice cream parlor would elicit the same reaction. Motherhood came with its own hot flashes, where warm glimpses of the past and present tumbled over each other without warning.

The absolute joy on her face was a sight to behold. "I am going to kill it! Gosh, I didn't think the opportunity would present itself so quickly!"

"Even an entry-level position there is a stepping stone to the big time!" Katie wrapped her arms around her daughter. "Look at you making all your dreams come true!"

"All those hours I spent after work and on the weekends was worth it!" Callie said, triumphant that her hard work paid off. "I thought I'd have to cut my teeth for at least another year or two."

"I guess Pixar knows brilliance when they see it." Katie beamed at her daughter.

"*Brilliance* is a stretch," Beckett teased Callie, pulling her in by the shoulders and skidding over the top of her head with his fist, making her hair stand up on end.

"Hey!" Callie laughed, wrestling to get away from him.

"Okay, maybe in this *one sphere*, you are brilliant." He grinned. "On the others, I choose to reserve judgment." He laughed. "But seriously, I'm thrilled for you Cal!"

"I can't believe it!" Callie said as tears gathered in

the corners of her eyes. "We are celebrating tonight!"

"Yes, we are!" Katie cheered.

The flight attendant invited them up the stairs and onto the aircraft, and an hour later, they touched down at the compound, were loaded into the golf carts, and taken to the main house.

———

Later that evening, Callie studied her reflection in the mirror, admiring her shiny waterfall of raven-black hair. It was smooth down her backless red gown that plunged so low the curve of her shapely bottom peeked out. She sipped at the champagne in the crystal flute and reveled in the first carefree moment she'd experienced as an adult. To be a breath away from her biggest dream coming true filled her with joy, and she was in the mood to celebrate.

Her stilettos clicked on the marble floors as she descended the staircase, heading closer to the music. The ball was in full swing and she was ready to cut loose.

She pulled another flute of champagne off the tray and sipped at it, scanning the room for familiar faces. Across the crowded dance floor, she locked eyes with the dark-haired Adonis she'd briefly danced with at the Spring Ball. She was the first to look away and check over her shoulder, sure he must be staring at someone else, but there was no one there. When she sought him out again, he'd disappeared. Disappointed, she wandered over to a table to set her glass down and then headed to the dance floor.

She was swaying in a sea of bodies as the music washed over her, and she let it take her away. Tipsy, she shimmied her hips and got lost in the moment, making deliberately slow, swooping figure-eight motions in time to the deep bass that resounded in her chest. She was effervescent as she tapped into the sensual power within that she rarely let herself indulge in.

After three more songs, a light sheen of sweat covered her body, and she gathered her hair into one fist to pull it up off her neck as she fanned herself. Callie helped herself to another flute of champagne from a passing shirtless waiter and picked her way down a pathway that led to a walkway lit by twinkling fairy lights. It was darker in the garden, and her ears adjusted to the soundtrack of the ocean as she stepped closer to the sea.

Curious at what lay around the bend, Callie continued down the path through the garden, where a maze of hedges stood eight feet tall. Sensing she was being followed, she whipped around, her gaze tangling with the dark-haired man she'd noticed from the dance floor. Overhead, two eagles circled and shrieked in the darkness, lit by millions of pinpoints of starlight. They swooped down and then shot back up into the air, seemingly circling the air above her.

"Are you following me?" she teased, biting her bottom lip. She wasn't usually so daring and flirty, but tonight the champagne emboldened her. Her eyes flicked to his, and his gaze was so magnetic she couldn't pull herself away.

"Perhaps," he whispered.

The eagles screamed, and Callie pointed up at them, still circling. "Looks like we have an audience."

"Does that bother you?"

Callie had to lean in to hear him and, focusing on his full lips, felt herself drawn even closer. Her inhibitions melted away as she took stock of the stunning man in front of her. He was elegant and refined, with tanned olive skin and hazel eyes framed by dark lashes. His pristine white shirt was open at the neck, and the remnants of his bow tie flapped in the wind.

Callie let out a nervous laugh and answered, "No." His eyes darkened, and he traced down the length of her jawline with one finger. An intimate act that sent shivers down her arms.

"What's your name?" he asked as he tucked her hand in his warm one and pulled it to his lips, delivering a soft kiss to the top of it. Every word that spilled from his tongue was sexy, accentuated by a hint of an accent she couldn't place.

"Callie," she whispered, feeling warmth rush to where his lips touched her skin.

"I'm going to kiss you now, Callie," he whispered with a roguish grin. Not asking permission, but taking it, and she felt a horde of butterflies release in her belly. The sultry air made her more malleable and let herself lean into him. His lips were warm and tender and barely brushed against hers. He wrapped his hands around her waist, and they trailed up her bare spine, setting fire to every inch he touched. She was delirious for several long moments, lost in his kiss. When she pulled away, her chest heaved in the moonlight. Confidently, he pulled her hand into his again and led her deeper into the maze. The privacy made her bolder, and she made a split decision to give in to it.

"Who are you?" Callie asked. Her head was still swimming from his kisses and touch, combined with the champagne she'd overindulged in.

"Christos," he answered as he pressed her into the hedge, making her gasp.

"Greek?"

He laughed, revealing a flash of white teeth. "Yes."

"I've always wanted to go to Greece," she confided, her nerves making her chattier than usual.

"We'd welcome a beauty like you with open arms." He cupped his hands together and brushed his knuckles softly across her cheeks, and Callie gasped. Slowly, his touch lingered down her neck, and then he gathered her hair in his hand and pulled it tight into his palm, tugging her head to the side and exposing her creamy collarbone. His soft lips traced down the length of it. "You are exquisite." He breathed into her ear, and the tickle of his warm breath on her neck made goosebumps race down her arms. It was a deeply pleasurable sensation that made every cell in her body roar to life.

From the other side of the hedge, Callie overheard a woman moaning in delight. She pulled away as her eyes widened in response, and his amused expression made him even more devilishly attractive. He held one finger to his lips, then grabbed her shoulder and turned her away from him to face the shrubs. Using his powerful hands, he pried apart the thick limbs to create an opening for her to peep through. Callie glanced back over her shoulder at him nervously before she leaned closer to the area where a shaft of moonlight illuminated a topless woman on the brink of orgasm. Her eyes were squeezed shut and her legs straddled around her companion. Callie felt need gathering in her core, and when Christos bent his gorgeous mouth to where her neck and shoulder blade kissed, she felt a wave of desire crash over her.

"Do not take your eyes off her," Christos demanded as he clamped down on her collarbone again. He pressed his hips to hers, and she could feel his length harden against her. She pressed herself back against him, desperate for the fabric that separated them to disappear.

Letting go of the hedge, he whispered in her ear, "Would you like to join me in my private cabana?"

She couldn't speak, only nodded. He nibbled on her earlobe, and when he sighed in her ear, she felt the last of her resolve melt away. Taking her hand, he led her to the exit of the maze and over to the collection of cabanas. Crescendoing with the sea, she heard animalistic, sensual sounds coming from the occupied cabanas. Callie brushed the embarrassment aside as she followed behind him, wallowing in her good fortune. He was the sexiest man she'd ever laid eyes on, and he wanted *her*.

Christos pulled her into an empty cabana that was lit by soft candlelight. A sumptuous bed lay in the middle of it, dressed in navy sheets and scattered with orchids. The roar of the sea was a soothing sound that centered Callie. Overhead, the full moon traced the outlines of his chiseled jaw from across the room. He stalked through the space that divided them, and she shivered with delight when she felt his warm hands on her shoulders. His fingers found the zipper of her dress, and she leaned her head back and moaned as his kisses grazed her shoulder blades. She felt the zipper slide and stepped out of the gown before draping it over a chair. Standing there in the cool blue moonlight, she was relieved when he sighed, and his response chased away her skittish tendencies.

"Your body is magnificent."

Unabashedly, she unbuckled his belt with her trembling fingers, then unbuttoned his shirt and ripped it off of him. When they were undressed, he carried her to the bed. She was soaked with desire, eager to see what sensations lay ahead. Christos was a *man*. In college, she'd only been with boys. This was the kind of earth-shattering orgasmic experience she'd yearned for and was a rite of passage into womanhood. She gave herself over to him freely, grateful for such an experienced companion.

The last coherent thought she had before lust consumed the rest of her brain was, "This is the beginning of my real life."

THIRTY-SEVEN

In her suite at the compound, Katie wrestled her curvy figure into the body conscious mermaid dress Zoya had chosen for her. Eyeing herself in the mirror, she gazed at her reflection. There was a knock at the door, and when she opened it, Frankie grinned, dressed in a turquoise sparkler. Standing next to her was an equally decked-out Zoya holding a bottle of champagne.

"You make an odd couple," Katie remarked as she invited them in. At her side, Arlo barked and growled at Zoya and then hid under the bed.

"I find Frankie delightfully tacky and unapologetically honest," Zoya said. Under the bed, Arlo growled louder and barked. "It's refreshing."

Zoya knelt down and whipped the coverlet up to look into his brown eyes. "Still holding grudges, I see?" Arlo answered by snarling and snapping at her, an act that only made her chuckle and get back to her feet.

"You did promise him his freedom on my birthday, and that was several months ago," Katie quipped, standing up for Arlo.

"Soon, darling. Soon," Zoya responded.

Across the room and out of earshot, Frankie popped the top of the champagne, poured the bubbly into three glasses, and brought them over.

"What are we toasting?" Katie asked.

"To the inner circle," Zoya said with a smile. "Frankie's found her place among us."

Frankie practically glowed in the presence of Zoya's praise.

"That reminds me." Zoya pulled out her beaded clutch and offered the Verity Oil to Frankie.

"What is this?" Frankie asked, holding the brown bottle up to the light. "CBD?"

"It's much more powerful than that." Zoya winked. "It's the Verity Oil that might have greased the wheels in regards to Sam's confession. Now that we're finished with it, maybe you could find a use for the remainder?"

"Whoa." Frankie looked down at it with greater reverence and a bit of trepidation, but her frugality won out. She never refused a gift.

"It's powerful, Frank," Katie warned her friend. "I don't know…" Katie was shocked Zoya offered it in the first place, and she was deeply conflicted. Her response hurt Frankie's feelings.

"You don't think I can handle it?"

"No." Katie tried to backtrack as Zoya wrapped her

arm around Frankie's shoulders and walked her over to the bed, laying it on thick.

"You know our secrets and have proven your loyalty to Katia and, by extension, me…" Under the bed, Arlo grunted and growled as if the word loyalty incensed him.

"Shut it, dog!" Zoya blurted then turned back to Frankie. "This oil acts like a truth serum. When it is administered near the brainstem of any ordin, it renders the person unable to tell a lie for twenty-four hours."

"Really?" Frankie said, awed by the bottle even more.

"I'd advise you to keep it under lock and key. It's much more powerful than you would ever realize. Ordins are notorious liars. The truth can hurt. Sometimes it's better not to hear it at all."

"Honesty has never been my problem," she said, laughing at herself. "Is there an oil that would give me a filter?"

Katie laughed. "That's the one she really needs."

"Never apologize for being bold enough to be yourself. Now that you are in the inner circle," Zoya stated, "you have the burden of keeping our secrets. Can we count on your total discretion?"

"Discretion is my middle name," she promised.

"Is it though?" Katie asked, her question infused with a teasing tone.

Frankie laughed at herself. "You got me. But this secret? I will take it to the grave."

"Speaking of secrets," Katie said, "Callie's

interview with Pixar, you didn't have anything to do with it, did you?"

Zoya's eyebrows shot up, and she pinched her lips together, busying herself by taking a sip of champagne. "Would it be a problem if I did?"

"I wish I had a fairy godmother like you!" Frankie enthused. "C'mon, Katie, who does it hurt?"

Katie was torn. "She thinks she earned it on her own. I know Callie, and it would crush her to learn it was preferential treatment instead of her skills that won her the opportunity."

Zoya sighed in frustration. "This is how the world works, darling. It's not what you know, it's who, and the sooner you accept that, the happier you'll be."

Katie pursed her lips but nodded. She never bought into the idea of reward without work and hadn't raised her kids that way.

Seeing she was conflicted, Zoya insisted, "All I did was give her a seat at the table. What she does with it is up to her."

"True." Katie found herself coming around despite her misgivings. "But it stays between us," she cautioned, and Frankie and Zoya quickly agreed.

"Should we join the others?"

"I can't wait for Harry to see me in this dress!" Frankie said. "Technically, I can't wait for him to see me out of it either!" She laughed.

Zoya smirked at the sexy remark, then turned to Katie. "And Katia, you are a vision in the Dolce and Gabbana!"

"Are you sure I don't look like a sausage in an undersized casing?"

"Of course not!" Zoya reiterated, "You're a bombshell. It hugs every curve."

Katie glanced once more in the mirror and saw herself in a new light. "Let's get down there before I change my mind."

———

Katie searched the crowd for the faces of her children. Lauren and Tom were carefree, swaying to the music on the dance floor, lost in each other. The sight made Katie grin. They had weathered their first storm together and come out the other side stronger than ever.

In the months since Sam's confession, Rox's charges were officially dropped, and they reinstated her as CEO at the Adapt4Heroes Foundation. Tom had also successfully campaigned for a reduced sentence for Keith Landers that did not include jail time. The media had a field day with the truth and labeled Sam the Band of Brothers Killer. His Medal of Honor was officially revoked and was to be awarded posthumously to Corporal Montgomery at an official award ceremony slated for the end of October. Thankfully, the media frenzy was starting to die down, and Rox moved back to her home in St. Pete. Katie's beach house was quiet again.

When the band stopped to take a break, Tom led a dewy Lauren back to the table.

"Whoa, Mama!" Beckett said as he joined them. "You are beautiful!"

"Thanks, buddy." She leaned over to kiss his cheek. "You're dashing in that suit."

"Have you guys seen Callie?" he asked, concerned, scanning the crowd looking for his little sister.

"She's out sowing her wild oats," Lauren said with a grin. "Instead of keeping track of Cal, who is an adult, by the way, why don't you do the same?" She extended her pinky finger to where a gorgeous blonde was eyeing Beckett. "B, I think you might have a taker over there." He glanced over to where Lauren was pointing and straightened up with an engaging grin.

"You make a valid point." Beckett ran his fingers through his dark hair. "Don't mind if I do." With a naughty smirk, he slipped away from their table. Katie glanced back over at Tom and Lauren canoodling with each other. Their bodies were pressed together, and he couldn't take his eyes off her daughter. Even in a sea of models and celebrities, Tom only had eyes for Lauren.

"You two look happy."

Tom grinned. "What's not to be happy about? I'm on the arm of the most beautiful woman in the room, and all is right again in the world with my mom." He leaned in and added, "Thank you for being there for her."

"Of course." Katie grinned. "She's an incredible woman, with a pretty darn incredible son."

Tom grinned from the praise and kissed Lauren's cheek.

"We hate to leave you to your lonesome, but…" Lauren's eyes darkened with desire, telegraphing her intentions to Tom. Not skipping a beat, Tom grinned and threw back the rest of the whiskey in his glass.

"I get it. Goodnight, you two." Katie laughed as Lauren led Tom away and disappeared into the house, headed toward their suite. She picked up another glass of champagne and sipped it, content to people-watch for the rest of the evening on her own. Enjoying time alone was a new skill she was working to gain, and she settled in for a lengthy practice session.

The next morning, they boarded the aircraft home. Callie was more relaxed than she'd been for months. She was whispering back and forth with Lauren while Tom napped in the seat next to her. Katie watched Callie's cheeks flush red, and they both collapsed into a fit of gut-busting giggles. Clearly, something steamy had happened last night to make her grin so wide, but Katie didn't want to know the gory details.

Next to her, Frankie's head was resting on Harry's shoulder. A string of drool dripped down her mouth, and Harry wiped it away with the sleeve of his shirt. She started to snore like a buzz saw, and it just made Harry grin even wider. The man was a saint who clearly loved her best friend.

Arlo was unusually forlorn, looking out of the window, and Katie reached over to pull him onto her lap. Surrounded by their joy, he was melancholy, and unfortunately, all she could offer him were chin scratches and liver snaps.

THIRTY-EIGHT

A week after the ball, Frankie dimmed the lights in her bedroom to set the mood. She had a special night planned. Having educated herself on all the pressure points in the human body by watching several short videos from a celebrity massage therapist, she felt mildly capable of being able to deliver a decent massage. She pulled her extensive collection of essential oils out from the cubby in her bathroom where they'd been relegated after her second failed attempt at a multi-level marketing business and lined them up in a row on the bedside table.

A giddy thrill crawled up her insides when she heard Harry's key slide into her lock and the door opened. She left the oils behind and walked out to the entryway with a wide smile that quickly faded when she laid eyes on Harry. His lips were pinched, and his shoulders hunched as he beelined to the fridge where he grabbed two bottles of beer. Popping off the tops with Frankie's phallic bottle opener, he offered one to her and almost drained his in one long gulp.

"Bad day?" she asked, picking up immediately on his tension.

"I should have warned you. The closer it gets to the anniversary of Jessica's disappearance, the harder it gets for me." He scratched at the five o'clock shadow darkening his jawline then added, "I'm not good company today. Maybe I should head home."

"Nonsense," Frankie said. "I'm not just here for the good times." She took a sip of her beer and offered, "How about a massage? I have it all set up in the bedroom. I was going to surprise you."

"I don't know," he hesitated. "I'm pretty tired."

"Not the kind that leads to sex, silly," she said with an impish grin that relaxed his face ever so slightly. "It might be hard to believe this, Willey, but you're not just a piece of meat to me."

Harry released a warm chuckle. "Come here, you." He pulled her into his arms and held her close. "You are the best part of my day. Even the bad ones."

"How about it? A massage will help you sleep like a rock. Besides, I've watched hours of TikToks and YouTube videos. I'm practically a professional now," she teased as she led him into her bedroom. Warm yellow light streamed from a bedside lamp, and she busied herself by pulling out a sheet and snapping it into the air. "Get undressed and lie on your stomach."

"Maybe you're right. I haven't slept much this week," Harry finally agreed. Deciding to give in to her impromptu plan, he kicked off his shoes near the bed then pulled his clothing off and folded it neatly into a pile. He stacked it on top of a pile of her clean, unfolded laundry on the dusty treadmill that occupied a corner of the room.

Letting out an anxious breath, he lay down, and she covered him with a sheet. Then she folded it to his waist, exposing his muscled back, executing the privacy technique she vaguely remembered a masseuse using on her during a Groupon massage years ago. She selected an amber bottle of oil from the lineup on her nightstand and squirted several drops into her palms, rubbing them together to warm the oil. Hints of lavender hit her nostrils at first, but the underlying scent was unfamiliar. She wrinkled her nose and reached over to the bottle again, holding it in the light as she studied it. "Do essential oils go bad?"

"Doubt it. Besides, it's not like I'm ingesting it," Harry said, his voice muffled into the bedding. "It's good enough for who it's for."

"You're right. It's probably fine," she agreed as she climbed on the bed and straddled his hips. Pressing her palms flat into his back, she leaned in, delivering consistent pressure from his waist to his shoulder blades, using the heel of her hands to dig into the network of tense muscles that formed his back. He sighed, settling into the pleasing sensation.

"I'll admit, I had my doubts about your skill level when you offered, but this is magnificent."

"I'm glad." She continued to make circles on his

lower back with her palms. She balled her hands into fists and dug in deeper as he wriggled on the bed in pleasure.

"Ooh! That's a tender spot," he groaned when she dug too deep.

"Sorry!" Frankie backed off slightly and stood. With one hand, she reached out and deposited more of the oil onto her palms. This time, she walked around to where his head lay at the foot of her bed. After warming up the oil with friction on her palms, she dug into the tension locked in his neck. Using her thumbs, she made firm circles around the collection of muscles at the base of his skull for several long minutes. Then she pressed her fists into the area where his shoulder blades met his neck, and with long strokes, pulling up toward his ears, she smiled when she heard him murmuring, "Uh-huh. Yep. That's the spot."

"You're putty in my hands," she cooed, feeling accomplished as she spent the next several minutes alternating between tiny circles and larger movements to dispel the tension in Harry's body. She was ecstatic to see him relax and melt under her touch.

"It seems silly to make two house payments when I already know you're the one."

"What?" Frankie pulled back as if she'd been jolted with a cattle prod. Subconsciously, her hand flew to the back of her neck, where she scratched an itch.

His voice was sleepy when he added, "I love you. You love me. Let's just do it."

"Do what?"

"Life… together," he mumbled into the sheet. "I want to marry you."

Frankie gulped as all her fears rushed to the surface. They tangled with excitement, giving her an off-kilter feeling that sent her reeling.

"You're so lovey-dovey today," she remarked, fascinated by this side of him, a drastic departure from the tense man he'd been when he first arrived. "Usually, you don't get mushy until you are balls deep into your second margarita."

He chuckled. "I've been tip-toeing around this conversation for months, afraid to tell you what I really think."

"Why?"

"Because I didn't want to scare you off." Frankie was glad when he turned his head and she could hear his muffled words more clearly. She didn't want to miss a thing. "Your NTM philosophy is legendary. I didn't want to rush in and ruin it."

"I am the one who always ruins things," she blurted truthfully and immediately wished she could take it back. Frankie usually preferred to keep her more vulnerable feelings locked inside. It was unnerving to feel so exposed.

Harry flipped over and rested on his elbow, reaching up to tuck a wayward red curl behind her ear. "You're more beautiful to me than Cindy Crawford."

"You had a crush on Cindy Crawford?" she asked.

"More than a crush! In high school, I cut out her face from a magazine and glued it over a photo of me and my ex-girlfriend." He laughed at himself. "I had it bad. What's the craziest thing you've ever done for love?"

"In my twenties, I once called every S. Wilson in the Tampa Bay phone book after falling hard for one after a drunken night at a music festival."

"How many were there?"

"Forty-seven," she admitted with a wince.

"Whoa," Harry whispered, stifling his laughter. "Your dedication to the mission was impressive."

"Unfortunately, Steve-o was not impressed," Frankie mused, "In my mind, it was a grand romantic gesture. But now that I'm hearing myself re-tell it out loud, I have to admit it leans hard into psychotic territory."

Harry's eyes widened and shame flushed Frankie's cheeks crimson. He reached out to touch her cheek and chuckled. "You're blushing. My blushing bride." He pulled her on top of him for a kiss, letting Frankie recover from the mortification. "It's a good thing we're older and wiser now." He laced his fingers through her hair. "I love every inch of you. Every freckle on your face, every dirty thought that flies through your head."

"You're different tonight," Frankie admitted, and her own honesty shocked her. She usually relied on hiding behind sexual innuendo and humor.

"Now it's your turn to tell me how you feel about me. Quid pro quo, woman!"

Frankie couldn't stop herself from responding with the most tender truth. "You're the most amazing man I have ever been with. I never thought men like you existed, and every day you prove to me you do. I want to keep you forever."

Harry rolled them up to a sitting position. "Then let's get married. I'm serious."

Frankie gasped. She never thought she was the marrying kind, but in record time, Harrison Willey was proving her wrong.

"Let's just do it," Harry said. "We can get dressed right now and go to the courthouse."

"Slow your roll. The courthouse isn't even open."

"Let's hop on a plane to Vegas, then," he suggested.

"We could." The words left her mouth before she could sensor them. Scared, she pressed both her hands to her mouth to stop any new dramatic revelations from escaping. What was happening? Where did all of her usual defenses go?

"Look, you've had a day. This is not the right time to make huge life-changing decisions," Frankie said. "I think we should table this until the morning."

"You're probably right, but I'm warning you, nothing will change. I'll want to marry you tomorrow as much as I do right this moment."

"I hope so," she whispered, then patted the bed. "Now hush up and let me finish." Harry chuckled and rolled back onto his stomach. Thoughts raced through Frankie's mind, and she was grateful when a few seconds later, she heard Harry snoring softly. She plumped up a pillow and, when he rolled over, gently tucked it under his head. In the warm light of the bedside table lamp, she studied his handsome face.

She'd already memorized every fine line on it. With one finger, she lightly traced the deep cleft in his chin. The stubble made it feel like sandpaper, and she felt a wave of love crash over her while she watched him sleep.

All her life, she thought love was difficult and elusive. Having been raised by her single mother who never missed an opportunity to tell Frankie how worthless her father was, it deeply entrenched the belief that men were selfish and unreliable. The men she'd chosen to date only further confirmed this belief. She'd ping-ponged from train wreck to train wreck, finally giving up in her late forties. That's why it was so astonishing to have met the love of her life at age fifty. He was the one she hadn't seen coming. The one who challenged every one of her fears and kissed away all her worries. It was the kind of love she'd read about in all her smutty books. She turned to them in moments of need but with a cynicism that book boyfriends didn't exist in reality. They were wonderful sexy escapes, but unattainable.

Now that she was dating her ultimate book boyfriend in real life, she was torn in two by the joy of finding him and the fear of losing him. It was a daily seesaw of emotion she felt forced to control as her feelings grew deeper.

She gathered up all the massage oils and quietly walked them back to the hall closet. Then she showered and crawled into bed with Harry and spooned him in the darkness.

THIRTY-NINE

The next morning, she was awakened by the scent of bacon and freshly brewed coffee. She reluctantly tugged the warm sheet off her body and stood on the cold floor, stretching to work out her usual daily body aches and kinks. They showed up when she turned forty-two, and now that she was fifty, she'd learned a few preventative morning stretches usually unclenched her angry knots.

She stumbled out to the kitchen in search of coffee, and seeing Harry sitting at her counter reading the newspaper made her heart lift. She walked over and hugged him from behind.

"Good morning, gorgeous," he greeted, brushing his lips to her temple. "Let me get you some coffee."

She sat down on the stool next to him and said, "I'll let you."

"It's only fair since you gave me that great massage

last night. Don't get me wrong; I loved your hands before, but now I love them even more."

She chuckled as he set the steaming mug in front of her. Taking her first sip, she grinned when she felt the caffeine seep into her soul. "You were saying all kinds of crazy things yesterday before you fell asleep."

"They are only crazy if you don't mean them," he replied. Then his chin jutted back and confusion lit up his features. "I'm a little loosey-goosey with the truth bombs today. My apologies."

A lightning bolt of understanding made hairs stand up on the back of Frankie's neck. She popped up from the stool and ran over to the bathroom cabinet. The amber-colored bottle Zoya handed to her at the compound was gone. She shouted from the bathroom, "Have you seen a brown bottle of essential oil I keep under the sink?"

"Yeah, I put it in with the others when I cleaned out one of the drawers last week so I could organize my toiletries. It smelled like lavender, so I combined it with the other bottle," he hollered from his perch at the stove. "I love you, woman, but you're a mess!"

Frankie pressed her palms to her lips to keep the grin from covering her face. Sitting down on the toilet, she ran through the sleepy conversation they'd had the previous night. With giddy excitement, she washed her hands and face and then returned to the kitchen where Harry was busy at the stove scrambling two eggs.

"Maybe you should call in sick today," she

suggested, wondering what the professional ramifications of the next eight hours would be.

"But I feel fine." He shrugged. "Better than fine, actually. I slept like a baby after the rubdown you gave me. I'm full of piss and vinegar."

She mumbled to herself as she walked over to him and planted a kiss on his bacon-greased lips. "That's what I'm afraid of."

FORTY

In mid-October, the moon was plump and waning, illuminating the water of the pool in Katie's beautiful backyard. Arlo paced the great room, tags jingling. He had a delicious secret. A secret that, if leveraged properly, could set him free. He wrestled with it for days since the discovery, weighing the implications of betraying Katie's confidence again.

Ultimately, he'd made the selfish choice. Impatient to reclaim his human form, he developed tunnel vision. Arlo wasn't content to live out his days as a companion animal any longer. He yearned to meet Katie, the woman he considered the love of his life, as equals. He wanted a real shot at a relationship with her and decided to put a plan in motion that would fast-track his desire to be with her. In his besotted state, he reasoned it was better to ask for her forgiveness than permission.

Arlo paced for an hour as he waited, torn up inside, wondering if he was making the worst mistake of his life. Distressed, he whimpered and cried as he expelled nervous energy, unable to sit or sleep. The evening gave way to darkness, and he tingled with anticipation when he saw Zoya's shadow fill the patio door. He rushed over to it, waiting for the few seconds it took for her to disengage the alarm system and unlock it to let him outside.

"Get down," she said, pushing him off. In his exuberance, he'd jumped up, and his paws landed on her skirt. He whined, then tucked his tail and sat, avoiding eye contact. She stood with her hands on her hips.

"Begin your report," she demanded, and her arrogance irritated him.

He sat down and refused to speak.

"Are you still pouting because I delayed your return to human form?"

"Among other things," he admitted with a growl.

"Get over it," she snapped.

"I have information." He dangled the secret in front of her like ripe fruit. "But I will not share it until you've fulfilled your promise."

"What kind of information?" she asked.

"I'm not falling for it." He sat on his haunches. "You will not want to be in the dark about this, though, I promise you."

Zoya cocked her head, studying the disobedient dog. "Your secret is that juicy?"

"Yes." He punctuated the reply with a bark.

"Out with it then, and I'll change you back."

"No way," he said. "Turn me back and *then* I'll tell you."

Their eyes locked on each other for several silent minutes, and Arlo refused to back down. He had to play hardball and knew it was the only leverage he had. Zoya broke their staring contest first.

"Fine," she acquiesced. "You've been useless to me anyway since Katie found out about our clandestine conferences." She knelt down and wrapped her arms around the fluffy dog. Harnessing her powerful energy, she focused it all on him. Golden sparks circled around them both, then swept Arlo into a funnel cloud and pulled him up off the ground. She stood and pressed both her palms outward to the spinning canine. Faster and faster, he whirled until he tumbled onto the patio, naked and shivering.

He let out a cry and stood looking down at his long human legs and forearms. His wavy brown hair threaded with gray brushed his shoulders and was in a shaggy, surfer style. Warm brown eyes filled his face. "I'm free," Arlo said, astonished at the transformation. He waved his fingers in the air and dragged a palm across his jawline, laughing in utter astonishment. He marveled at the miracle of his physical body, and relief washed in when he realized his mind was fully intact as well.

His gaze flicked down his torso, taking in his tanned skin and complete nakedness. He quickly covered himself with his hands, and embarrassment flushed his cheeks red.

"Would it be too much to ask for a pair of pants?"

She rolled her eyes and then snapped her fingers, and a faded pair of well-worn Levi's adorned his muscular legs. Converse tennis shoes and a pair of socks appeared on his feet, and an aqua-colored Salt Life T-shirt covered his heavily muscled shoulders and softened belly.

"Happy now?"

"Yes," he confirmed, clearing his throat. He was still getting used to his human voice.

"I did my part. Now, you must fulfill your end of the bargain. Chop, chop. Time is money."

"Of course." He was eager to be on his way. "A child has been conceived."

She wrinkled up her forehead. "Are you certain?"

"Without a doubt." He pointed to his nose. "Dogs can detect the change in a pregnant woman's pheromones long before it shows up on a pregnancy test."

"How far along?" Zoya asked.

"Three to four weeks."

Zoya considered this revelation and mentally did the math in her head. A pregnancy now would result in a late June or early July delivery. If the baby born was female, she would be the new supernatural female in their bloodline. Since their mortal coven only spanned three supernatural generations, the birth of a baby girl meant Zoya's impending death. It was the beginning of the end. The revelation tied a knot in her throat, and Zoya swallowed hard against it. She always knew this moment would come, but until that night, it had been an abstract concept. With Arlo's confirmation, she couldn't help but feel her end-of-life countdown begin. Stunned by the discovery, she staggered to the table and sat down, weighing her options. She would have to move her timeline up considerably. The eternal coven would be passing judgment on her desire to reincarnate within the next year, and there was so much to do to ensure she'd be granted the chance to be born again and reunite with Sally's soul.

Seizing his opportunity to escape, Arlo sidestepped her, afraid to say anything more or draw attention to himself. Leaving her distracted and seated at the table in shock, he walked down the stairs and around the house under the cover of darkness, pleased with himself. Strolling away from Katie's stunning beach house, he whistled as he walked, a spring in his step. It felt incredible to be walking on two legs again.

FORTY-ONE

A few days later, at Kandied Karma, Katie walked through her duties on her normal shift in despair. She'd had two sleepless nights without Arlo, and without needing to ask, she knew Zoya had freed him. Part of her was thrilled and overjoyed that her best friend was free, able to live his new life on his own terms. The other part of her was depressed. Living alone in her silent house without his companionship left a hole in her heart a mile wide.

She distracted herself with work, and the hours flew by. Katie was at the door, turning the sign to closed, when a familiar face made her smile. Instead of locking the door, she swung it open wide. Typically unflappable, Davina was surrounded by a muddy red aura that had Katie squinting to see her properly.

Stress.

Katie brushed the warning aside since stress comes with the territory of any divorce attorney.

"Davina!" she said. "It's good to see you again."

"Sorry to drop in right before closing time," she apologized. "I was having a client meeting across the street, and when I saw your sign, I just had to swing by. I've heard so much about the truffles!"

Katie grinned. "Well, they *are* legendary. I don't blame you at all. What can I put together for you?"

"How about two gift boxes for clients and one for me?"

"Anything special, or a sampler?"

"Whatever you recommend," Davina said, pulling out her phone that had been chirping a series of unceasing notifications since she walked into the shop.

"You got it," Katie said as she folded three boxes together and walked down the glass case, making selections for her. Davina was distracted and tapping out replies. Katie tried to connect with the litany of disjointed thoughts that hovered around Davina. It was a stressful mis-mash that was hard to comprehend.

Send the letter of engagement to the mayor.

The Samson deposition is tomorrow. I've got to get Amy to keep her emotions under control.

Shit! I have to call my sister back. I can't believe it's been almost a year since Mom died and we've only spoken once.

"You seem a little preoccupied." Katie made an observation.

"My apologies!" Davina said, waving the phone in the air. "This thing makes my clients feel they have 24/7 access to me."

"I was married to an attorney for years. Believe me, I get it."

"Of course," she said, finally tucking it away into her Kate Spade bag and pulling out her credit card. Katie reached up to take it from her hand, and her fingers brushed across Davina's. A wall of heat surged up her torso to the top of her head, and she jerked backward. A flash obscured her vision. A red apple rotted before her eyes and rolled off the corner of a desk. A string of black pearls broke apart, hit the ground like rain on a tin roof, and bounced away. Confusion welled up as she felt beads of sweat roll down between her shoulder blades.

"Are you okay?" Davina asked, concerned.

"It's just a hot flash." Katie shrugged. "They can come out of nowhere."

Davina's eyes shot up, "Black cohosh and evening primrose have been a game changer for me!" The lawyer shared, leaning in to add, "We get the hot flashes and night sweats, and men get silver fox status. It's criminal."

Katie laughed. She wasn't far off from her assessment. "Here you go." She handed the shimmering gold gift bag with the three boxes of truffles tucked inside off to Davina and watched her walk out the door and over to her car. Her next assignment from Karma had arrived, and all she had to go on was black pearls and a rotten apple.

———

Thank you for reading "Flash Point: Midlife in Aura Cove." Check out the next thrilling installment of this hilarious and heartwarming series! In a Flash: Midlife in Aura Cove. Order here.

In the hallowed halls of Aura Cove High School, Principal Adrienne Thorne is a beloved beacon, guiding teenagers toward their destinies. The school board's decision to elevate her to Superintendent feels like a mere formality until an ominous email threatens her career and reputation.

During a routine truffle stop by her estranged sister, Davina, a reading from Karma spurs Katie and the coven into action. Bound by a mission to rectify the past, they join together to salvage Adrienne's future.

Meanwhile, Zoya shares a revelation with Yuli that will shake the mortal coven to its core. The next successor in their supernatural legacy has been conceived, triggering a cascade of events forcing them to confront their deepest fears and embrace the impending transformation that awaits them all.

Escape to Aura Cove for another captivating battle of good versus evil and wicked female empowerment.

Order In A Flash Here.

Also Available on Amazon, BN Nook, Apple iBooks, Kobo, Google Play and many international booksellers. Or request it from your local library.

Like FREE Books? Enter to Win a Gift Card to My Bookstore   https://tealbutterflypress.com/pages/join-our-email-list-and-win

There's a new winner every week!

READ MORE BY THIS AUTHOR

Use the QR code below to access my current catalogue. **Teal Butterfly Press is the only place to purchase autographed paperbacks and get early access.** Buying direct means you are supporting an artist instead of big business. I appreciate you.

https://tealbutterflypress.com/pages/books

Also available at Barnes and Noble, Kobo, Apple books, Amazon, and many other international book sellers.

Find My Books at your Favorite Bookseller Below.

Books by Ninya

Books By Blair Bryan

ABOUT THE AUTHOR

 I've always been a risk-taker, so at 44 I decided to write and publish my own books. It has been a roller coaster ride with a punishing learning curve, but if it were easy, everyone would do it. I write under the pen names of Ninya and Blair Bryan.

I love to travel and a trip to Scotland with a complete stranger was the inspiration for my memoir. I also seem to attract crazy experiences and people into my life like a magnet that gives me a never-ending supply of interesting storylines.

If you love a good dirty joke, a cup of coffee so strong you can chew it, and have killed more cats with your curiosity than you can count, I might be your soulmate.

Visit me online www.tealbutterflypress.com

Let's connect in my facebook reader group, **The Kaleidoscope: Teal Butterfly Press' Official Author Fandom**

Made in the USA
Monee, IL
05 February 2024

52405720R00225